Butter Pecan

By Angela Moore

Butter Pecan
by Angela Moore

Cover by: Nathaniel Grady
Edited by: Tess Rowing
Copyright 2016© Angela Moore
ISBN: 978-0-9909903-4-5

Published in the United States of America
Worldwide Electronic & Digital Rights
Worldwide English Language Print Rights

Acknowledgements

A very special thanks to my editor, Tess Rowing.

Your Patience and Sacrifice Have Not Gone Unnoticed!

In Loving Memory of Harold Anthony Ward

Born November 25, 1977

Killed by the police on July 6, 2006

"Come to me, all you who are weary and burdened, and I will give you rest. Take my yoke upon you and learn from me, for I am gentle and humble in heart, and you will find rest for your souls. For my yoke is easy and my burden is light."

Matthew 11:28-30

Table of Contents

Chapter One

Sincere...

I'm a workaholic, and my week was one from Hell. Not just because of work but because of work and play.

To occupy my time, I've always worked two jobs. Though I'm financially stable and don't have to work at all, old habits are hard to kill.

FedEx is my fulltime job and I put in part-time hours at my mom's clothing store.

Yeah, I gotta lotta slack from my boys for working there but hell, it was a sure fire-way to meet the ladies.

Twice a week I worked at the store. I didn't do shit but help stock, and didn't even need to do that. My mother's establishment was fully staffed, and I worked as a courtesy. From time to time I was needed and helped on the floor. That's usually when I got into trouble.

I was a young man with raging hormones. For my own good, and to keep the peace between me and Mom, I stayed in the back as much as possible. But when duty calls, what's a brotha to do?

It would be while working at my mom's boutique that the spiral of craziness would began. I must admit, it was partly my fault.

Mom always told me to never shit where you eat, but dayyymn, Veronica was a firecracker. Momma never consulted me when it came to her business. I was glad 'bout that, because I woulda hired every employee based off looks, never considering their brains. Veronica woulda been a sure hire.

I met Veronica on a rare occasion when I was needed on the floor. She was a college student who had to take an exam, and was running late for her shift. Mom asked me to hold the fort down until Veronica arrived. I had no problem with that.

While hanging summer dresses on a rack, Ms. Smarts made her appearance. I was mesmerized.

When that fine specimen of beauty and brains walked into the store my heart did a somersault. Veronica was more than pretty, she was absolutely stunning.

I wasn't into superficial, weave-wearing, long press-on nail, fake eyelash-having chicks. I like my women au naturale, and all-natural she was.

She had two long, kinky French braids that were parted in zigzags down the center of her head. She wore a turquoise choker, an Indian tribal belly shirt and tight jeans. Her skin was a dark chocolate and flawless.

The gods were looking out for me that day because after she walked into the store the door caught on a rock and didn't shut. She had to turn around to close it. As soon as I lay eyes on her round, apple bottom butt, my dick jumped.

Damn!

My lusting ass missed the rack and dropped the dresses.

Shit!

I guess she'd seen me as well, because as I bent to pick up the dresses she politely sashayed her round mounds right past my head. As she did, Veronica looked down at me and her eyes screamed sex.

When I stood up my eyes shot past her to my annoyed mom, who was looking directly at me. She didn't look happy.

"Thanks for filling in Sincere, I'll see you tomorrow."

My momma shut that shit down real quick.

Mrs. Fleming . . .

As I watched my son make google-eye moves on the new hire, Veronica, I feared for him. Not just because of the girl; Because of life. Plain old, everyday life in the city of Indianapolis.

I gotta keep my eye on that boy of mine, Sincere. The ladies flocked to him like stink on manure. He was smart, independent and handsome, handsome, handsome! The spitting image of his father. That meant he never lacked female companionship, which equates to trouble.

Lord, how I hated thinking about his dad! Thoughts of him made my stomach turn, but not so much in a bad way. It's a love-hate kind of turn. I loved, and will always love my husband. It was the way he died that made me want to vomit - A topic for another day. But I could say this; He made sure I didn't want for nothin'. Ever.

Though we didn't have money to spare, my husband and I were financially sufficient. While still newlyweds we bought our first home, along with the car of his dreams; A brand spankin' new Cadillac. We were comfortable and happy. That's all that mattered.

Charles, my husband, had always known that I'd wanted to open my own clothing store, and had actually considered getting a second full time job to make it happen. I had been totally against that.

I wanted my man at home more than I wanted that store and wasn't willing to sacrifice our time together for my desires. I was glad I made that decision. Unbeknownst to me, every moment we spent together would be cherished ones.

Now, my son Sincere is my heart. When he was a baby he was the reason I got out of bed everyday. Although he didn't know it, he was my motivation. Circumstances that were out of our control had forced me into a deep depression. During that period, I'd been lost, confused and felt totally defeated and abandoned. At times, when a new day would begin and I'd feel the sun kiss me through my window, I wouldn't want to open my eyes. It was too painful. But then I'd feel Sincere squirming next to me and as if on autopilot, the tears would begin to fall. 'Don't open them. Keep them closed'. I'd tell myself. I'd say it numerous times trying to think my way out of my reality. It never worked.

I'd force my eyelids opened, look over at the tiny replica of my deceased husband and then slowly take in a calm deep breath. Almost instantly I'd feel revived, rejuvenated and ready for war.

After wiping away my tears, I'd pick up my son and whisper in his little ears 'They picked the wrong black man to kill baby boy. Let's go fight for some justice.'

Never in a million years could I have known that I'd be once again saying those words. Never!

Sincere...

Since I'd gotten a visual of whom I was filling in for, the next time I was needed on the floor to occupy her spot, I made sure I was at the front door acting like I was doing somethin' while actually doin' nothin'.

Hell, I'd seen the lustful way Veronica looked at me and was determined to make sure she knew that I knew.

Mom was always cock blockin' so I had to be on top of my game. I acted as if the clothes I was rearranging were the most important things in the world while watching the clock, and store entrance.

When I saw Veronica walking towards the establishment I quickly looked up and saw my mom taking care of a customer. Veronica's timing was perfect.

Veronica walked in and as she did our eyes locked. In that instant I knew I'd be between her thunder thighs that night.

"Sincere Fleming?"

Mom was calling my name but she was too late. I already slipped Beauty and Brains my number.

Seven hours later Veronica was rolling her tongue around the tip of my dick.

Before I even spread her wings, I let Veronica know what was up.

"You know we just friends right?"

"I'm down with it."

Hell, that was all I needed to hear.

"Leave the choker on."

She smiled, and did anything I asked.

After a devastating breakup, I was never a one-woman-man kinda fella and wasn't about to start. So, once Veronica realized that I wasn't the committing type, and the statement I'd made about us just being friends was true, she clowned.

As a rule I hardly entertained women at my house. It was my sacred sanctuary. As a handsome bachelor, I knew women saw dollar signs whenever they crossed over the threshold of my immaculate three bedroom ranch-style home. I kept my place so pristine that I used to make everyone take their shoes off at the door. I'm not as anal anymore but I still keep my place in top-notch order.

They way Veronica was behaving was another reason I rarely entertained at my crib. It helped to curb incidents of madness.

"Sincere, you better open this fucking door or I'mma sincerely kick yo ass!"

It'd been two weeks after I'd hit it and she was acting a fool.

She'd been blowing up my phone, and I'd been ignoring her calls.

"Sincere!"

Shit, I had another 'worthy' babe in the crib and Veronica's ass had just blown my top. My new friend was shitty too and I didn't blame her.

"I'm ready to go, Sincere," she said, while Veronica was pounding the door.

We were hiding in my bedroom. I looked at her out of the corner of my eye.

"Exit at ya own risk, 'cause I ain't openin' shit."

She rolled her eyes and loudly popped her gum.

An hour later, I couldn't hear Veronica's nonsense. She'd bounced, or so I thought. Of course, now that I was safe, I did what brothas do and tried to talk my companion out of her panties.

"So, are you ready to do this?"

I flashed my million dollar smile, showing off my dimples to get some brownie points. She looked at me like I'd lost my damn mind.

"Look, I told you that she's crazy. I ain't never even touched that girl. I met her at the club, and that's all she wrote," I insisted. "She just won't leave me alone."

Home girl looked bored. I counted my losses and walked her to her car. Just as she pulled off, Veronica came speeding down the street and came to a screeching halt in front of my house.

Aw, shit!

Like a runaway slave, I ran my butt inside, locked my door, then waited for the ruckus to restart. When it didn't, I released a long, deep breath.

After fifteen minutes of nothing, I walked to my window and peeked outside.

Veronica was gone.

Later that night while sound asleep, I'd learn that there were a few embers still burning in Veronica's heart.

I was having a bomb sex dream when instead of an orgasm I damn near had a heart attack. Not the kind of death I was looking for.

A big-ass brick shattered my bedroom window with a loud crash, and my house alarm started blaring.

Now ain't this some shit!

I hopped outta bed and ran to my livingroom window. Her ballsy behind wasn't even scared or trying to hide the fact that she'd done it.

As I looked through my blinds, I saw Veronica sitting in her car with the engine running. When she saw I was looking, she gave me the finger, and slowly drove off.

Veronica began having trouble concentrating in school, and our work weeks were strenuous as hell.

When she couldn't take my flirting with the other workers no more, she quit because she knew my behind wasnt goin' nowhere.

After all that drama, a drink was in order. That's when I met Sabrina.

It was dark but my eyes quickly adjusted to the atmosphere. I'd been scanning the congested scene for a minute. Fine sexy babes were everywhere. As me and my boys made our rounds my eyes latched onto absolute fineness. I quickly took a detour from the fellas and went on the hunt.

I was downtown at Club Sparkle, mesmerized by her beauty and shiny-ass lips. Like a stealth cat, I eased next to her.

"What's your name baby girl?"

She turned in her barstool and looked my way.

"Seems it's baby girl, since that's what you called me."

I liked that come back and smiled, showing off my deep dimples in approval.

Instead of her being mesmerized by my good looks, she turned her head and finished talking to the girlfriend I hadn't noticed.

There are a lot of distractions in this club, but I only had eyes for her. She was truly beautiful.

Ebony Exquisiteness.

"What's your name, for real?"

Just as she was about to turn my way, another sly cat cut in on my play and asked her to dance.

What kinda shit is this?!

I played it cool and watched as she accepted his invitation. As she walked out onto the dance floor she didn't even look my way, and that did something to me. I was always the center of attention. I placed myself in the seat she'd vacated and waited.

Seven long songs later, she skipped her sweaty sexy behind back my way.

"Excuse me." She said.

I didn't move. She was in such a good mood that she smiled. I saw her pretty, deep dimples.

Sabrina...

When he'd asked me my name and I'd turned and looked into his pretty brown eyes I knew I was in trouble. That man was magazine fine. And when he flashed his million dollar smile, showing off his deep dimples, my silly heart skipped a beat.

After I got over his pretty-boy looks, I replied to his statement and resumed talking to my girl.

The request to dance came right on time. I made my exit but while I danced with this faceless guy, I watched my other suitor through my peripheral. When he sat in my seat I knew he'd be there when I got back. The anticipation took my breath away.

I knew his type: Straight-up ladies' man and whore. Been there and done that. Hell, that was the story of my life. I'd had men come and go but the last straw came about a year ago with Tyrone.

He was best friends with my cousin's man. After she begged me, I finally allowed her to introduce us.

Tyrone turned out to be a really a cool dude. If we hadn't dated we probably would've been friends for life, but we did date.

At the time I thought he was the complete package. Brotha-man was such a gentleman I just knew I was in a fairytale. Tyrone was extremely patient with my shortcomings and Lord knows I had a few. He was handsome in a Denzel Washington kinda way. Tall with broad masculine shoulders that you wanted to wrap your arms around and hold onto. They screamed strength and protection. He kept his hair in a very small Afro, never a hair out of place, and dressed immaculately. He always wore a different, new cologne that was tempting and tantalizing. Although he wasn't arrogant, his pores secreted money. As a partner in a very successful lawn care business, I wouldn't expect anything different. But, like most men, in time I saw his true colors and true intentions.

"Just one time Sabrina," he said, trying to weasel his way into my pants again.

"Your beggin' is a real turnoff, Tyrone." We'd had this conversation before.

He paused and tried a different tactic, "You know we're going to be together forever..."

I cut his butt off, "No the heck I don't." He'd been trying to get my goods for almost a year. When those words rolled off my tongue, he clicked.

"You bitch!" He was mad.

I was amazed, "Bitch?" I said. He's asking for my goods and he thinks calling me a bitch is gonna get him there?

"Yeah, bitch!" He thought he had something on me. "I dun wined and dined yo stuck up ass all these months and you ain't gave up no fuckin' pussy!"

Stuck up ass?

I thought a lady should never use profanity but he took me there. The entitlement to me. How dare he! I still gave him a chance to leave. "I never asked you for shit! Now get the fuck out!"

Did his little dick-ass just lunge at me?

"You owe me!" In a split second he went from Denzel to demon.

No he didn't! I didn't owe shit. I evaded his grasp and ran towards my bedroom. He followed, enraged.

"You fucking tease, get yo ass back here."

Just as I made it to the door he grabbed me by the back of my neck. His grip was heavy and painful and the fight flared inside me. I turned around screaming and swinging. "You punk ass nigga!" I clawed his face with my manicured nails. "Get yo nasty hands off me! Get off me daddy! You freak!"

I'd turned into another person and it was His fault. "How you gon' try to take shit that don't belong to you huh?" I screamed at my daddy. "You ain't shit!"

He was backing up, arms in front of his face as I clawed at him with every intention of taking his eyes. "Get off me you crazy bitch!" He yelled.

I was blinded by my sadness, my pain, my life, my everything. "Fuck yooooou!"

I beat him so bad he sued me for his medical bills. I got off, temporary insanity. At least daddy gave me something.

Sincere...

She ignored my boldness and picked up her drink. While standing she opted to chat with her girlfriend. I would not be deterred.

I politely turned in my chair towards the bartender to order a drink for baby girl, the invisible girlfriend, and myself. Finished with that, I spun in my chair to scan the crowd.

I see all kinds of chicks I'd kick it with, but when I saw Veronica's crazy butt, that shit got real.

I quickly turned back towards the bar, looking into the mirrors that drape the back wall.

When I spot Ms. Psycho, she's looking right at me.

Shit!

I shift my gaze to baby girl and she met my eyes through the mirror. She smirked as we watch Veronica make her way towards me. Spinning in my chair, Veronica walked between my legs and looked at baby girl.

With venom in her throat she spoke. "You know he ain't shit."

Baby girl smiled.

Veronica looked at me, smiled her damn self, then started licking and kissing my neck. I was frozen. After a few moments I heard baby girl say, "Well, looks like somebody's packin'."

I swallow because I hadn't even realized my dick was hard.

Veronica stepped back and looked me in my eyes, "You don't love me no more Sincere?" she crooned.

I look at Veronica like I wanna kick her ass even though my mama taught me better.

"Baby girl and Sincere. Hmmm, that has a nice ring to it."

I looked to my left. Veronica, with a frown on her face, looked to her right.

"What do you think Shanika? You think those two go together?"

All three of us looked at Shanika, the invisible friend.

"Naw, I like Sabrina and Sincere better," she smirked.

I raised my eyebrows. "So your name is Sabrina?"

All eyes on me.

Guess that was the wrong thing to ask, because none of the looks were pleasant ones. I didn't care.

With an extended hand I introduced myself, hard dick and all. "It's really nice to meet you Sabrina."

My cheek stung as a ferocious slap struck my face.

I looked at Veronica's retarded ass. She slapped me so hard that I didn't have a choice; The force turned my head in her direction and just as I looked at Veronica, Sabrina walked off.

I gave Veronica a real calm look that caused her to choke on whatever words getting ready to float out her throat. I watched as her face took on the look of shock when security tapped her shoulder and asked her to leave. I wasn't paying attention to Veronica.

I was on a mission.

I scanned the crowd but didn't have to look long. I saw Sabrina walking towards me and Ms. Invisible. When she got to the bar, I opened my mouth to explain myself but she halted me with closed eyes and a raised manicured finger. It was pretty too.

"Don't. Please don't."

She opened her sexy lids and gave her attention to the bartender.

"I'd like to order the drink that he paid for, please."

When she said the word 'he' she didn't even look my way, just tilted her head in my direction.

I turned to face the bar and when I did, I caught her staring at me through the mirror. She tried to act as if she hadn't been looking, but it was too late, I'd caught her.

"She's my ex, Sabrina." I explained, "we haven't been together in a very long time."

She ignored me.

While waiting for her drink she turned, facing the crowd. I turned too.

"You don't seem like a woman who's about playin' games. So, I'm not about to play with your intelligence. Although we weren't together I was still hittin' it from time to time."

Hell, mama always told me that honesty was the best policy. If Sabrina believed me so be it. If she didn't, it was all the same to me.

"I, therefore, can't put all the blame on her. We both wanted each other so we hooked up."

Sabrina smelled really good. As her scent floated into my nostrils her fragrance was a tease to my nares.

She let out a tired sigh.

"Here ya go ma'am."

As she turned towards the bartender, she reached into her pocket for the tip, but I beat her to it.

"Tip's already been taken care of."

She lay down a five dollar bill anyway.

"Will you look at me?"

"I'm good. Think I've seen enough for one night," she sipped her virgin drink.

I open my mouth to speak.

"Damn, nigga! Can't you tell she don't wanna be bothered?"

That was Ms. Invisible and I treated her as such.

"Look Sabrina, you're a very beautiful woman."

"Tell me something I don't know," she took a sip.

A nice young chap boldly walked over to ask her to dance. She put down her drink and politely accepted.

Now ain't this some shit!

I watched as she sashayed her happy butt onto the dance floor, losing her and her rescuer as they were absorbed by the crowd.

As I strained to see where they'd gone I could feel Ms. 'Invisifriend' staring at me.

I downed my drink and went in search of baby girl.

Sabrina...

Sincere, huh? Guess that's what he was trying to be by telling me about Veronica. Too bad it backfired.

Sincere...

I tapped the young chap Sabrina was dancing with on his shoulder, when he turned in that direction I eased between him and Sabrina.

Oldest trick in the book, and he fell for it.

When he acted like he was mad, I raised one of my thick eyebrows. He scrammed. I turned my attention towards Sabrina and started moving to the beat.

Her eyes were closed. She was dancin' offbeat and it was sexy as hell. With a big smile on her face she did a crazy spin like she knew she was the shit. She was in a zone and I liked it. The song changed and Tupac's 'Gangsta Party' came on. She turned her back to me, dropped it like it was hot and I stopped dancing. I rolled in laughter; She was hilarious and my gut-deep howl was evidence of how funny she looked.

I was glad the music was loud because I didn't want to snatch her out of her moment. I savored all of her unsynchronized, corny movements. I knew she could dance for multiple songs. I was shocked when the third song came on and she still had her eyes closed, dancing in her own world - She didn't want anyone pushing their way in. Although I stood there as her partner, I got the feeling the only thing she was dancing with was the music. I put my hands in my pockets and watched.

Her ass was comical. She couldn't dance worth shit but I drank in the sight of her.

Sabrina was a mahogany bombshell with oval eyes, a small pointed nose and a cute, pouty mouth. Her skin was unblemished and her body perfect. She danced offbeat, hips swaying to a melody all their own.

Yeah, I'd checked her out while at the bar, but now I was up close and personal. I liked what I saw. She started turning in a slow circle. When she raised her arms her Wonderbra lifted her perky breasts, and her hips continued to sway off-rhythm as if on autopilot.

When I took a step closer her back was to me. I placed my hands on her hips. She turned around, probably to see who she was dancing with. Her eyes widened in surprise, her body grinding close to mine. She grinned after a moment and slid her hands over my chest, then into my pockets to pull my hips closer and started grinding.

Damn she was fine!

That's when Ms. Invisible became visible. She tapped Sabrina's shoulder and said something in her ear. Sabrina's brown eyes, the kind that drew you in, suddenly weren't so bright anymore.

Her smile disappeared. She slowly let down her arms and stopped dancing. I thought I was in trouble.

She looked confused, then I realized she was looking over my shoulder. She immediately became agitated. That was my cue to turn around.

"Not tonight Tyrone," she said.

The music was so loud I barely heard her, so I knew he hadn't.

Although a halfway decent looking cat, I could tell that something was off as he approached. "I just wanna talk to you Sabrina." He said in a pleading voice.

He treated me like Mr. Invisible and acted as if I wasn't there.

Just as he was about to reach out to her, someone who looked as if they were a relative gently took his elbow and led him off the dance floor.

I turned back towards Sabrina and homegirl was ghost.

Sabrina...

I didn't realize I was dancing with him at first, but I had to admire his persistence. So I slid a little something-something in his pocket. He was interesting, that was for sure.

Sincere...

The club was packed, making it hard to find her. Something told me that Tyrone was what ended her night. I looked towards the exit and lo! She and Ms. Invisible were headed towards the door.

As I made my way in their direction, a bunch of females who knew me from my past exploits at the club got in my way. It was as if fate knew that if I left the club I'd never be seen again. They were almost right.

"What's up Sincere? Leaving so soon?" Michelle was a sexy roadblock prohibiting my exit.

"Yeah, as soon as you get outta my way."

She wasn't as easy to dodge as the others. She pouted and crooned in a voice like a woman from those late-night commercials, dripping with lust. "Now why you gotta be like that?"

Her beautiful caramel breasts spilled from her tank top. My eyes had been on the door that led me to my prize, but she stopped me in my tracks.

"Like what?" I asked, irritated at the delay, yet interested in the hot woman in front of me.

She walked into what little personal space I had left, making sure her two perky mounds touched my body, "All rushy, rush, rush."

I leaned, draping my arm around her small waist, "Ain't no rush..."

My response was aborted when Too Short's 'Blow The Whistle' came on. When the first whistle blared, it sounded like a traffic cop directing cars to go in the opposite direction after a bad accident. I looked at the door that led outside.

"I'll be right back." I said, no longer paying attention to Michelle.

"I've heard that before."

I stepped to the left and so did she. My eyes shifted to her. "I'm serious. I'm coming right back. There's something I gotta take care of right quick."

My exit was a few steps away and Michelle was making sure I didn't walk out and conquer in my pursuit of new pussy.

"You don't do anything quick, Sincere."

I got frustrated and when a look of unimpressed calm replaced my amusement, she stepped aside.

When I finally made it out Sabrina was nowhere to be found. I looked left and right, not knowing what direction she'd gone.

The sidewalks were packed with party-goers, chicks in their cliques and brothas laying it thick, trying to score for the night.

Standing a foot above everyone else because of the back step, it wasn't hard to scan the crowd. Michelle may have made me miss my chance of locating Sabrina.

I shifted my search to the cars inching through traffic - that's when I noticed a gold Infinity driving past.

Sabrina?

She smiled, waved and continued to creep right past me. I put my hands in my pockets in frustration, pausing when there was something unfamiliar against my hand.

The next day I gave her a call.

Sabrina...

My cousin Shanika couldn't wait for me to pull off after the clusterfuck of an evening.

"He sure had a lotta nerve!" She was hyped up, digging in her purse for some gum.

"He sure in the hell did," I gripped the steering wheel, angry and running my mouth, "the audacity of him to come at me at a club. And how did he know I was even there? It's like he can smell me or somethin'. Like he knows how to spot me outta a crowd of thousands. He must have lost his mind cause ain't no way he don't know I'mma call about that restraining order I got on him. Yeah, it was probably a coincidence that we were there at the same time but he didn't hafta come up to me. Hell, the restraint says he's not to be within sixty feet of me. I can't wait to call them tomorrow."

She plopped some gum into her mouth.

"Girl! Ain't nobody talkin' bout Tyrone's crazy ass. I'm talkin' bout that fine piece of chocolate that was snoopin' round you all night. The nerve of him!"

I'd known exactly who she'd been talking about but didn't wanna go there.

"He was on you like white on rice! Damn, he was fine. And his dimples." She paused. "You didn't give him your number did you?"

"Now why would I do a foolish thing like that?" I was lying, but I didn't want to hear it from my beloved cousin.

I felt her looking at me. Instead of speaking, she popped a bubble. Just as I was turning my head to look at her she was turning hers to look out of the window.

"Cause Sabrina, I know how you can be and I just want the best for you."

My cousin loved me like a sister and she was right, there were times when I could be a little naive.

I reached over and placed my hand on her shoulder.

"I love you cuz-cuz, and I can assure you that after Tyrone, you have nothing to worry about."

Sincere . . .

The following day I rang Sabrina, but she didn't answer. That was cool by me. I'd had plans to help Mom at her store and knew I wouldn't have a lot of time to talk. Her not answering was a godsend.

The second day, after getting off work at my FedEx gig, I called her with the same result.

When she didn't answer on the third day, I concluded she didn't respond to calls she didn't recognize via her caller ID, so I made sure I called at least once a day.

It would be a week of persistent calling before she'd pick up.

"Hello?"

"Now how you gonna get to know a brotha by not answering your phone? " I couldn't believe she slipped her number in my pocket and refused to talk to me. I guess she was playing hard-to-get.

"Excuse me?"

I repeated myself.

"I've been busy and I don't answer calls from unknown numbers. Who is this anyway?"

"You know who this is. I know you remember my voice."

For a long time she said nothing and neither did I. I heard her moving around as if walking from one room to another.

"What do you want from me Sincere?" She sounded tired.

"Nothing Sabrina. Absolutely nothing."

"Is that riiiight?"

It was my time to be quiet. God knows I wanted to spread her wings. "That's right baby girl, nothing at all."

"Whatever Sincere. All y'all after is pussy and mine ain't up for grabs."

I acted as if her statement hadn't affected me but her boldness caught me by surprise. "Well I'm not y'all' so you can cut that out."

She laughed, "Did you reeeeally just say that? Ya dick was on swole last week and you tryin' ta tell me that sex ain't what you want? Brothaman please."

I changed the subject, "Do you always elongate your words?"

"Do you always elongate your dick?"

I smiled, "You gotta smart little mouth."

"And you got weak game."

"When are you going to go out with me?"

"In your dreams."

"Well, that means we've already been on our first date, so when's the second one?"

"What time are you going to bed?"

My smile got bigger and I shifted gears. "You're a very beautiful woman."

"I know. Look I'm about to get ready for this date."

"What time am I picking you up?"

"So I'mma hafta chat with you later."

"Bet you don't even realize you gave me permission to call you again."

"Don't get it twisted homeboy. Every word that flows out of my oral cavity has been accounted for so on that note, holla."

Click!

I liked Sabrina.

Sabrina...

After hanging up from Sincere I picked up the anatomy book I'd taken with me to my bedroom and finished studying.

Sincere...

I was laying at the crib in chill mode while talking to Sabrina. As soon as I hung up from her I sat up, put my phone on private and called Veronica.

"Hello," she sound sweet as honey but I knew better. I kept her hanging on a string and didn't say shit, "Sincere?"

Cricket cricket cricket.

"Look baby, I'm sorry about the other night."

She heard me sigh.

"Sincere?"

"Look girl it's been over a year. You got one more time Veronica and I'm not playin' wit yo ass. What you did last week was so wack and foul."

"I know baby, I know."

I got mad, "Stop calling me baby! Look! Lose my name and the fact that you know me. I ain't been with you since last year."

She changed with the quickness, "Well yo DICK sho' wants me to remember your damn name and number."

"Do you want me to get at yo ass for harassment? Huh? How would yo people feel about that? Get ya damn mind right and leave me the hell alone!"

After officially breaking it off, Veronica stalked the hell outta me. It got so bad that I had to sit-down with her folks. They assured me they'd keep her in check, which was a damned lie. Like me, she was an only spoiled-ass child. The only thing her parents required of her was college, otherwise her wish was their command.

I knew if I tried going to them again nothing would happen. I had no problem filling out paperwork though. I'd done it before and would sure as hell do it again. I softened my tone. "Veronica, I've moved on."

"With who? That stuck-up bitch that paid you no mind the other night?"

I'd had enough of the madness. I hung up.

She called me right back.

What was messed up was this was my seventh number change since I'd left her. And I called her private. How in the hell did she have my number?

Damn!

The next morning I was at the courts asking for the paperwork. Although Veronica lived alone, I made sure a copy went to her parents' house.

The whole ordeal was tedious. By the time I walked out of the congested courthouse my head hurt. At that moment I realized that all pussy wasn't good pussy because Veronica's psychotic ass had become an unwanted burden in my otherwise simple life.

With time to burn I drove over to my mother's shop and hung with her for a few. We chit-chatted awhile about nothing but when she saw me eyeing one of her workers, although not dressed for labored work, she put me to use and threw me in the back. Her female staff was now able to work without the distraction of their boss' sexy son checkin' them out.

What she had me do was lightweight. With a clipboard in hand, I went into the dungeon and took inventory. Time quickly got away from me. By the time I'd finished my task Mom was closing up shop, counting the drawer.

She was tired. Without much resistance, I took the money from her hand and shooed her out of her store. After making sure she was secure in her car, I ran back inside, counted the money, locked up, made the deposit and went home. When my body hit my bed, it transitioned into chill mode. I pulled my phone from my pocket and saw that I'd had numerous missed calls. I'd forgotten to turn it back on after leaving the courthouse.

Oh well.

As I scrolled through my list, the name and number I longed to see wasn't there. I flipped onto my back and called Sabrina.

I hadn't expected an answer, but she did, "how was that date?" I asked.

"Entertaining," she drawled, like she was disinterested.

"I had to get papers on homegirl."

"Who?"

"You know who."

"So, you got that effect on women?"

Next topic, "How was your day Sabrina?"

She didn't answer.

"I asked how…"

She cut me off, "I heard you the first time. I just don't like being ignored."

"I'm not ignoring you."

"Well, you didn't answer my question so I count that as ignoring."

I played dumb, "What question?"

Silence.

"I'm serious Sabrina…"

She cut in on my word dance again. "I am too."

After clearing my throat I answered. "No, just her." That lie came out way too smooth. I was almost ashamed.

"You gonna answer that?"

I was so caught up on trying to figure out if she could read through my bullshit that I hadn't heard the beep of my call-waiting. After taking a quick peek at my caller ID I asked, "Answer what?"

She was over it, "Look Sincere, I'm not the one okay? I don't have time for the games and since I'm not the type to beat around the bush I'll let you know that I don't mind being your friend but I have nothing else to offer."

Damn, she sound just like me. I sat up. "That's all I want, is to get to know you Sabrina."

She laughed, "That's what they all say but when they realize that all I want is true friendship they either stop calling or accept what is and we become really cool."

I wondered who the hell "they" were. "So what you sayin'? I wouldn't be your only friend?"

"Sincere?"

"Yes?"

"When I say 'friend' that's what I mean. No benefits, and yes, I have more than one."

Damn.

I didn't visualize Sabrina as a hoe, so I had to clarify some shit. "You're telling me that you don't sleep with any of those so called 'friends'? And just so you know, I'm not trying to be placed in the category of 'they'. I'm not feeling that."

She wasn't amused.

"Sorry for ya, but when that chick started licking all over you and ya dick got hard as a rock, you kinda placed yaself in that category. Not to mention that you just received a call and tried acting as if it never happened. I see now I'mma hafta place my 'Sabrina Yoke' around your neck."

That sounded kinky. "What you mean by that?"

She laughed, "You ain't no different than 'they' were when we first met, so I'mma need to tame you."

"I like the sound of that," I sensed her smile.

"When I say 'tame' I mean that I can show you better than I can tell you about the real meaning of the word friend". She paused for a second, "Sincere, when I say I have friends that's what I mean. These guys look out for me and make sure I'm okay. They've accepted their position in my life and we've become very close. I guess you can say I've got a band of brothers. And when I do come across a guy that I might find myself attracted to..."

"So you're not attracted to me?"

She ignored that question, "I run every conversation and situation by them and they give me feedback. Tyrone..."

"Tyrone?"

"The guy from the club."

"Oh." I'd forgotten all about dude. Hell, I got a quick synopsis of their relationship that night and knew he wasn't a threat.

"Anyway, he had best be glad my boys weren't there. It woulda gotten real ugly."

"I'd have protected you," my phone started ringing again.

She laughed. "You are a mess Sincere. You gonna get that?"

I didn't even look at my caller ID, "Naw, we're good."

She was prompt with her response, "Aww. You won't be hard to tame. You're a quick learner."

All I could do was smile.

Chapter Two

$\mathbf{I}$t took a while but Sabrina finally let me take her to dinner.

Months had passed with nothing but phone conversations keeping us connected.

When I saw her pull into the restaurant parking lot I was glad I allowed my patience to overrule my jealously. When Sabrina said she had friends, she wasn't lying. It seemed like during every phone conversation, one of those brothas were cutting in.

The first was the impatient brotha.

I was on a deliver at my FedEx job when I'd given her a call. I knew that shit wasn't allowed but hell everybody did it. There was something about Sabrina that made me want to break all the rules.

I'd been discussing how hot it was in my truck when she interrupted me.

"Can you call me back Sincere? This is Malcolm."

"Who's Malcolm?"

"My friend. And he doesn't like waiting so I'll chat with you later."

I looked at my phone when I heard the dialtone. "Well damn!"

I may have liked breaking the rules for her but she sure in the hell didn't break them for me. Not when it came to her 'friends.'

Next was the one she had dated in her younger years.

It was a couple of weeks later when again, I was breaking the rules while delivering a package. I'd made it to the address and saw someone sitting on the porch. That was my cue to get my ass off the phone pronto. Just as I was about to tell her that I'd hit her up later, she beat me to the punch.

"Hey, you remember me telling you about Cyprus?"

The package was forgotten, "Hell no!"

"You know the one I said plays the guitar? The one who used to play me to sleep every night. Anyway he just called, so can you call me back?"

We were just friends so I couldn't say nothin'. "That's cool. I'll hit you up…" She hung up before I could finish.

I'll be damned.

Or that aggressive ass, Rusty. She hardly answered when he called.

I was making a run to the grocery store, when mid-sentence, one of her words was cut off, which let me know that her other line was ringing. I asked

"You gonna get that?"

I could feel her smile, "Answer what?"

I pulled into the store lot, found a spot and parked, "Don't try to play a Sincere. You know you hear that beep sound."

"Naw, we're good. Besides I'd rather talk to you for a change."

Her response let me know it was Rusty.

"Well you know he ain't hangin' up until you answer."

"I know."

Ya see, Sabrina was a special kinda girl and it took a man like myself to recognize it. Just as she was aware of my behavior changes while chatting, I was aware of hers.

When I'd ask about her family, she'd always pause before answering. She took so long with her response I thought she was lying. Family matters were not her favorite subject so she kept her answers short and to the point.

During the infancy of our friendship I treaded upon those shallow waters. We were both at our respective cribs chilling when I began the 'getting to know you better' questions.

"Are you an only child?"

"Nope."

"Cool! How many siblings do you have?"

"Plenty."

I coughed, "Okay, what about aunts and uncles? You have any?"

"Yeah, a few."

"So, are they here in the city?"

"Yep."

"I'm just trying to get to know you Sabrina."

"That's cool."

"Well, you said that your parents were dead that's why I wanna know about your aunts and…"

"Look Sincere, my parents are alive and well they're just dead to me."

Subject dropped.

When her other line rang I'd hear her quietly clear her throat. Although not loud, it'd be loud enough to notice. It was almost like she was giving herself a signal.

Most of the time it was that worrisome Rusty calling and I'd ignore the interruption just like her, but I noticed.

Our most interesting convo was the ONE we had about sex. At this juncture of our friendship I was making daily calls just to say hello. We'd have lengthy talks but when it came to the subject of sex, she was adamant in her stance.

When I initially brought up the topic, I was at home flicking through channels with the volume on mute. Although the playoffs were on I didn't want to miss a word that floated out of her mouth.

She on the other hand was at the library when the subject was broached, "I don't talk about sex."

"And why not?"

"Because I don't have it."

I had been lying down, I sat up. I needed clarification. "You don't have what?"

She didn't answer.

"So you tellin' me that you don't have sex."

All of a sudden it sounded as if she was on the move. As if gathering her things to leave.

She tried evading the question, "So how many dates have we been on?"

Her ass thought she was slick. "Just like you don't like to be left hanging after asking a question, neither do I."

I could tell that she was walking.

"So we're going on how many months of talking?"

"Two, which means we've been on forty-five dates."

"Somebody can't count."

"I can count just fine. So when are you going to answer my question?" Shit, I wanted to get to the meat of the subject.

"When are you going to ask me out?"

"I've been asking you out for the last sixty days and you ain't budged."

"I thought you said it was forty-five."

She got me. The subject of sex was history. My mind was on the fact that after all this time, I might actually get to see her again. "Who gives a damn about the mental dates I've taken you on? Are ya 'boy friends' gonna let you up for air tomorrow night?" Yeah, I was being petty but didn't give a damn.

I heard her get into her car. "They surely will."

I was happy as hell. "Are we going to continue this conversation on our date?"

She responded to that real quick, "Where are you taking me?"

This girl had secrets and I was determined to have her reveal them to me, one delicate moment at a time.

The occasion had arrived. My second physical encounter with the mysterious Sabrina was upon me and she was well worth the wait.

I dressed to impress, making sure my image would forever be engrained in her memory. I wore black slacks, cream colored polo vest with a crisp white shirt underneath. The outfit was complete with a brand new pair of loafers.

I made reservations for Ruth's Chris, the kind of place that served fries in fancy glass cups. It was intimate enough to drown in her beautiful brown eyes while not crowding her, giving her some personal space.

I had to admit, a brotha was a little nervous. Sabrina was like no one I'd ever met before and things moving in slow motion had never been a part of my conquering repertor.

She beat me to the restaurant. When I walked inside and saw her standing in the entryway, my heart melted. Sabrina wore a sexy multicolored, retro dress, black and red western boots and a red headband. She'd been on her phone but hung up when she saw me. "Sincere?"

The smile that spread across her face let me know that she was pleased with what she saw.

"Hello there baby girl."

She smiled, and put her phone in her purse. I wondered which one of her 'friends' she'd been talking to, but when she walked my way and embraced me all thoughts of their needy asses vanished.

We were escorted to our table. I pulled out her chair and watched her plump bottom ease into her seat. After sitting we stared at each other, made small talk and then scanned the menus. Once our orders were placed we started sipping wine. My tongue began to get loose, "So, besides Club Sparkle what other clubs do you go to?"

"I don't do clubs," she said while we waited for our food.

"I can tell."

She was shocked, "What's that supposed to mean?"

"Girl, if I was Ray Charles and used my hands to follow your moves on the dance floor, I'd have thought you were white."

"Was I that bad?"

"You were so bad that I promise to never take you out dancing again."

We both laughed. When we quieted, she looked away at the deep red decor of the place. "I don't get out much" she said.

I smirked, "With all those friends? You got ta be kidding me."

"I'm serious. Even with all of them, I'm a homebody."

I leaned back in my chair. "You don't call men, but your phone is always ringing. You must be a high commodity." Although I noticed that she didn't like what I'd said I continued, "You don't do clubs but funny how that's where I met you."

"I was there only because my cousin begged me."

Yeah, right.

I frowned as I looked her in the eye. "You ain't havin' sex, but got a body that screams otherwise, and you dress sexy as all get out."

"I've paid a lot of money to be comfortable with the skin I'm in."

"So what? You saying you walking around with fake body parts?"

"Um, no. I'm not saying all that."

I let that response slide and continued, "You're secretive as hell when it comes to your family, who I wouldn't know exist if I hadn't hounded you. The list goes on and on. Tell me Sabrina, what do you do?" I was serious. The few months we'd been talking on the phone let me know that I was dealing with a peculiar woman, and I wanted to know more.

Sabrina didn't miss a beat. Baby girl leaned in on her elbows, with sadness in her eyes and vulnerability in her voice she whispered, "I love Sincere. And I love hard."

Since I wasn't up for no love games I switched gears, "Why is it that you never ask me any questions?"

She sat back and got comfortable, "Because, I'm the one doing the interviewing."

That made no sense, "But you never ask me anything."

"Exactly."

This woman was a piece of work. "Exactly? What's that mean?"

"It means that if you're asking questions, you're interested."

I lay my hands across the white tablecloth, dark skin standing out starkly, "Hold up, hold up." I tilted my head to the side as I thought about this game she was playing, "If I'm asking all the questions and you're not, that means that I'm interested and you're not. What's up with that?"

"Not necessarily, Sincere. When going on an interview, the interviewer asks the questions, not the applicant. My role in this is dual."

I liked that answer. I grinned, "What am I applying for?"

Her light brown eyes met mine, dead serious, "Rusty's position." When she saw the look on my face she burst into laughter.

I didn't see anything funny. Just as I was about to give my retort, our a la carte food arrived. We both ordered lamb. I was about to pick up a tender leg when she cleared her throat. I looked from our steaming meat; she had both her arms stretched across the table, ready to take my hands. "Will you do the honors?"

I looked at her like she was crazy. "The honor of what?"

She dropped her hands onto the table, shaking the silverware and looked at me with shock.

I smiled, reached across the table to put her soft hands into my rough ones. I closed my eyes, bowing my head. "Heavenly Father," I started, the familiarity of the words comforting, "I'd like to thank you for this opportunity to come together to break bread. I ask that it nourishes our bodies and keeps us healthy. It's in Jesus name I pray, amen." I looked at Sabrina, waiting on my accolades.

Without looking my way she mumbled that my prayer was kinda impressive and then dived into her food. Although I was starved, I couldn't help but watch as she picked up her fork and meticulously sliced into her meat. Granted I hadn't noticed her hands before but at that moment I had. They were small, flawless, and a turn on. "For you to be so conservative you sure wear some sexy polish on your nails."

As if I hadn't said a word she continued eating keeping her eyes on her plate, "Yep."

Okay, I may not have paid attention to her hands but I had immediately noticed her lips. They were glistening just as bright as the night I'd met her.

"How do you get that lipstick to stay on while eating?"

"Very carefully."

Damn them shits were sexy. After picking up a piece of lamb that had slithered off her fork she licked her fingers and I watched as her tongue curled around her tiny fingers. My eyes couldn't help but travel down to her neck. When she swallowed, I saw her little throat make room for her food. I was hungry for more than what was on my plate.

She started cutting up her asparagus, "Are you going to eat or sit there and watch me?"

"Watch you."

She smiled.

"Do you always eat one item at a time?"

After she finished chewing she answered, "I surely do."

My stomach growled so I picked up my napkin, placed it on my lap and for the remainder of dinner we ate in silence.

Later that night, as I replayed the conversation and meal through my mind, I noticed that not once, while eating, did Sabrina look at me. She kept her head down the rest of the time and cut her food in exact portions.

This girl had secrets. I was determined to reveal them one delicate moment at a time.

Sabrina...

As soon as I got home from our dinner date I called my cousin Shanika, excitedly pacing the house. "I can't believe I told him so much so soon!"

She sounded bored. "It was bound to happen." I could practically see her filing her nails. "So, where'd he take you?"

I'd called her on a high but she'd deflated my enthusiasm. I reached for the house phone, dialing in my number so it set off the call-waiting. "Hey cousin, I'mma hafta call you back. Malcolm is clicking in."

"Since when have you gotten off the phone with me for any of them?" She was both amused and annoyed.

She was right. I always talked to her no matter who was calling. "He sent me a text while out and I hadn't noticed until now, it must be important. Gotta go. Love you." I hung up before she could respond.

I felt bad for deceiving her but I didn't want my cousin messing up my vibe. It had been a long time since I'd been on a date, and I refused to allow anyone to take my joy.

Shanika...

My precious Sabrina and I have experienced a lot of similar tragedies. One is that we were both molested. Our fathers are brothers, and both those sick bastards preyed on their daughters.

The act was brutal, and we've dealt with those experiences in extremely different ways; Sabrina chose to keep her legs closed and fell in love with education. I chose to open my legs wide and fell in love with no one.

When I found the power my pussy held, I used it to survive.

I don't want for shit, and made sure I never did. I kept my body on point - Swimming an hour a day three times a week assured me that it stayed that way. I ate healthy as hell, and as ratchet as I am, I learned four languages and didn't go on no college campus to learn that shit either. Rosetta Stone was a bad bitch.

On the other hand, my cousin has made love to books for years and it paid off. Her ass got hella degrees, and she's smart as all get out.

Although she didn't pay for her crib, she maintained it well and invested a lot of money into transforming it to fit her unique personality.

It didn't hurt that she had unflinching help in her roommates, who would turn the world upside down to make sure she was straight. Without so much as a kiss, Sabrina was able to achieve what I laid on my back to get, and I ain't mad.

I actually love fuckin', but I wasn't doin' that shit for free.

Now, I always kept a close eye on my cousin. I had to.

It seemed that, because of the pure way she conducted herself, men thought they could run over Sabrina. Most figured that they could keep her on the sideline while they fucked the night away with other bitches. They were wrong.

When Sabrina found out about their indiscretions she cut the relationship off like it had gangrene. When she was through, she was through.

I watched those men damn near beg Sabrina to give them a second chance. She never did. I commended my girl for that. So when my strong, precious cousin started letting some of them move in with her, I had to do a double-take.

Sabrina had a band of brothers that lived for her. They were her chastity belt, and I must admit, I saw that as a little weird. How in hell you gonna live with men who broke your heart? That shit didn't make crazy sense, but to each their own.

I concluded that they all must need each other, 'cause ain't no way the niggas I dealt with would go for that. Even more crazy was when she met new guys, some actually accepted that shit! They're educated niggas too. My cousin must have the bomb game 'cause them fools be stuck like glue.

When pretty boy Fleming walked up to my cousin at the club, I smelled trouble.

Sincere Fleming. Who didn't know about that nigga? One of the finest representatives of fine, dark chocolate that ever walked this earth. That man was the epitome of tall, dark and handsome. I heard his tongue and dick game were on point too.

Not my type. A little too clean-cut for me. I like real roughnecks, no matter the country, and although Sabrina and I were attracted to the opposite type of men, I knew Sincere wasn't her type either. His butt was a straight up hoe and hadn't been in a steady relationship since Ramona's ass.

Yeah, I know about Ramona. She dipped into a few of the men I conquered. It wasn't for money, either. It was for straight up dick. That was just how she got down and eventually her ways caught up with her.

On the low, everyone knew Ramona's son, Brice, wasn't Sincere's. You couldn't tell by the way that man took care of that child though. That nigga Sincere laced Ramona's pockets on a regular, and she had plenty of material things to show for it. But, it was the time that man spent with that little boy that people envied.

Everyday I came across men who wouldn't spend two seconds with a child that had their blood pulsating through their veins. That wasn't the case for Sincere. Little boy Brice didn't look nothing like that man, and Sincere took him damn near everywhere he went. Showing him off to the world, like a proud papa.

Despite his good qualities as a parent, he had no good qualities as a man. Sincere was a dog. I knew, but Sabrina didn't.

The night at the club, when I yelled at Sincere for going hard for my cousin, most people may have thought that I was throwing salt on his game. They were right.

As sick as it sounds, the first man Sabrina ever fell in love with was her own damned father. Because of that relationship she wouldn't know how to handle her emotions when it came to men.

She fell in love too easily; found herself in some bad situations. The worst was Tyrone.

Unlike Sabrina, I could read niggas and knew Tyrone had been purchasing her all that shit to get some sex. Though most men respected her celibacy and got their rocks off elsewhere, Tyrone was different. He brought the pussy subject up way too much, and while at the Underground listening to some live music, I told her so.

"Cuz, I'm telling you," I told her, "Something's just not right with that nigga. He wants you waaay too bad."

"Stop being so paranoid," Sabrina shrugged me off, "He's just a guy who expresses his feelings differently."

I could not believe my ears. "A five thousand dollar Gucci purse? Now you know as well as I do that ain't no nigga nowhere going out like that."

"Cyprus did."

"And his ass is crazy too."

She giggled.

"I'm serious girl." I couldn't be mad at her, but I was worried. "Both them fools are nuts. You better mind your p's and q's when they're around."

She thought that shit was funny, but I didn't. Niggas like Tyrone were ticking time bombs, and when Tyrone detonated I was right there for my fam. She'd called me hysterical.

"Can you believe his ass actually chased me to my damn room?! Oh my God Shanika! All I could think about was daddy! That's why I fucked his ass up!"

Sabrina hardly ever cursed so I knew she was at her limit. As she spoke I wanted to scream "I TOLD YOU SO!" but held my peace. Instead, I envisioned the drama in my head.

That wasn't my first rodeo with Sabrina and her men issues. I was certain that it wouldn't be my last.

In spite of her ignorance I would always be a listening ear for my cousin. Like myself, Sabrina had to learn her lessons about men on her own, and that meant with Mr. Fleming as well.

Ramona...

Sincere has been in and out my life for years. We met in the middle of the semester in second grade. He was my new neighbor. The first time he rode the bus to school he sat next to me, and we became fast friends.

He always had a gentlemanly persona about him. Like an old man in a young boy's body. That's what made him cute. As far back as I remember he was always my champion. He was also the love of my life. We were ten years old and in the bedroom I shared with my thirteen-year old sister Cathy when we got curious and started exploring each other's bodies.

"Feel them Sincere. They startin' to really poke out."

He placed his boyish hands on my little breast nubs and felt, "They feel kinda like mine but softer," he observed.

"I know. I wonder when my mama is going to get me a bra."

He didn't answer. His eyes were glued to my little titties.

"Pay attention Sincere! I'm serious," I whined, "All my sisters have bras but me, and I cain't wait to get one."

I pulled my t-shirt down, walked over to the dresser and turned towards my friend. "You wanna see one?" I asked with an impish grin.

"Hell yeah."

I laughed and pulled out one of her lace bras. I handed it to Sincere. He felt it as if it were a fragile piece of expensive silk, then brought it to his nose, "She smells good."

I snatched the bra out of his hand and laughed when he protested.

"Hey! I wasn't finished with that."

I walked to my best friend, dropped my Cathy's bra, lifted up my t-shirt and placed his hands on my breast, "Now squeeze."

He did.

"I'm not going to show you any more of my sister's bras. You don't need those when you can have these."

With drool seeping out of the corner of his mouth he was speechless. Instead of answering, he nodded his head.

Our first time having sex was clumsy. It was my idea not his. On multiple occasions I heard my sister screwing one of the many boys she'd sneak through our bedroom window, so I functioned off what I'd heard her doing.

My parents and siblings trusted Sincere. He had become like part of the family. Dad treated him like the son he never had since there were only girls under our roof.

Because of that trust Sincere and I were left alone a lot. During one of those moments I would broach the subject of sex to Sincere. It was summer break, and we were in my living room watching cartoons.

"My sister had another boy over last night."

"So?"

"So? So I heard them doin' it."

He didn't answer. He was so engulfed in the cartoon that he ignored me.

"Did you hear what I said? I heard them doin' it. It was funky too."

"I don't care about that."

What Sincere didn't know was that I'd found myself getting aroused lately; The sounds I heard those boys make while screwing my sister turned me on. Especially when they had their orgasm. The power my sister's pussy held to make those boys moan became intoxicating, and I wanted to see if I could make Sincere feel the same way. He was making it hard.

I needed his attention on me and not that stupid TV. I took a different route.

"Have you started getting hair down there yet?"

"No. Why?"

"Because I got some more. You wanna see?"

"Not really."

I hopped off the couch and turned off the television. With my hand on my hip I stood in front of it.

He was pissed, "What you do that for?"

"Sincere! I'm trying to talk to you but you won't listen."

"Because we're supposed to be watching cartoons. You know how I get when my shows come on. Now move."

I ignored him, "I was trying to tell you that I got some more hairs but you weren't paying attention." I started taking off all my clothes. That was something I'd never done before. Sincere had seen my body parts, and I his, but we'd never stood totally nude in front of each other. After stripping, I stood in nothing but my socks. He could barely talk.

"Where's those extra hairs?" He asked, probably for lack of anything else to say.

I bent at the knee and looked down. I placed my hands on my twat in search of the new hairs I knew weren't there. "I know they in here somewhere."

As I looked, Sincere's shadow covered my body and I raised my head. He was standing in front of me, a serious look on his face. I was kinda scared.

He placed his shaking hands on my bare shoulders and brought me close for a kiss. His lips touched mine and although our lips were closed his felt wonderful. I pulled back and swallowed. "I think you're supposed to put your tongue into my mouth."

He nodded and came in for practice number two. Our mouths were still closed, and when he tried putting his tongue into my mouth our teeth clacked together.

He huskily whispered, "Open your mouth Ramona."

So I did. He again placed his lips on mine and he slowly slid his tongue inside. It felt good. As the pressure of his hands on my shoulders increased, I placed my hands on his thin waist and we pulled each other close. Our heads were on autopilot. We tilted our heads to allow room for more exploring. His tongue on mine was new, soft and comforting. Because I didn't know when my parents or siblings would be home, I broke the kiss, picked up my clothes and led Sincere to my bedroom. After locking the door I turned to find him totally in my space. I walked around him, grabbed his hand and led him to my bed.

"We need to hurry up Sincere."

He stood dumbfounded. "For what?"

"We about to have sex, boy."

He looked confused. I lay back on my bed and then pulled him down on top of me. After bringing his lips to mine, any reservations he had about sleeping with me were out the window.

I whispered "Pull your pants down."

Without hesitation he did what I asked. I leaned upon my elbows and watched. When I saw his thing pop out, my eyes got big.

"What?" He asked, sounding concerned.

I'd seen Sincere's dick a number of times but it was always semi-hard. What I was beholding at that moment was a full-fledged erection. I was having second thoughts. Then memories of my sister causing those boys to make those noises crossed my mind.

"Nothin'. Come on."

When my sister did her business it was dark in the room, but so dark that I wasn't able to see their body movements. I recalled my sister and those boys and instructed Sincere on what to do.

"Okay, now get between my legs."

I opened my legs and he did as instructed. Still on my elbows I told him to put his thing into my private part. I watched as he took ahold of his hairless shaft. It was standing at total attention.

It took numerous tries before he was able to get inside. When he did, I watched as his face changed from worry to pure ecstasy.

"Oooooh shit!"

That was the same thing I'd heard the boys screwing my sister say and I felt empowered. I watched as his face took on different expression. The sight I was beholding was a beautiful one. It's sad to say, but I wasn't able to watch for long. When Sincere dropped his full weight on top of me, I felt a sharp pain that caused me to cry out.

"Ouch Sincere! It hurts. Get up! Stop!"

I tried pushing him off me, but Sincere was not having that. He had me in a stronghold and held me close as he went in and out.

"Ouch! Sincere!"

"Ahhhhhhhh! Oh shit!"

I held on tight, praying that it would be over soon. To my surprise, I didn't have a long wait. As the pain subsided, I started enjoying the feel of Sinceres dick. I liked the sounds he was making, too. I slowly opened my eyes and looked at Sincere. His mouth was wide open and his eyes were closed tight. I saw some spit coming my way and turned my head to the side. It landed in my ear and just as I was about to push him away, he held me tight, started pumping real hard and then let out a deep groan.

"Oooooooh! Mmmmmm! Oooooooh!"

His grunted moan caused me to wrap my legs tightly around his waist, and I never wanted to let go.

When he was finished he lay on top of me, breathing hard and fast.

"Get up Sincere. You're heavy." He didn't move. His heart was beating rapidly and it wasn't until it'd slowed down that he climbed off. Putting an arm over his eyes, he lay on his back next to me.

"Let's get dressed and finish watching cartoons." He said - I could only see his lips moving.

I hadn't moved either. I could not believe that I'd just had sex. Although not the best experience, it wasn't the worse. I thought about my parents. "We need to get a move on, Sincere. Somebody might come home."

He slowly rolled out of bed and stood, almost tripping over his pants. Once they were up and fastened he watched as I put on my clothes. When I looked into his eyes I saw desire. I turned away in pain.

When I did my eyes got big. "Oh shit!"

His eyes followed mine and spotted the big red dot on my bedsheets. I was sore down there and didn't wanna budge but after seeing the blood stain I went into panic mode. I put my pain to the side and started getting a move on. "Help me Sincere."

He stood stock still.

I rambled as I ripped the sheets off the bed, "It's nothing. I heard my sisters talking about how the first time there would be some blood. Come on! We need to hurry up before somebody comes home."

When he remained immobile I exhaled loud and hard, then continued snatching up my white, bloodstained bedlinen. Taking the sheets to the laundry room, I threw them into the washer, dumped in a whole lotta bleach and set the hot cycle. After replacing the sheets with clean ones, I went into the living-room where I found Sincere on the couch watching cartoons. I cautiously sat next to him.

Although we had our eyes on the TV, I knew neither of us were watching. We were both thinking about what had just happened.

We said nothing for a long time, drowning in our thoughts. He was the first to speak and it was without words.

When he got enough courage, Sincere took my hand into his and squeezed. That's when we became boyfriend and girlfriend.

Our relationship was a turbulent one. We would both discover that there are a whole lotta other pussies and dicks out there and cause each other a lot of pain. I inflicted the initial blow.

We were sixteen and the only souls at my house when all hell broke loose.

"Who you been with Ramona?"

"Sincere I promise you that I haven't been with nobody. I swear."

"My dick has been itching for days and it hurt when I pissed. My boy had to tell me what it was all about. Now who the hell you been with?"

He was irate.

"Sincere you know where I am at all times. If we ain't together then we on the phone. I don't have time to sleep around 'cause you always around."

He raised an eyebrow. "So what? You sayin' you don't want me around?"

"No, no, no. I'm just sayin' that we're always together. It leaves little room for either of us to go behind the other's back."

He was quiet for longer than was necessary and then his face softened. "You know what? You're right. We are always around each other."

He picked up his Levi jacket that lay on the couch, then walked to the mahogany front door he'd become so familiar with. Placing his hand on the doorknob, he dropped his head and then opened the door to leave. With broken eyes, he turned and looked at me.

"You told me that you were going to the mall with your sister the other day. I know that I'd told you that I was gonna chill at the crib but I didn't. My boy called and wanted to go workout on the court, so we did. While there I saw your sister on the sideline. I don't know where the hell you were, but I know where she was not." He left.

That one incident shifted our relationship forever. Sincere never trusted me again.

We would break up and make up a lot. I tried over and over again to prove myself, but to no avail.

I knew, deep down, Sincere loved me, but he could never bring himself to trust me, no matter the circumstance.

When I found out that Sincere stepped out on me, it broke my heart. I was hurt not only because it was with one of my closest friends, but also because the heffa went around talkin' about his good lovin' to anybody who would listen. All I'd asked was for him to put her in her place. He wouldn't. The shit was killing me.

When I could take it no more, I called it quits.

He'd parked in front of my house after school. We'd been arguing the whole way there.

"You just gon' let Phyllis run her mouth about yo dick like that Sincere? Everybody and their mama know that we together and you just gon' let her disrespect me like that?"

"Ramona! I cannot control what that girl do!"

"You shouldn't have ever fucked her in the first place!"

He got that stupid calm look on his face, "And yo ass shouldn't have ever gave me a damned disease!"

He always threw that shit up in my face, "It happened one damned time Sincere! This bitch running around town talkin' bout you hittin' it on a regular! How in the hell am I supposed to cope with that in school? Huh? I am the damned laughing stock of our city."

"I'm going to need for you to calm yo ass down! Now how in the hell do you think I feel when I'm up in my boy's face all the time knowin' he know what you gave me? And I took you back after the fact. My shit ain't no different than yours. It's just more people know."

"Why her Sincere?! Why in the hell did you have to fuck her? All these bitches out here jealous of our relationship and you choose her dirty ass to creep on?"

"She came at me! I wasn't payin' that chick no attention! Just like you told me I'm tellin' you it was just that one time! Now drop that shit!"

Sincere very rarely yelled, so I knew he was at his wits end but so was I. After bursting into tears I screamed, "I cain't do this Sincere! I just can't!"

"Cain't do what?"

He looked shocked.

"THIS! US! IT'S OVER!"

"You sure you wanna say that?"

I started hitting him, but not hard enough to hurt, my hands small against his broad, still-growing chest.

"What do you mean? That bitch is fucking bullying me with her words! I cain't take it no more."

Sincere held me in his arms. While squeezing me tight, he told me over and over he was sorry. Deep down I knew he was. I also knew that there was nothing he could do about that trick going around talking about my man, but I had to try. He had been my last resort at silencing her.

My sisters and me kicking her ass hadn't worked. In spite of the black eyes we'd given her, Phyllis continued to use her tongue to cut me deep. The wounds sliced me to the white meat. It was too much for me to handle.

Sincere and I broke up. We would numerous times, but somehow always managed to cascade back into each other's arms. That is, until Sabrina.

Sincere...

Ramona was, and will always be, one of the most beautiful women I've ever known. Even as kids she held a rare sensuality about herself. Although a skinny rail with big kneecaps when I first met her, she grew sexier with age. In our teens, her measurements were perfect. Long slender neck, perky firm breast, thin waist with childbearing hips. Having Brice did nothing to hide her sexuality. I loved kissing her ebony skin. Her hair was sandy brown while growing up, the auburn color she dyed her hair kept her looking youthful. Breathtakingly beautiful on the outside, the woman was treacherous and corroded on the inside.

I was at Ramona's checking on my little man. I know he's not mine. Hell, we both know. When his half-breed ass slithered his way out of her revolving-door pussy, my heart broke into a million pieces.

For months she had me believing she was pregnant by me. After delivering, she saw the look of shock on my face and broke into tears.

"His daddy is dead, Sincere. He died soon after I found out I was pregnant. I'm so sorry. I was scared and didn't know what to do. I'm so sorry."

I was paralyzed.

Stuck, I felt sick to my stomach.

Did she just say what the hell I think she said?

Although the entire damned staff had heard her confession of admitted betrayal, the doctor had the nerve to ask me if I wanted to cut the umbilical cord. I turned my head in his direction and looked at that red, slimy creature they called a child and wanted to run out of the room. I couldn't believe Ramona! Her words suckerpunched my gut and I damned near couldn't breathe.

"We don't have much time, son."

What Ramona didn't know was while she was throwing her theatrics at the head of the bed, at the foot of the bed her doctor whispered something in my ear.

"Blood don't make you a father, young man. I've watched you cherish this woman and her unborn child. She is who she is, but don't let that dictate who you are."

I looked at Ramona's trifling ass and shook my head.

Turning back to the doctor and looking at that baby swaddled in his arm, I took the medical scissors out of a nurse's hand and cut the umbilical cord.

As they sucked snot out of his nose and mouth and cleaned him, I took a step to the side. I watched as the staff held and cared for him as if he were a precious jewel. I looked up at his mother.

All I could do was continue to shake my head.

Damn!

Ramona and I had been through some doozies, but this took the cake.

As I walked to the head of the bed I noticed that her legs were still wide open. I watched as the doctor tried putting some closure to a hole that would take a miracle to give decency. I eventually shifted my gaze and looked down at that beautiful woman, and couldn't stop shaking my damned head.

What kinda shit is this?!

She paid me no attention. I looked from her to her baby and knew I witnessed Ramona falling in love. At that moment she was a changed woman, but it was too late.

With her eyes on her new baby she reached for my hand and held it.

"He's perfect Sincere. He's absolutely perfect."

I followed her gaze and had to agree.

Although he was as red as the blood that had seeped out of her vagina while giving birth, after cleaning him up and placing him in the baby warmer, from where I was standing, he was truly handsome.

"Sincere?" I hadn't noticed that she'd turned her head and was looking at me. "Well, you know we agreed to name him Sincere Junior." As soon as she'd said those words she yelled out in pain. We both looked between her thighs.

"Ouch! Be careful down there. That shit hurt!"

Guess what she said had affected somebody other than me.

I looked at my once upon a time best friend and let her know how I felt, "Sincere Junior? You changed all that, Ramona."

The doc between her massive legs coughed his approval of my response.

She smiled in understanding and then turned her head to look at her son. "Brice. Brice Alexander Fleming. How's that sound?"

When she said the last name she cautiously turned her head back towards me. She had a worried look on her face. It was warranted. I smiled, kissed her on the forehead, popped off my sweaty latex gloves and walked over to the baby warmer.

I looked upon my new son, squirted on some hand sanitizer, took his little pink hand into mine then sat.

As I rubbed the back of his soft skin I looked at the woman I still loved. As she beheld me trying to bond with a child that wasn't mine, she cried.

"I'm so sorry Sincere."

I turned my head back towards the baby. "You're good Ramona." I said, "You're good and yes, I think Brice Alexander Fleming fits him."

Quickly, one of the nurses handed me a fresh pair of gloves."Congratulations Mr. Fleming. Would you like to hold your son?"

I snapped those gloves on and watched as she gently placed my boy into my arms. Although nervous as hell, I held him securely but felt some kinda way. His ass was definitely mixed. Brice had red skin with straight, charcoal-colored hair. If I hadn't watched him come out of Ramona's pussy, I'd have sworn he was a white baby.

As I looked at him I started to feel uncomfortable. My ass was black as night, holding a baby that would never look like me. Just as I was about to abandon ship, Brice started squirming. I nervously looked around and was rescued by a nurse.

"I think somebody is hungry. Time to go to mama." She carefully took him out of my arms and walked towards Ramona.

The nurse asked, "You are still nursing aren't you?"

I answered before Ramona could, "She sure in the hell is."

Ramona looked at me like I was crazy and I looked right back at her.

I removed my gloves, washed my hands and watched as the nurse instructed Ramona on how to nurse. As I stood next to the bed I still had feelings of reservations. They surfaced when Brice latched onto her titty and started eating. Ramona was damn near as dark as me, but had gotten darker with pregnancy. Seeing his extra light skin next to her dark tone caused me to grimace.

I looked at Ramona. Her lids were barely opened.

"You better wake up and feed this baby."

She didn't budge but neither did Brice. I pulled up a chair, reached across Ramona's bloated stomach and found Brice's little hand.

I placed his tiny pale fingers around my big black index finger. As soon as I did he gripped it.

"Alright," I grinned at my son, "Somebody's gotta strong little arm." I watched as my son opened his blue eyes for the first time. I realized the very first face he'd ever lay eyes on was mine.

I thought my heart would explode with love.

Like magic, all the anger, animosity, and bitterness dissipated. Poof. Gone. "Hey there little man. Welcome to the world."

The shattering of my heart, knowing Brice wasn't mine, reversed and healed with an innocent look. Brice forever solidified my co-parenting friendship with Ramona.

Mrs. Fleming. . .

I did it alone, and I think I did good with my son.

Becoming a single parent wasn't by choice, but after his father's death I chose not to remarry. I didn't want my son being raised by another man. I just couldn't stomach it. Besides, nobody compared to my Charley. Nobody.

I've always kept the line of communication open with my boy and the realities of this world clear.

"Tell me if you're having sex Sincere. There are certain steps you need to take to make sure that you don't make no mistakes, if you know what I mean."

"I know what you mean mama."

I was also blunt when it came to girls, "Don't be out here disrespecting these young ladies. We have it hard enough without the male species adding to the traumatic experiences we have to endure in this thing called life."

"I wouldn't do that. You raised me better."

"Well, I hope so."

Ramona didn't sit well with me. When my son brought Brice to see me confirmed why. Before I could even get the words out he stopped me.

"I see the same thing you see but he's mine."

That settled that, and I had me a brand spankin' new grandson.

Sincere...

I had a key to her house and dared any of her 'friends' to say something.

After letting myself inside, I walked over to Ramona who was sitting on the couch and gave her a kiss on the forehead.

"'Sup Sincere?"

"Nothin' but the rent. Where my boy at?" She didn't answer as I walked back to his bedroom, just kept flipping through her Ebony magazine. I knocked lightly two times then opened his door.

Brice spun around in his chair.

"Daddy!"

I ain't gon' lie, there were days that the sight of him made my stomach turn and I wondered what he would have looked like if he had been my blood. I loved him true enough, but the thought was deep in the back of my mind and would surface from time to time.

"You doin' ya homework?"

I sat on the edge of his bed and pulled his desk chair close to me. His excitement put a grin on my face.

"Yep! Did mommy tell you that they wanna skip me up a grade?"

Hell to the naw! I was gonna get with Ramona bout that. I looked at my pale, blue eyed son, with the straight black hair and smiled, "They do? Well boy genius I'm not surprised. What did you eat for lunch today?"

Brice was on the chunky side. I did his grocery shopping to ensure he had a good diet, but Ramona's childish behind rewarded him with junk food. Even for stupid shit like cleaning up his room.

"Mama made me a good chicken salad with those cranberries I like. Can you get some more when you go to the store?"

He always got excited when it came to the subject of food.

"Yeah, yeah. What else?"

"Some apple slices and celery with peanut butter. And of course my water."

"That's what's up. Now let me see that homework."

We finished his schoolwork, ate a light dinner as a family, then Brice and I watched a movie in his bedroom. Brice was five and bright as hell. I knew he got those smarts from his daddy because although Ramona wasn't no dummy, she sure in the hell didn't have his academic skills.

When he was falling asleep, I woke his little butt up and told him to go brush his teeth and get into the tub. As he started taking off his clothes I asked my boy something that I'd never asked him before.

"Hey son, what do you want to be when you grow up?"

I watched as Brice yawned and walked towards his bathroom and replied, "A policeman."

I froze.

After tucking my son into bed, I went into the living room and sat next to Ramona, "Where's ya man at?" I teased.

"You know where he is."

"Come sit on daddy's lap."

She smiled, put her magazine down and lay her head on my thighs, "Not happenin'."

I laughed, "Girl you better get yo' ass up on this dick."

She lifted her hand and playfully touched my hardness, "Where's that crazy ass Veronica?"

I didn't answer.

"Her ass is like a plague." Ramona complained. "Even after all this time she won't go away."

I looked at her full lips. She was doin' too much talkin' so I shut her up with a kiss. She tasted of peppermint. When she moaned I deepened the kiss and started rubbing her breast.

"Damn girl you feel good." I lifted my head and pulled her up onto my lap. She had on a skirt with no panties - Her prearranged attire when she knew I was strolling through for an extended visit.

She straddled me, then rose up on her knees when she felt me going for my belt, "Hurry up. I've missed you."

She didn't have to tell me twice. After pulling down my pants I reached into my back pocket for a condom.

"Sinceeeere?"

I paid her whining no attention. She had a man and I didn't know who else she had goin' up in her. I was not trying to have a repeat of when we were younger.

"Don't start Ramona."

She shut up, and once the condom was on immediately mounted me, "Ooooooh yes. Yes. I miss this shit boy."

I put my head back on the couch and let her ride. Ramona was an excellent lover. Although she had some whoreish ways she also had the bomb pussy.

"Oh Sincere! You know your shit's good." She was slow riding the dick and the familiarity of her sex started to hit my brain.

"Ride that shit girl." I took her shirt, pulled it up and started sucking on her braless breast.

She threw her head back. "Yes baby. Mmmmmm. Yes. Suck on them titties boy."

The more I sucked the faster she rode. Her shit was sopping wet and smelled like ripe fruit.

"You the only man who can make me cum. Make me cum Sincere. Please baby. Take me there."

Yeah right.

I placed my hands on her fat ass and started rocking her back and forth, "You like that shit Ramona? You like this big black dick?"

She grabbed onto my shoulders and tried to increase the speed. Not happenin'. I was rocking her in slow motion. As I did I could hear the wetness of her fluids and that shit turned me on. I opened my eyes, looked at her long, succulent neck and went in for the kill. She stopped all movement.

"Cut that shit out Sincere. We ain't kids no more and I know how you get when you excited. Tame that shit or we stop."

I ignored her and licked her throat. She let out a soft moan. As I started up my pace I kissed her softly on her face, lips, neck and ears. She trembled, grabbed the back of my head and we devoured each other's lips. Round and round her hips went and I met every rotation with raised hips.

"Fuck that shit Sincere. Tear this pussy up. Oh yes!"

I wanted to eat her out so bad but didn't dare. Her scent had my mouth watering. "Whose pussy is this? Huh?"

"Yours always Sincere. Always." She opened her eyes and I saw the girl I'd fallen in love with. "I'll always love you Sincere. No matter who I have in my life I'll always love you."

I placed my lips onto hers knowing the things she said were true. I felt the same, but I'd die before I spoke it so I told her in my dick strokes.

"Yes! Yes! Yes! Oh Sincere! Please! Please! Please!"

I pounded that ass. She turned into an animal, just the way I like her. "Fuck that shit nigga." She knew I hated that word except when having sex. Before she screamed out in pleasure I put my mouth onto hers, not wanting our son to mess up our moment. She held onto me tight and as I felt her pussy grip my dick, I reciprocated the gesture and came long and hard. "Oh shit Ramona! Oh shit girl. Oh shit!"

Afterward we held each other tight.

"I love you Sincere." She kissed my eyes. "I'm so sorry. So, so sorry." She kissed my cheeks. "I have always loved you."

We kissed deeply, allowing our heartbeats to normalize. Once my dick was soft I lifted her off me and placed her on the couch.

"Make sure you spray that spot where you sittin'. Don't want my son around your juices."

"You are such a buzz kill."

I ignored her and slowly took my condom off and held it tight as I fastened my pants. After making my way to the bathroom, I flushed the condom and cleaned myself off. I looked up to see her watching me. "When were you going to tell me about them trying to skip Brice?"

"He don't give me time to tell you shit!" She looked frustrated. "But yeah, they wanna do that foolery but I told them no. He's already the youngest in his class."

I put the dirty face towel into the clothes hamper, zipped my pants and walked past her to the front door. She was right behind me.

"Make sure you feed him right."

"I am Sincere."

With my hand on the knob, I spoke over my shoulder.

"And before I come back, I want you to talk him outta wanting to be a policeman. I don't know where the fuck he got that shit from but it needs to get got!" I left her house in a huff.

Ramona...

As soon as I locked the front door I went into my son's room and woke him up. "Brice, what did you say to your daddy? What in the world did you say to him?"

My boy rubbed his eyes in confusion. "Huh, mommy?"

I knew that Brice didn't know any better but I also knew Sincere never used the "F" word.

After placing my too-big son on my lap, I rocked him back to sleep. I knew first thing in the morning we'd have a discussion on why he didn't want to become a policeman.

Sincere...

It would take me two days to get over what my son said, and three to pick up the phone. "You miss me?"

Sabrina laughed, "Sorry my man, but naw."

That kinda stung. "Maybe it'll help if I told you that the days I haven't spoken to you I took you out on dates."

"Is that riiiiight? So where'd your dreams take us?"

"That's what's crazy. During all the dreams we dined on sandy beaches."

"Now that sounds interesting."

"It was, man. And you were teasing me by wearing a sexy ass swimsuit showing off that banging body."

"Now I know that was a dream."

"Don't tell me you don't wear swimsuits?"

She laughed again, "Naw I'm not going to say all that, but I will say I don't like showing my body. I believe that that's something that should be reserved for my husband. Gotta leave something to the imagination."

She don't leave nothing to the imagination with all those tight ass clothes she be wearing. "True, true. A sneak peek never hurt nobody."

"I totally disagree but anywho, how was your week?"

I let her have that one, "It was cool. Helped Mom out and consistently wore that black uniform. Same crap, different day. I cain't believe it. You actually asked me a personal question."

"Desperate measures my friend."

"Okay, okay." I sat quietly for a minute wondering if it would prompt her to start a conversation. It didn't. "You know, we've been chatting for a while. Would you like to meet my mom? We can go to the clothing store, then get a snack or something."

"Sorry, Sincere. I promised Walter that I'd help his son with his homework. Maybe another time."

"Who in the hell is Walter?"

"Excuse me?"

Baby girl had way too many friends. I was kinda feeling Sabrina, but not so much those men. All those 'friends' had me thinking it may be time to move on.

"Look Sabrina, I think you are a mysteriously cool chic but I'm not feeling all those friends..."

"And why not?"

"Because… shit. I'm not used to taking a number and that's what I gotta do with you."

"Didn't nobody tell you not to call me for two days."

I smiled. "Oh, so you been keepin' count?"

She got quiet and I let her. I wasn't interrupting her silent zone either. Hell, it was time for her to do some talking for a change. But after five damned minutes I 'bout gave in.

"Walter just text me. I suppose we can meet at your mother's store and then chat for a while afterward."

Homegirl had been keeping count. The smile on my face broadened. "You better be glad I find you intriguing. I was about to drop yo ass like a hot potato."

She let out a hearty laugh. I knew I had to tread lightly so with caution, I asked, "You gonna let me be a gentleman and pick you up? Or do you not ride in cars with men?" I'll be damned if her ass didn't get quiet on me. This shit was for the birds.

"You can pick me up. Just give me a few to get myself together."

With that answer my heart skipped a beat. For some reason, I knew Sabrina was stepping out of her comfort zone. "Thank you baby girl."

After giving me her address, without saying goodbye, she hung up the phone.

Sabrina...

After hanging up on Sincere, I made my rounds through the house. I set it in order, then got ready for Sincere to meet my friends.

Chapter Three

Sincere...

I hopped into the shower and made sure I was looking and smelling good for Sabrina. After checking myself one last time in the mirror, I made my way to my Land Rover. I put her address into my GPS and began the trek towards Sabrina's private world.

I consider myself a patient man, especially after all that Ramona had sent me through. But I wasn't so sure I had what it would take to wait on Sabrina's secretive ass. I've come across some peculiar women, but none like her. She required a special kind of patience. With all the panties being thrown my way I wasn't sure I had what it took to figure her out. I just hoped she wasn't another basketcase like Veronica.

After a forty-five minute drive with nothing but the sound of my thoughts in my head, I finally made it to Sabrina's house.

Angela Moore

I pulled into her circular driveway and was thoroughly impressed. "This is the shit!"

Her crib had to be worth well over a million dollars. With the precisely manicured lawns, I knew she was laced with bread.

Now I see why she is so secretive.

I took off my seatbelt, and got out of my truck. Before I could reach the front porch I was greeted by a very pale outstretched hand.

"You must be Sincere. Glad to meet you, I'm Cyprus."

Like a ghost he appeared. I hadn't noticed him coming out of the house.

What kinda shit is this?!

As soon as he said those words it reminded me of Ramona's stank ass. I did not want to shake that man's hand, especially if it had in any way touched Sabrina. Then I saw her peeking out the window so obliged and mumbled "Sincere it is, my man. Sincere it is," while walking to the porch. I did a quick scan of the man. He was one of those surfer boy types. Sandy blond hair, fair tanned skin and piercings blue eyes. He had the physique too.

I reached for the screen door, but missed it because it was opened by another man. "Hey Sincere!"

He was drying his hands on a dish towel. He too was a handsome man with dark skin, a keen, straight nose, full lips and light brown eyes. His head was shaved bald.

"My name is Walter, and this here is my son Junior."

I looked down at a little boy that looked just like his daddy and again Ramona popped into my head. I didn't even shake that brotha's hand. I just walked in looking for Sabrina.

Frustrated, I asked, "Where's the lady of the hour?"

This is some bullshit and I definitely don't like the way it smells.

All three stood in the entryway staring me down.

Surfer boy answered, "She'll be down in a second."

There was something about the way he said that that didn't sit well with me.

"Naw, I just saw her in the window. Matter of fact, I'm out."

Just as I said those words, she came skipping down the stairs. She snatched a jacket I hadn't notice was on a chair, grabbed my hand and pulled me out the front door.

"See you guys later, and Junior, be nice to your tutor."

She led me back to my truck, and I watched as she waited for me to open the door. I wanted to tell her to skip her butt back up to her Three's Company household, but stopped.

She was looking and smelling delicious. While she looked at me with her pretty brown eyes I opened the door. "You better be glad you're cute."

She thought that was hilarious.

As I ran around to my side of the truck I took a quick look at her house. I'd be damned if there weren't three men standing on her front porch looking at me with envy. Where that third one came from was a mystery.

I fastened my seatbelt and didn't inquire about the circus I'd just beheld. Figured I'd save that for another day. She thought otherwise.

"Sorry about that?"

I played brand new. "About what?"

I glanced at her. She was looking out the window, "Nothing."

She was captivating. Sabrina was beautiful, and her innocence charming. I knew that even if Sabrina lived with fifty men, none of them would ever have the pleasure of touching her body. Although her presence dripped seduction she didn't focus on it. She let men do that. Instead, she flaunted undeniable perfection. She knew she was tempting, but she wasn't arrogant about it.

I liked that. I press play on my CD player and let Eric Benet coast us to my mom's shop.

After parking in my reserved spot, I opened Sabrina's door and led her into the store. Mom was nowhere to be found, so I showed baby girl around. I could tell she was impressed with my fashion knowledge so I lay it on thick.

When I got to the new season of winter dresses, she was in heaven. In an instant she was engulfed in women's favorite pastime: Shopping.

As she browsed, I made my way to the front counter. Just as I was about to ask about Mom's whereabouts, she walked out of the storage room with a handful of boxes.

"Woman! What do you think you are doing?" I took the merchandise from her hands and placed them on the counter.

"I'm no cripple, Sincere."

I paid her no mind and started opening packages. They were filled with bracelets and earrings. I started putting them on their respective shelves.

Forty-five minutes later Sabrina came towards me with the desired items she wanted to purchase. I hadn't forgotten about her, I just knew how women were when it came to shopping. I saw it every time I worked the storefront.

"See anything else you like?"

She took a pair of earrings out of my hand and placed them with her other items. "Surely do."

Her smile made my day.

Mother cleared her throat. She knew Sabrina wasn't a "regular" customer - My mom knew her child and she also knew my type. "Oh my bad. Sabrina, this is my mother Mrs. Fleming. Mommy, this is Sabrina."

Did I just call my mother 'mommy'?

I hadn't called her that in years. I shook that off and beamed with pride as approval slid across Mom's face.

"Hello there Sabrina. Glad to meet you."

Sabrina warmly accepted the hand that was extended towards her. "My pleasure Mrs. Fleming. Sincere speaks of you often and it's great to finally put a face to a name."

Mom was pleased, "Are you finished with your shopping? I'll be glad to place these items to the side if you'd like to continue."

"I think I'm about through..."

"You can put those on my tab..." Before I could finish they both looked my way.

"What tab son?"

"That'll be charge Mrs. Fleming."

They left me hanging and walked to the checkout.

For some odd reason I wanted to have Sabrina all to myself. It wasn't as if I didn't want my mother to meet her. I was cool with that.

It's just that, I realized that once she was out of my presence she'd be around all that extra testosterone. I wanted to stand out from the crowd. I knew that couldn't happen with a lot of people around. Including my mother.

Sabrina's tab came to over seven hundred dollars. When she had her receipt in hand, I grabbed the other and slowly pulled her out of the store, telling my mom that I'd call her later.

"That was kinda rude Sincere." We made it to my vehicle and once she was secure, I slammed the door on that comment.

She continued when I climbed into the driver's side, "I'm serious. I wanted to talk to your mom some more. I was going to ask what kind of cereal you liked as a kid."

I started my truck, "Captain Crunch."

We looked at each other and burst into laughter.

Although it was a brisk Fall day, we went to an ice cream shop close to my mother's clothing store. Sabrina's suggestion. Once inside we placed our orders, took our seats and got to lickin'. Ice cream may not have been a wise choice, so to get my mind off her luscious lips, I asked a question to which I didn't really want an answer.

"So what was up with them boys?"

She smiled, got up and went to ask for a bowl for her ice cream. She knew whom I was talking about. As she made her way to the counter, the sway of her hips were like a gentle breeze. I hadn't realized that there were mirrors throughout the parlor. When I did, she was watching me watching her. She didn't look happy.

Oh well.

I watched her walk back too. I couldn't help it. Sabrina was sexy as hell. She sat and took a spoonful of ice cream.

"They're my roommates."

What kinda shit is this?

I wasn't happy with that answer and she knew it, "Roommates?" I asked skeptically.

"Yes, roommates. I have a seven bedroom, eight bath home. At one time they were attracted to me; now we live together."

"At one time?"

"Yes Sincere. At one time. Anyway, just know that they are truly my friends and we love each other very much. They've all crossed my life and played a vital part in my becoming the woman I am today."

I wasn't impressed. "Is that right?"

"Yes it is. Just like I'm sure you'll play a part as well."

"Whatever." I started squirming in my seat.

She looked like she was holding back a laugh. "Why you say that?"

"Because just from what you're telling me, everybody who somehow affected your life ends up living with you. I'm cool on that."

She let loose her laugh. "It's not like that. I'll tell you about it one day."

"I bet you will. How are your classes coming along?"

"Great. Malcolm is helping me with my anatomy class."

"Why couldn't he help homeboy's son with his homework?"

"Aren't you observant. And homeboy's name is Walter. He couldn't help him because he doesn't have the patience."

"I bet he doesn't."

She laughed at the frown on my face. "So, how long has your mom had her shop? I think I've been in there before."

"Since I was a kid. She's been evolving. I keep telling her that she should open another one but she won't. It's like her firstborn and I think she feels she'll be abandoning her if she opens another."

"Why does she call it 'Justice'?"

I'd been asked that question many a day and never answered truthfully and I wasn't about to start. "Who knows. I never asked and she never volunteered. I just assumed that it's a name she'd have given her daughter if she had one."

The same generic answer I'd given over the years - I'd mastered that lie, and shifted the focus of the discussion. "I see you're opening up and starting to ask me questions."

"Is that what I'm doing?"

"Yep. So I'mma take advantage of this moment of kindness and repeat a question I asked before. Tell me again why you don't have sex."

A crooked smile spread across her perfect chocolate face, "Never told you the first time."

"Really? I coulda sworn you had."

She started eating her melted ice cream and didn't stop until she was finished. I'd smashed mine while talking. After wiping nothing off of her mouth she reached across the table, took my hands into hers.

Although her response was serious, she didn't look serious stating it. "You sure you want to know the answer to that?"

"Of course I do." I was anxious to know why she felt her pussy was worth a brotha waiting for.

"First off, I'm trying to get to heaven."

With God knows how many men living with you? Yeah right!

"And secondly, I haven't had sex since I was eight years old. Since my dad decided to take something so valuable from me. The least I can do is remain pure until my wedding night."

I know I shouldn't have but I let her hands go and sat back as if I'd been bitten by a scorpion.

I barely got an audible 'what?' out.

"Yep, you'll be my next houseguest." She thought that shit was funny, but I didn't and I told her so. "Sincere I'm not making light of what happened to me. Never that. But your response is just about the same I've received from Cyprus, Malcolm and Walter. That's why they all live with me. Guess they're trying to protect me from the evils of the world. But they shouldn't worry, I always have Roscoe with me."

Another one!?

"Now who in the hell is Rosco?"

She started cracking up. I didn't see that as being funny either. "This my friend is Rosco." She pulled back her leather jacket, displaying a small pistol in a holster. "And he goes everywhere I go."

Sabrina stood and put our trash in the garbage. She then walked to the counter to order some ice cream to go.

As our eyes met in the mirror, I knew that just like Cyprus, Malcolm and Walter, I wanted to protect Sabrina but on a different level.

Not only did I want to protect her from the dangers of this world, but I wanted to protect her heart and claim it as my own. Before I could, I knew that I had some dirty laundry that needed cleaned, and it needed to be cleaned fast.

I ain't gonna even lie, Ramona was not the only one I was hittin'. As a handsome, single, twenty-four year old, financially secure man who had hella options, I took advantage. The first young lady I cut ties with was Phyllis.

I know it was dog of me. Even after all these years I was still messing around with her, Ramona's number one enemy. I couldn't help it.

In my mind, every time I slept with Phyllis, I was getting back at Ramona. It may sound crazy but I never got over Ramona messing around on me. And giving me a disease on top of it.

Eventually I realized making that move only reminded me of Ramona's infidelity. It wasn't healthy. I did what I thought would medicate my disappointment.

Ramona was my first love, and first heartache. Those emotions had been new to me. I didn't like how they felt but repeatedly inflicting myself with their pain didn't help matters.

It wasn't hard to to end it with Phyllis, she was a booty call. A means to an end, someone I used to add insult to injury.

The next two were also easy. Crystal and Kenya. They were 'whenever the moment hits me' calls and neither ever said no. My sex game was top notch and they knew it. Every female I touched, except for Ramona, I made them feel like they were the only woman in the world.

After breaking my heart, Ramona was denied that luxury even though it would be through our sexcapades that I'd gain most of my sexual skills.

She wasn't the only woman I'd learned from either. I mastered the art of eating pussy from the sexiest older woman I'd ever known. Her name was Karen. She taught me well.

"You've gotta treat a woman's pussy like a delicate rose."

As I watched her use both her hands to spread her hairy peach, my dick got rock hard. "First I want you to smell it."

She was on the edge of her bed with her legs wide open, me on my knees between them. I could smell her nectar from there, and willingly rushed forward to do as I was told.

"Slow down Sincere. Don't sniff like you smelling some damn SpaghettiO's. Take ya time, boy. My stuff ain't goin' nowhere."

I swallowed hard and then slowly placed my nose over her twat. I thought I was going to nut she smelled so good.

"Good boy. Now, gently place your tongue on my clitorus. You remember where I told you that was?"

I shook my head like a starved dog.

"Good. Now lick it." As she watched I did as I was told. "Gentle, gentle." I slowed my roll and lightened up on the pressure. After a few good licks she said, "That's it baby, that's it. Now open your mouth and softly suck on it."

Her shit was hard as hell. I took her erect clit into my mouth and sucked. I looked up at her, watching her watch me. When I saw her eyes go to half-mast I lightly grazed her clit with my tongue. She let go of her wings, fell back onto the bed and cried out in pleasure. I sucked harder on her pearl and came on myself.

We had many lessons like that which placed my pussy-eating skills at a ten. A skill reserved for a select few, like April. Now that chick's pussy was intoxicating. She was a big girl too, super thick, almost fat, but I could handle that ass. I don't know what it was, but something about her scent made me want to eat her out forever. The pull and desire was almost animalistic.

We always got busy at her condo, never my house.

I'd walk in and she'd be butt ass naked.

After taking a shower I'd lay on her bedroom floor. Homegirl needed leverage.

"Come sit on my face April."

"Only if you promise not to squeeze my thighs so hard. You left bruises the last time." She knew whether I left bruises or not she was going to squat. We went through this every time.

"I promise, April. Now get ya ass over here." She crawled on her hands and knees, place her big thighs on either side of my head and hover her pussy over my nose.

"Don't move." She knew the drill. She'd stay in that position for as long as I needed her to. "Okay. Come down just a little bit."

She placed both hands above my head and brought her hips down. I played with my dick as I smelled her mouth-watering goody-good. When I couldn't take anymore I spoke with a hoarse throat, "Bring that shit to daddy."

April teased my tongue with up and down motions of her hips, until I grabbed her thighs and dragged her onto my face.

I didn't eat everybody out and I had good reason: Not everyone was worthy. Mostly because you cain't trust just anyone.

Of all the chicks, April would be the one I hated parting ways with. Especially since I got a weekly dose of her comforting remedy.

Deep down, I knew Sabrina was worth it. I just needed to reduce her 'friends list' to a distant memory.

Sabrina...

The few times I went out with Sincere were refreshing. Sadly, those times reminded me of my singleness, and I realized that I was kinda lonely.

I had plenty of houseguests, but that's all they were. Everyone of them would abandon common sense to be with me again, but I didn't go backwards, only forward. Some may find it weird living with not just one ex but four. Not me.

Cyprus, whom I dated off and on in high school, is my security.

Malcolm is my handyman. Dated him for about a year. Couldn't tolerate his insecurity.

Walter is my mechanic. Actually, he's everyone's car guy. I'm the only one he doesn't charge. He was my man the longest - A solid three years. Caught him cheating and he's been trying to get me back every since.

Rusty's crazy butt is my extra. Whenever one of the other guys would hop into a halfway decent relationship and abandon the house for a while, Rusty was on hand to pick up where they left off. He knows enough to keep me safe, the house functioning properly, and my car running smoothly. We were in it for about a year and a half.

He was a little too possessive. Why I allowed him to move in has a simple answer: He fell on hard times and I stood there to catch him. He's back on his feet, but liked hanging with the fellas so I said he could stay.

Walter I dated for a short three months. Within that short period of time he made me feel like I was the only girl in the world. And still does. He's a sensitive jewel and I don't know what I'd do without him.

I've had male friends come and go. Most couldn't deal with my living arrangements. Their issue, not mine.

Those runaways didn't stick around long enough to learn that I have a few phobias. I'm sure they stem from my childhood but there's nothing I can do. They're engrained into my soul and no amount of therapy can extract that kind of fear.

My major phobia is being alone. After that, is the dark.

I grew up in a tri-level Victorian style home. The house was so big that we only used three of its five bedrooms. It would be in that ghostly place that my tormentors abandoned me.

"Sabrina we'll be right back."

"Please don't leave me. Daddy please."

"Don't say a word. Not even a whimper. The neighbors might hear you. Now, if you stay quiet, mommy and daddy will reward you when we get back."

I wanted to burst into tears but didn't. His reward was sex, and hers was allowing him to do it. I would long to ask them to leave on the lights, but knew they wouldn't.

"If you get hungry there's food in the corner to your left."

They slammed the door shut, an ominous click echoing in our empty house. Sometimes they'd leave me home for days. When my parents started having other kids, my siblings, I was in charge of keeping them quiet while they were gone. Even if they were infants.

I knew I had issues but they were warranted. For someone coming from a dark pit, I'd done quite well for myself. Blessed with brains, I swallowed knowledge like air. Always at the top of my class, I left Cyprus in my tracks and graduated high school in tenth grade.

I had every Ivy League college on my heels but stayed local. Had to look out for my siblings.

Because I no longer had distractions from the superficial kids in high school, I excelled even more in college. A contributing factor was a professor who observed both my potential and struggles. He invited me to stay with him and his wife, and I gladly accepted.

My siblings were left with our parents, but I had to make a better way for us all. It wouldn't happen under my parents' roof.

Sadly, every child born in that household ended up on drugs, prostituting, or institutionalized. Except for me. I got lucky and was out before the rage-filled beatings started.

Through the years, I spent many days with an outstretched hand, trying to get my brothers and sisters to safety. I was heartbroken time and time again; They'd been conditioned and feared the normalcy that a semblance of sanity offered.

Although I'm able to stretch my neck and breathe through the suppression my parents placed around my throat, the memories still choked me. That's when my friends are there to help. They are the select few brave enough to stick around.

I just don't think pretty boy Sincere has what it takes to do the same.

Sincere . . .

I started going in hard for Sabrina. She was everything I wanted and more. I knew it was going to take more than conversation to win her over so I willingly went out of my way to prove to her that she was special. I took her to dinner, the theater, sporting events, The Jazz Kitchen for live music, to my mom's shop whenever the opportunity presented itself. And although she always tried refusing the jewelry I got her, my sad puppy face would persuade her in my favor. But the day I'd given her a four-carat, white, gold tennis bracelet was one to remember.

We were at a local park. Sabrina placed her big round derrière in the seat of a swing and asked me to push her. What made her request so unique was the fact that we were in formal attire.

My job had thrown an elegant retirement party for the supervisor of our location and all were invited. Of course I'd asked Sabrina to accompany me and I must say, baby girl didn't disappoint. She was absolutely stunning in a emerald green dress and silver stilettos. While driving home from the festivities she'd asked if we could stop by the park. Of course I obliged. She anxiously got out of the car first, not waiting for me to open her door and then patiently stood as I locked up.

We walked up to the swing set in silence, hand in hand. When she let go of mine and squeezed her butt onto the small sliver of leather, she started swinging her legs not making any progress.

"Push me Sincere."

I looked at her like she was crazy, "What? In these damn expensive clothes?"

She was still swinging her legs back and forth, "Boy quit whining and push me. You're not going to sweat out your tux."

I rolled my eyes in my head, took off my Ralph Lauren jacket and gently placed it on the swing next to her. After rolling up my sleeves, I stepped behind Sabrina and started softly pushing. As I did she began swinging her legs again.

"Faster Sincere."

I kept my pace. "Nope."

She giggled like a child. "Scaredy cat."

With a smile on my face I replied, "Yep. Cain't have my baby gettin' hurt. I need you in one piece."

"Whatever Sincere." Although she swung her legs in and out, because of her dress, she could never get the momentum she wanted. "Alright, you can stop pushing now."

"Too late. I got a rhythm started. You gotta swing until I tell you you can't."

"Is that riiiiight?"

While softly pushing, I walked around to the front of the swing. Sabrina was absolutely stunning.

She smiled. The sun shining on her glossy lips was super sexy.

"That's right baby girl."

"And what if I stopped myself? What you gonna do about that?" With her heeled feet planted on the ground she stopped herself.

I stepped back and crossed my arms. "You've been a very bad girl Sabrina. You're in trouble now."

I watched as she bent down and took off her shoes. Before I could get another word out she leaped from the swing and tried running away. Just as I about to follow she tripped over her dress and fell.

"Sabrina!"

I immediately got to my knees to make sure she was ok. When I realized what I thought was crying was actually laughing, I sat my butt next to her.

"Girl you tryin' ta hurt a brotha. You cain't be doing that goofy shit."

She thought the shit was hilarious. Once she got over herself she put her face in hands and screamed. "Talk about embarrassiiiing!"

That made me laugh.

She hit me on the knee. "It's not funny." She lay on her back, placing her arm over her eyes. "You should have pushed me harder."

"I couldn't. You smelled too good."

Shielding her eyes from the sun Sabrina looked at me. "Huh?"

"Your perfume. If I'd have pushed you harder it would have really gotten to me so I left well enough alone."

She smiled. "Oh." She held out her hand. "Here, help me up."

I got to my feet and helped her to hers. When she went to take a step she limped. "Oh shoot Sincere. I think I sprained my ankle."

Out of reflex I put her arm around my shoulder.

"Sike! Race you to the car." With her shoes in one hand she used the other to raise her dress and then took off.

I grabbed my jacket off the swing and then went after her. Although I could have won, I let Sabrina have her moment. She rubbed it in my face too. As she reached for the door she sang, "Slow poke."

I slapped her hand. "Woman! Don't you open that door." With her face flushed from running, Sabrina looked like a blessed new day. I opened her door and then bent at the waist. "Madam."

Sabrina giggled but froze when she motioned to get into the car.

"Oh my goodness. Sincere."

In her seat lay the bracelet I'd wanted to give her at dinner but hadn't had the opportunity.

I stood and watched as her small petite hand went to her mouth. "My goodness!" She looked at me over her shoulder. She looked as if she wanted to cry.

"Shhh. Don't cry Sabrina."

She turned into my arms. "I'm not. I mean I won't." Sabrina held me tight. That was a first.

"Why did you get me that Sincere? I mean, I know that bracelet cost a lot of money." She let out a frustrated breath. "Thank you Sincere. I didn't mean to sound ungrateful. Thank you."

The joy I saw on Sabrina's face was priceless and well worth it. Then with caution she asked a question I'd been expecting. As I pulled back from Sabrina and began putting the bracelet on her wrist she whispered, "Look Sincere. I know jewelry. I know this was expensive."

"Hold your arm out Sabrina. I want to see the diamonds glistening in the sunlight."

She did as I ask yet continued. "Sincere, how could you afford to get me such an expensive gift? I mean…"

I cut her off. "I stacked up my coins from my mother's shop. Now stop asking so many questions, you're spoiling the moment."

With her arm still stretched out, Sabrina quickly kissed me on my cheek and like the jewel she was, began admiring a gift that didn't come close to putting a dent in my bank account.

With the goal of winning Sabrina's heart, mind and very being I left no stone unturned.

Hell, I'd not put forth a lot of effort for a female since Ramona and I had to admit, I thoroughly enjoyed it. Sabrina was fun, smart, and a breath of fresh air. Nothing I'd ever encountered in a woman before.

Yeah, I saw some red flags but who don't have issues? On the real, she saw mine too and baby girl didn't hesitate to call me out on them either. Especially whenever I was driving. More than once she asked, "Sincere? Why do you always freeze up when we're around police or police cars?" To which I'd always reply, "Cause." Then change the subject. That topic was not up for discussion.

Although it was eating at her to get an honest answer she never pressured me, and I was grateful for that.

While on the pursuit of happiness, I kept her as far away from those damn dick-slinging friends of hers by occupying as much of her time as I could. Anything to keep those mice from my pussy cat.

I have to admit, being with Sabrina brought a different kind of intimacy out of me; I was experiencing feelings for a woman I'd never had sex with - the closeness and connection was foreign and new. Her boundaries were a challenge as well. As a man who was used to getting what he wanted when he wanted it, what Sabrina introduced me to was a growing appreciation for women. Shit, I still had my hoein' ways but I was getting better and I didn't want to take a chance of The Dicks getting in the way of my progress.

Now, when it came time for Sabrina's studies, I let it be known that I was there for her. I loved being in her company and if helping Sabrina with her lessons allotted me more time with her, I was definitely down.

We were having a early lunch at Subway when I let my intentions out the bag.

"I don't mind helping."

She put down her sandwich.

"Well, this is a medical class Sincere." She had me on that one. As I tried coming up with a plan B, her lips curved as she kept mocking me, "I see you want to be of the utmost assistance. Why don't you enroll?"

I looked at her sideways. "Excuse me?"

She thought that was funny. "I'm serious. Why don't you enroll in school and we attend together? I know I'm ahead of you but I don't mind shifting my major until you catch up. It's not as if I have anything else to do."

I ain't gonna lie, Sabrina's willingness to make such a profound move on my behalf was a big turnon, but a brotha wasn't about no secondary education. Helping her was one thing but me attending myself? Naaa.

She didn't know but, thanks to my pops, I was financially set for life. I didn't need to work, but it gave me something to do. It also gave me access to women I wouldn't otherwise meet.

Like most men I always had sex on the brain and it didn't matter its class. That's when it hit me: *Shit! I could be introduced to another class of pussy on a college campus via a damned classroom.* Although it was bad to think that way, especially since I was trying to gain Sabrina's trust, I could not just shut off desires that had been active for so long overnight. I mean, I'd been having sex on a regular since I was ten. At that moment, Sabrina's suggestion gave my dick a change of heart. I still played hard-to-get.

"I don't know Sabrina. I ain't touched a book since I was in high school. And job manuals don't count."

"I'll help you Sincere. I got you."

And she did. That woman handled everything like it was a walk in the park. When it came time to talk about paying for classes, she asked me if I needed to fill out financial aid forms. I told her no, and that my job would be reimbursing me for my courses. I'd be paying out of pocket.

"Do you need any help paying for them Sincere? I don't mind helping and you can just pay me back when your job does."

I hesitated before answering. I already knew what I was going to say, "You would really do that Sabrina? It won't be putting you out will it?"

"Of course not. I'm all about education and don't want money being a reason you can't attend."

So I let her pay. Only two people knew about my stash. Mom, and Ramona. I kept it like that for a reason. A young black man with a bank account with over six figures in it is not for the public to know. Especially since it's blood money.

"Thank you Sabrina. I promise to pay you back as soon as my money comes." That's how I became a twenty-five year-old college student.

She majored in nursing, so I decided to as well. Figured I'd get some medical questions I'd wondered about answered. Because I'd been out of school for so long I had to start with the basics: Math, reading, interpersonal studies, and psychology. They weren't hard classes but they were time-consuming. I didn't mind because where I fell short, Sabrina stepped right in with her promised help.

Her ass was smart too. She was so smart that at times I thought she was frustrated with my lack of ability to catch on. More than once she assured me that wasn't the case. We decided that the campus library would be a neutral place for me to study. So, while stumbling over some algebra, I lay the cards on the table.

"I can always find someone else to help me Sabrina. It's really no big deal." It was a big deal. I was certain that there wasn't a finer, sexier tutor out there. And it kept her out of the company of those monkeys.

"No, no. That's not necessary. Now let's start again…"

That's how a lot of our initial study sessions went. Most of those classes were like rocket science to me. Once I got the hang of things and followed my studious tutor's advice on taking notes and studying, it was a wrap.

I aced my classes. Even when I didn't need Sabrina's guidance or help anymore, I didn't let her know that. When I learned the periodic table for chemistry Sabrina and I wrote the elements on flashcards. We'd gone over the symbols numerous times. She made sure I studied them and would surprise me with pop quizzes via text with either a symbol, name, an atomic number or whatever, and sometimes I'd get it wrong just to hear what she'd say.

"Sincere, how is it that you knew the symbol for Rhenium yesterday but not today?"

I smiled on the inside and gave my sad reply, "You know I'm trying. There's just so many to remember and I get confused."

She got quiet for a few minutes, then showed mercy. "Alright. Just try to remember the techniques I told you about. Your test is in a couple days and I don't want you to fail. You've worked so hard."

"I will, I promise. You've worked so hard at helping me that I don't want to disappoint you. I'll try harder." That was the only time Sabrina ever phoned me. She did make one exception on test day.

"Hello."

"Hey Sincere. I just wanted to tell you that I'll be praying for you. I know today is the big day and I have every bit of confidence that you'll pass with flying colors."

I lay it on thick trying to keep her on the phone as long as possible, "You think?"

"Heck yeah! You got this."

I heard a male voice in the background and it drew her attention from me. I politely pulled it back, "Can you go over the table with me one more time? I just want to double check to make sure I'm on point."

"But of course we can."

So we began. I knew that periodic table like the back of my hand. I'd done exactly what Sabrina had told me and studied everywhere; At work, home, while taking a shit, at my mom's spot, eating dinner, wherever. No matter the location, I always had a flashcard in my hand.

Some may have called me petty for playing slow with Sabrina. Oh well. They can call it what they want but I wanted her, by any means necessary.

While I caught up with Sabrina in medical classes, she took a culinary course. That was all well and good, until she told me she was cooking her newly learned recipes for her permanent houseguests. I tried to put a stop to that shit.

I made plans to shoot some pool at a sports bar with some of my coworkers. On the drive there I decided to give baby girl a call. I wish I hadn't.

"How was your day Sabrina?"

"Great! Learned how to make a new shrimp scampi. It was delicious so I decided to make some for the boys."

I didn't like that answer, "You got me over here getting jealous."

"And how is that?"

"You all Chef Boyardee over there, and I'm always at home alllll alone starving."

She laughed, "Sincere, you ain't missin' no meals."

"I might not be missin' no meals, but when you're not around I surely miss you."

She got quiet.

"I miss hearing your voice. I miss your encouragement. I miss your presence. I miss your scent. I miss everything." I was trying to lure her from that lion's den, but my words were true, "I miss you Sabrina."

"Sincere?"

"Yes?"

"Can I tell you something?"

It was my turn to get quiet. With Sabrina living with all those dudes I didn't know what she was going to say. The tone in her voice made me worry. "Sure Sabrina. You can tell me anything." I regretted saying those words as soon as I said them, assuming that she was going to tell me something I didn't wanna hear. Something about one of those dicks she lived with.

"I." She hesitated, as if debating on whether to say it or not. Then she whispered, "I miss you too."

I had to strain to hear. I turned down my radio. "What did you just say?" I'd been sitting in the parking lot of the sports bar.

She giggled and whispered louder, "I said I miss you too Sincere. Can I tell you something else?"

"Hell yeah. I mean, sure you can."

She started cracking up. When she finished she continued to stage-whisper, "Wherever you call and I see your number on my caller ID, my heart skips a beat."

"A beat? Hell, you call so rarely that if by some miracle you do call, and I see your number, my shit don't skip, it stops."

She thought that was hilarious. Once she calmed down we were both quiet, "Sincere?"

"Yes?"

"I want you to know that I'm a piece of work."

I don't know why she thinks she can scare me away. "Well, I want you to know that I'm a hard worker, so there shouldn't be any problems."

I could feel her smiling through the phone.

My chemistry test was the next day. I aced the exam, then asked Sabrina to meet me at the movie theater.

We'd decided that pass or fail, we would end the night on a high note. When I pulled into the theater she was already there, which worked well for my plan. I got out of my truck, and with my head down, made my way inside. Out of my peripheral I watched as she stood and walked toward me.

"Sincere."

I looked up as if seeing her for the first time. "Oh, hey Sabrina."

She placed her hand on my arm. My face told a thousand lies. "So? How did you do?"

I put my head down and shook it.

"Oh Sincere, I'm so sorry. You'll do better next time. Maybe you over-studied or I pushed you too hard."

The self-doubt with which she spoke made keeping a straight face hard. "It's not your fault Sabrina." I placed my hand on top of hers. "Well, maybe it is." I said, "Because there's no way I could have gotten a hundred percent without you." I looked into her sad brown eyes, watching as they transformed from defeated to ecstatic.

She acted like a little kid. "What?! You passed? Oh my gosh you passed." She jumped up and down while clapping her hands showing off her pretty pearly whites. "You passed!"

Sabrina was so happy that people were looking. By the time she calmed down, she was out of breath. "Oh, Sincere."

She beamed like a proud parent. In her excitement she walked close to me, placed her hands on my face and gave me a quick kiss. That shocked the hell outta me, but I recovered real fast and pulled her into an embrace. Her chest was heaving against mine, and that shit felt so damn good.

"Sincere?" She must have known what I was going to do because she quickly licked her dry lips.

I slowly brought my mouth to hers and savored her sweet taste, moistening hers with mine. I took in everything about the creature I was holding.

Her firm breasts on my chest. Hot breath on my cheek. The clumsiness of her tongue. Her hands reaching around my neck. The way her fingers locked behind my head. The soft moan which escaped that I swallowed. How she took a step back when she felt my hard dick. I pulled her right back into my space.

I held her close and whispered into her ear, "Don't embarrass me Sabrina."

She was clueless and tried to pull away, "Huh?"

I looked down at her. "You can't move yet, baby girl. Not yet."

Then it clicked. "Oh. Okay. I won't."

She started shifting with discomfort at being so close to my hardness. I looked somewhere other than her beautiful face. "I'm sorry. I didn't know it was going to happen. Just give me a minute."

"You're fine. I do live in a house full of men."

That got my dick deflated. I looked down at her, "So what? You saying that you lookin' at dicks all day?"

She laughed. By then my dick was soft as cotton.

"You so silly Sincere. Come on let's go watch this movie."

Shit, I was serious.

"And by the way, you win an Academy Award for your performance, young man. I'm real proud of you Sincere. I knew you could do it."

"I just wanted to surprise you and say thanks. If it weren't for you I wouldn't have passed..."

She cut me off, "You know, deep down I got the feeling that you weren't having as many troubles as you let on. I've watched you catch on to a lot harder subjects and..."

It was my turn to cut her ass off, "Now, back to those dicks you around all day, every day."

All she could do was laugh.

I was finally able to convince Sabrina to cook for me at my crib. It took some coaxing but she eventually relented. The menu consisted of some spicy Jamaican jerk chicken with jasmine rice and fresh grilled green beans.

"Girl you gonna make me marry you."

"In your dreams."

I wiped my mouth with the elegant napkin she'd brought, "I gotta go to dreamland for that too huh?"

"Pretty much. I'm not on the market."

"Whatever."

"I'm serious Sincere. After all that I saw my parents go through and put us through I decided that marriage was not for me."

I put my fork down and stared at her. "You're serious aren't you?"

"As a heart attack. You don't know the hell I've been through."

"Enlighten me."

She did, and some of the things she told me made the hairs on my neck stand. "Well damn!" I was speechless and she knew it.

"Everybody don't get the story. I've had plenty of men flee once they've heard it." She looked sad, but okay, "You know those dicks you always talking about? The ones who live in my house? They have helped me tremendously. They're the select few who have helped me through my traumatic experiences. I'm never alone. I'm never in the dark. There's always food. Someone is there to motivate me to get out of bed when I don't want too. A couple of them can even tell when I'm on the brink of a depressive episode. And yes, I take antidepressant meds. With what I've been through, I think that's okay."

I'd seen some red flags but didn't know the causes. Under the circumstances Sabrina was doing exceptionally well, considering her life's catastrophes. "Well baby girl, I really don't know what to say."

She put a crooked smile on her face, "There isn't anything to say. The only task you have is to be understanding and accepting. I don't need a whole lotta questions opening up old wounds. Just silence."

Damn!

Across the table sat one of the most put-together women I'd come to know. I would have never imagined her being traumatized the way she'd been.

"Well, I'm in it to win it baby girl."

She kinda smiled. "I've heard that before."

"Naw, I'm serious. Next to my mother, you're one of the strongest women I know. I've watched my mom heal from some very dark and trying times. It's been a phenomenal transformation. She's whole, she's complete and successful. And that's without a man. I'd just like to be there to witness your transformation, but on a more personal level. A more intimate level."

She sat back in her chair.

"Not the physical Sabrina. The mental, spiritual, and intellectual. Don't get me wrong, I am a man and find you more than attractive. I also find you appealing and interesting and just an all around fabulous woman."

She still wasn't persuaded, so I kept it real.

"Look baby girl. You know I ain't got no problems getting a woman." I placed my hand on my chin and turned my face from side to side as if showing off my good looks. She laughed. "Never have and never will." I paused, wondering if I should put it all out there. "Look."

I was about to do something I'd not done since Ramona. I had some reservations about what I was about to say, especially since she lived in a house full of men. I trusted her. With that in mind I took a leap of faith. I took her hands into mine.

"Look, Sabrina. I've had one girlfriend my entire life and she damn near broke me down. We have a son who's five, about to be six."

She was shocked. "I didn't know you had a child."

"I do, and his name is Brice. Other than the women who are close to me, you're the only one I've told about him. I don't think it's anyone's business. On the real, I knew I wasn't going to be introducing any of those women to my mom, which meant they weren't good enough for introductions with my son either."

She didn't respond.

I guess it clicked that she was pretty special to me, considering I'd already introduced her to my only parent and was speaking to her about my boy.

Mission accomplished.

I let go of her hands and sat back in my chair and went in for the kill.

"You were a diamond in the rough, Sabrina, but underneath all the dirt of your life you came out shining and glistened your way right into my heart. Now I ain't gonna front. I had a few lady friends when we met, but they're history baby girl."

I couldn't believe I'd just lied like that. Shit was easy too.

April's pussy still had me on lock. I was on a regular sniffing and licking her. No less than once a week. When Ramona's jealous butt got mad at me for rejection, her ass greeted me at the door butt naked.

Temptation's a mo-fo!

"What I'm trying to say, is that I find you worthy."

She raised an eyebrow.

That did NOT come out right! "Let me start that over."

"Please do."

"I want you in my life exclusively."

"Is that riiiiight?"

"It most definitely is."

She leaned in. "And why have I been found 'worthy' of such an honor?"

"Because you're everything a woman should be..."

She cut me off. "I'm not getting rid of my friends."

"I wouldn't ask you to. They're a vital part of your healing process." *What kinda shit is this?*

She started bit her bottom lip. "You promise not to hurt me?"

"I don't hurt women." As soon as I said it, I bit my damned tongue. The shit hurt so bad, my eyes and mouth started watering. I played it off by picking up my water and took a long, deep drink. Shit!

She turned her head and stared out the dining room window. I wiped my eyes and down some more fluids. Once I'd recovered, I drew her attention toward me.

"I'm already a better man because of you. But I know I have to take it slow, and I'm cool with that."

She shook her head in agreement. For the first time since meeting Sabrina, I saw true vulnerability.

Sabrina...

Before I left his house I asked for a few days to think.

I wasn't dating anybody, and wasn't sure if I wanted to. My life was comfortable. Though I got lonely at times, it was just in passing, nothing I had to expediently deal with.

I liked Sincere. I liked him a whole lot, and that kinda scared me. He was smart, emotionally secure, and didn't display too many weaknesses. He had a steady income, his own place, a car and absolutely adored his mother. He was the total package.

I still wasn't sure that I'd be someone he could handle. Most men couldn't. My roommates, bless their souls, were dear to me. But they were so freaking competitive for my attention that at times I felt like a mother. But it went both ways. I needed them and just as much as they needed me.

The fellas relied on me mainly because I was their perfect excuse whenever they wanted out of what they thought was going to be a happily-ever-after relationship.

When they realized it wasn't going in that direction, I was used as the straw that would break the camel's back. They'd tell those women how beautiful, smart and intelligent I was which would cause a disturbing domino effect.

Cyprus told me about a girlfriend he'd tried numerous tactics to break up with. Nothing worked. Knowing that if he mentioned me his mission would be accomplished, he set his plan into motion and went for the jugular. It did not go well.

"Sabrina's just able to stimulate me in ways you wouldn't understand."

"I got something to stimulate you!"

That day he came home with a bruise on his cheek.

When Walter found out his girlfriend was bisexual and polyamorous, he threw me under the bus. When he initially learned about her sexuality he found it sexy. After six months the thrill wore off. He just couldn't stomach sharing his lady friend with a woman, or anyone else. Walter also couldn't stand that his companion constantly started her sentences with the last word spoken to her. He welcomed using me as a means of an exit.

"You know." Walter said to his girl, "I don't think this is going to work out. Sabrina has had another one of her episodes and I really need to get home."

"Home? What the hell do you mean home? Your ass is home, you lived here for two damn years!"

"I know but I really need to be there for Sabrina."

"Sabrina? Why does everything go back to Sabrina? Is she the reason you're leaving? Are you guys back together?"

"We're not back together, but she'll always be a part of my life. Look baby, it's just time for me to move on."

"Move on? Move on to where? Is it my sexuality? Tell me Walter. Just be honest."

"Not at all, Sabrina needs me, and being under the same roof allows me to focus on what's important."

"Important? Why don't you think what we have is important?"

Walter said that after thirty minutes of the 'ring around the word' game, he packed his belongings with her riding his heels. When he could take her breathing down his neck no more he snapped.

"Leave me the fuck alone!"

"Alone? How in the hell do you expect me to leave you alone when you're fucking leaving me?!"

He eventually slammed her own door in her face as he stormed out of what was once their home. Because of those situations, women I never met hated me. It was because I had access to the men they loved. Their issues, not mine.

Sincere was a tad bit different.

From what I could tell, he was a real man. I knew I wasn't the only one with a dark past. But he wasn't ready to divulge some things about his life.

I understood. Because of his honesty, I believed that a man, for once, had my best interest in mind.

Sincere...

With Sabrina out of the way I had to take care of Ramona's dick-thirsty butt. Instead of calling beforehand, I snuck up on that ass. Didn't want no door prizes.

When I walked in, I saw her on the couch watching PBS with Brice. She was surprised as hell.

"Sincere?" She looked at our son, then at me. "You should have told me you were coming."

"This ain't that kinda visit." I sat on the other side of Brice who took my hand into his. He was so engulfed in the educational program, he couldn't stop what he was doing to give me a proper greeting. I was cool with that. I could tell my unexpected visit had taken Ramona aback. She was uncomfortable.

As soon as his show ended, Brice jumped his big ass onto my lap and I welcomed it, "Daddy!"

"Sup little man? You about ready for bed?"

"Aww, but you just got here."

"I know. But me and ya mama got something real important to talk about." I looked at Ramona.

She picked up a magazine, flipping pages like she wasn't ear hustling. That woulda been dandy if the magazine were rightside up. I snatched that foolery from her hand.

She gave me an offended look, "You play too much Sincere!"

"Girl please. The stupid thing was upside down and I got some things I need to talk to you about."

"Why didn't you call? I coulda got ready." She looked at Brice who was still on my lap, acting like a big baby.

"I already told you this wasn't that kinda visit. Now, I'm about to take Brice to the back to get ready for bed. When I come back out here I don't want to behold no B.S." I tried hard to curve my cursing around Brice, even though I wanted to give her a tongue lashin' with the way she was actin' the fool. "Better yet, come on. We are getting him straight together." I stood and put Brice's heavy behind on the floor. When I saw that she hadn't moved, I put a calm ass look on my face. That got her butt up.

We got Brice together, tucked him in bed, and read him a bedtime story. After turning out his light we went to the living room and sat on opposite ends of the couch.

Before I could get a word out she spoke, "Who is she?"

"It doesn't matter."

"Yes the hell it does if she's going to be around my child."

"Don't you mean 'our' child?"

"Stop playing with me Sincere. What's her damn name?"

I watched as Ramona's breathing started to increase. She was about to have a panic attack. "Relax Ramona. It's not that deep."

"Yes it is. You ain't never turned down my pussy, which means you getting some on a regular from somebody."

"I ain't even hittin' it."

"I knew it! I just knew it! I know she's gotta be some kinda special if you turning mine down and ain't getting' none from her. And you're here in the middle of the week. Since you started school you ain't never been here on a Wednesday. What's her name Sincere?"

As soon as my name left her mouth a tear dropped from her eye.

"Come on now Ramona." I moved to embrace the woman I still loved.

Ramona knew how I felt about her, which was the reason she was behaving the way she was. Ramona had always been there. It didn't matter if she had a man or not. If I called she put everything on the backburner. She also knew that since her, I'd never had a girlfriend or a real relationship.

I'd plenty of female acquaintances, held them down a month or two. But I'd not been in a committed relationship since my first love. Ramona knew that.

"Don't leave us Sincere," she said against my chest. "Please don't."

Her words made my heart hurt. "I'm not going anywhere. I promise." Shit, I didn't know if I was going anywhere or not. I just needed her to calm the hell down.

"Yes you are Sincere. I feel it. I feel it in my gut." She pulled away and went into the kitchen. She came back out blowing her nose into a napkin. When she sat, I pulled her head to my chest and held her close.

"I think she might be good for me Ramona."

"I don't want to hear about it Sincere." She sounded defeated.

"Her name is--"

She sat up, "I don't want to know."

I pulled her ass right back down, "Stop being childish."

"I'm not."

"You are, and you actin' like a two year old."

"How do you expect me to accept the fact that I may be losing the only man I ever loved?"

"The same way I accepted and love a child that ain't mine."

That shut her ass up. I turned her by her shoulders to face me, and looked into her pretty brown eyes. "Ramona, it was bound to happen. She makes me happy. Although I don't owe you any explanation as to what I do with my life, you are, and will always be, an important part of who I am."

The tears kept streaming down her face.

"I deserve that, Ramona. Don't you wanna see me happy?"

"No."

We both laughed. "Well, I want to be happy and I want to see you happy. You gotta good man. If he wasn't he wouldn't be around my son. Don't take that for granted. Learn from your previous mistakes."

She knew exactly what I meant by that statement.

"We're still young. We've got a whole lifetime ahead of us and we need to embrace it."

I barely heard her when she whispered, "What's her name Sincere?"

I looked at that beautiful woman and exhaled long and hard not wanting to say the name that would seal the coffin.

"You can tell me. It's alright."

I took off my shoes and repositioned us. I sat with my back against the arm of the couch, with one foot on the floor and the other leg along the length of the sofa. I put Ramona between my legs with her head against my chest. With my arms wrapped around her waist I began.

"Her name is Sabrina. She's absolutely beautiful."

"Prettier than me?"

"Yep."

She hit my arm and laughed. "Continue."

I told her everything I positively adored about my Sabrina.

Ramona...

I knew this day would come. It was my fault.

Sincere always loved me. If he didn't, he wouldn't do the things he do, and he wouldn't come home to what's familiar. That's all the confirmation I needed to solidify knowing where his heart truly lay.

God knows I loved that man from the time I knew what love was. When we were teens and he didn't want me anymore, that's when I learned what true love meant. By then it was too late.

I can't deny Sincere has developed into a very good man. Although Brice isn't his, you cain't tell him that. He treats him like his flesh and blood. I know out in public, people assume that his mama is white. It takes a strong brotha to take unwarranted, biased stares.

Sabrina was a lucky woman. I didn't want to admit it.

Actually she's more than lucky; she's blessed. I wish her and Sincere my very best. He deserves it.

Chapter Four

Sincere...

I took my time with Sabrina and slowly pulled back those layers. While watching her blossom into a pretty rose, I set out to evict her roommates, one swinging dick at a time.

The day was bright and sunshiny. We were having a picnic in a park, both lying on our stomachs. I absentmindedly picked at the grass. She watched.

"Sabrina?"

"Yes Sincere?"

"Are we dating?"

She turned onto her back and through squinted eyes, looked at me, "I don't know. Are we?"

I smiled. "Well, considering we spend all of our time together I'd say we are."

"Hmmm."

I stopped picking at the grass and continued. Looking down upon her. "And when we're not together we're on the phone."

"Okay?"

Because of her emotional attachment to her roommates, I knew I had to tread lightly, but at the same time I needed her to see my perspective where they were concerned. While watching a dog run after a frisbee I continued, "Well Baby Girl, if we're not dating I'd say we're pretty close to it."

"Isn't a man supposed to ask a woman to be his girl? I know the game hasn't changed that much."

She had me there.

"True, true. But on the same token, before taking that leap of faith with someone, a man and woman have conversations that may be uncomfortable. Some even difficult."

"What kind of conversations Sincere?"

She gave me my window of opportunity. I cleared my throat. "How do you think it makes me feel to pick you up and I'm greeted by another man who's not your father or brother?"

"Never really thought about it."

I looked over at her. I said with a little extra baritone, "Well I have."

She snickered at me.

Damn! I hadn't meant to get caught up so quick. Oh well!

"How do you think I feel when we're on the phone and I hear a deep voice in the background. Do you know that I strain my ears every time that happens, trying to figure out which one had invaded on my time?"

"Naw, didn't know that."

"Well I do. Can I ask you to do something for me?"

She'd been lying next to me but sat up. "I'm not getting rid of my friends."

I know you're not, hell I am! "Wasn't going to ask you that, so slow down."

As she looked at some kids playing hide and go seek, she said nothing. After a few minutes she turned her head towards me and shaded her eyes from the sun with her hand.

"Lay back down Sabrina."

"Yes, you may ask me something."

She didn't lie down, so I sat upright. "Look at me, please."

She did. Placing her hands in mine, I held them tight. Although a little nervous, I had to get the shit off my chest.

"Imagine this. You call me and while we're talking you hear a high pitched giggle or a soft feminine voice asking me a question. Or let's say I get manicures, and one of my roommates is a manicurist, and every week she's touching on my hands and feet."

She tried to pull her hands out of mine and interrupt me. I wouldn't allow her to do either.

"Just listen." I licked my dry lips. "So, envision me living with three beautiful women that I've had previous relationships with. It doesn't necessarily have to be a physical one. It could be that we were attracted to each other, and found that our personalities automatically clicked. Let's assume that, by some chance, I'm not attracted to them anymore. Not sexually, and view our relationship in a sister, brother kinda way. But they're still attracted to me."

I let that sink in for a minute. Simply speaking those words caused me to become a little tart. When she opened her mouth to speak I beat her to the punch. "Or how about one is a masseuse and gives me a massage to relieve my stress on a weekly. If we were a couple, how would that make you feel?"

That was her opportunity to respond. She didn't take it. Instead, she placed a troubled look on her face. "I gotta be honest Sabrina, as a man, I ain't feelin' other dudes doing what I'm supposed to be doing. Better yet, doing something you and I should be accomplishing together. That shit just don't sit well with me. Not at all."

She snatched her hands out of mine and stood to leave. I stood too. "Hear me out. Damn!"

She raised both of her eyebrows and I raised mine. When she tried to take a step around me I blocked her path. Sabrina exhaled loud and hard. When I reached out to take her hands into mine she pulled away but not fast enough. I caught one and held onto it tight.

"I ain't asking you to do shit you don't want to do. What I'm saying is that I like you a whole lot, Sabrina, and the thought of those horny ass men parading around you all damn day and night just does something to me. And don't come at me with that 'I told you what the deal was' bullshit cause I ain't tryin' to hear it. Shit dun changed. Hell, my feelings have changed. You can call me selfish for wanting you all to myself but, I do. I don't want no nother nothin' around my woman without me being there. I know I'm being possessive as hell, but I'd hope you wouldn't want it any other way."

I started getting a major attitude. I dropped her hand.

"Do you know I faked not knowing so much shit in school just to get you away from them and close to me?"

"Yes, I do."

I pretended not to hear her. "I went to school for you Sabrina. So we could have something in common. So we could spend more time with one another. I rearranged my whole damn life for you. If that don't speak volumes, I don't know what will."

I couldn't believe I'd poured my heart out like that. I wanted them dicks out our lives. I calmed down. "I'm not asking you to get rid of your help. I'm asking you to at least consider a different alternative to what you got going on. I don't know how long I'll be able to tolerate other men getting friendly with my lady."

Sabrina sat back down, bent her legs at the knee, wrapped her arms around her legs and started biting her nails.

"I'll be back." I turned, put my hands in my pockets and went for a stroll. Baby girl needed some time to think, but I also wanted to clear my head and get my jealousy in check.

As I walked, I visualized the emotions that had crossed Sabrina's face. They weren't all good. I knew she felt she needed those men in her life, but I knew she didn't. They'd been her cushion for so long that they'd crippled her. How would she ever know that she could breathe without them if she never got out of the water? Sabrina was a well put-together woman who had an inner strength that superseded that of a lot of people. Baby Girl is the truth!

One thing was for sure, knowing that I was outnumbered, I was tired of competing for ALL of her attention.

Walking to the middle of a small bridge I looked over the railing at the fish. I wished I'd grabbed some bread. People were on either side of the little lake throwing morsels to the ducks and fish, drawing the creatures to the surface to enjoy an easy meal.

I stood watching, when I felt her presence.

"So, are you saying that you love me Sincere?"

I turned and faced her. Sabrina wore a pretty sundress with those stupid-ass western boots she always wore. She was absolutely breathtaking.

"I can't say that I love you Sabrina. I will say that I think I might be close. Hell, I don't know."

We leaned on the rail, people-watching in silence. We stayed like that for a long time, engulfed in our individual thoughts. When I got tired of seeing the same people pass, I grabbed her hand.

"Come on. Let's get back before the ants walk off with our food." We walked to our picnic area hand in hand, and lay on our blanket.

She was on her back and I was on mine with an arm shielding my eyes from the sun. Just as I was about to doze, she placed her hand on top of mine and squeezed. I knew then it wouldn't be long before The Dicks vacated her premises.

BYE BYE BITCHES!

Sabrina . . .

I knew everything Sincere said was true. No, I would not like it if the shoe was on the other foot. What was I to do?

I was at a loss as to how to handle the situation. Not because I didn't want my friends to leave, but because I was terrified of being alone. The memories of hearing nothing but the sound of the house breathing crippled me. The periodic car door slamming, wishing my parents were coming home.

The dreams were the worst. I needed someone to wake me when they came:

I was four in a huge mansion by myself. Because of the shadows, I was scared to move. Those ever-present overcasts visited like clockwork, slowly making their appearance when the sun rose, then slowly vacating when the sun set.

At times I thought someone was in the house and ran into the room where I thought I heard a noise. Nobody was there. The shadows would be though.

Sometimes they taunted me and danced around me in a circle. I was paralyzed and pissed and shit my panties. In my four year old voice I cried, "Leave me alone! Leave me alone!"

But they wouldn't. Instead the wind outside would blow, inviting the tree shadows to join the dance. It felt like the branches picked at my skin.

I fell to the floor and sang myself to sleep, "Leave me alone! Leave me alone!" over and over.

When I had those dreams, I climbed from my bed and ran into Walters'.

He'd feel my presence and scoot over. Then I felt his strong arms hold me tight, a kiss on my forehead, smell his stale breath as he told me I'm safe and that everything is going to be alright.

If I told Walter to leave, who would hold me at night?

Sincere...

Three months after our talk under the beautiful blue sky, The Dicks were still in her house. It was time for a sit-down. We were at her favorite place, the damn ice cream shop.

I knew I was asking a lot, and actually felt bad for taking it there that day at the park, but I couldn't help myself.

I also knew that she had deep-rooted issues from her childhood, I decided to kill two birds with one stone.

"Sabrina?"

"Yes, Sincere?"

"I think I have a solution to your problem."

"You mean your problem?"

I ignored her. "How about you come stay at my place."

"Not even a possibility."

I was offended. "You know that was not the response I was looking for."

"It's the truth. Look baby."

"Did you just call me baby? Now that's a first. Don't think that's going to get you dialogue brownie points."

She laughed. "Be serious Sincere."

I stopped playing and gave her my undivided attention.

"It's not a possibility because I'm attracted to you."

"You're saying you're not attracted to those dicks that live in your house?"

"Stop calling them that. And no, I'm not. That's what makes it so easy."

"For you."

"Maybe, but that's beside the point. I like you a lot. Don't think that because I'm celibate, I'm not attracted to you physically."

"Really?" That was news to me. Sabrina hardly showed physical affection. I usually initiated it.

"I'm serious."

"I am too. Girl, you hardly show a brotha any love."

"That's because I'm in love with you."

As she stood to leave my eyes were as big as plates. I grabbed her by the arm, "Hold up, hold up, hold up. Where do you think you're going?"

She couldn't look at me. "I should not have said that. Those words should have never left my mouth."

"It's okay Sabrina. No big deal baby girl. A brotha is loved by many." She was so downcast I needed to crash the moment.

When she smiled and lightly punched my arm, I was glad. "You know morally I can't do that. It'll be too tempting."

I know those words did not just come out of her mouth.

With gentleness I coaxed her into sitting back down. "You mean to tell me, living with four men is more moral than living with one?"

"You know I don't like them like that."

"That's not the point, because they like you like that. Tell me what the damn difference is?" I was digging at straws but I had to get her out of that house and into mine.

"I am the difference. I control what happens in that house, not them."

"Just like you can control what happens in mine."

"It's not the same Sincere. I have not been touched by a man in a very long time. Honestly, I've not thought about a man in a sexual way in a very long time. Then you came along."

I cut her off, "So you think about us doing the do?" Couldn't help myself.

"I think about us in a lot of ways. Which is why I can't move in with you." She dodged that bullet.

"I have a big ass, three-bedroom house. There's plenty of room for us to live around each other."

"And what about when I walk around in a tee-shirt and panties?"

"So you tellin' me that you walk around those dicks with a tee-shirt and panties on?"

She started laughing, "Of course not silly. I just wanted to see how you would react."

That shit wasn't funny and my lack of response let her know so.

"Anyway. Let me think about it okay? Give me a few days."

"You've had three damn months."

"That's three months with no options Sincere. Now you've given me one."

Her reply made me happy. "So, what you sayin'? You really gonna consider my suggestion?"

She rolled her eyes and walked away from me.

Sabrina saying she was going to think about moving in with me was music to my ears; I hated the fact that she lived with those extra penises. I needed her at my crib to tame my doggish ways.

I was still making my weekly visits to April, so I figured Sabrina being a persistent presence would curb my appetite.

I didn't like stepping out on Sabrina, but April's liquid fire was like a damn drug. Considering I wasn't getting nothin' from nobody else, the release she gave me was heavenly.

Sabrina...

It was time for me to talk to the boys. I cooked their favorite dish and nervously watched as they indulged. After dessert, I asked them to retreat to the den. They each obliged, and drank coffee, wine or smoked a cigar. After they settled, I bluntly announced my intentions.

"I'm moving out." I couldn't come up with a better way to tell them.

Walter was the first to speak. "I'm not surprised. You're hardly here as it is."

"You can't move out!" That was Rusty. I raised an eyebrow at him. He stuttered. "Well, what about us?"

I frowned, rolled my eyes and with as much calm as I could muster up replied "I think we're all grown, Rusty."

Malcolm shut his needy butt up with a good question, "When are you leaving, sweetheart?"

Now that was something I hadn't thought about. "I don't know. It'll be soon though."

"Is it Sincere?" He asked.

"Duh." I said. Everybody laughed but Rusty and Cyprus. Malcolm seemed genuinely happy for me.

"It's about time." Malcolm said kindly, "I thought you'd end up living here with us forever, dying an old virginal hen."

His words warmed my heart but when I looked at Cyprus it grew cold. "I just wanted you guys to know." I continued, "I've not thought everything out, but I'd appreciate it if you guys continued to stay here and sustain the upkeep of the house. You never know, it might not work out."

"Don't talk like that," Walter said, "You gotta speak positive. I do have a question. Have you been to where you're going to be staying? Will he, you know. Be there for you at night?"

I wanted to answer Walter's question but Cyprus interrupted me.

"I've heard enough of this madness." He stormed out of the room. I was quick to follow him but surprisingly, Rusty, stopped me. "Let him go. He'll adjust. We will too."

He looked so sad when he said that that I hugged him. "Thank you, Rusty. Thank you all for understanding. Y'all just don't know how much your support and backing means to me. You're the family I never had, and, your approval means more than you'll ever know."

My three friends arose and we embraced in a group hug. As we did I couldn't help but stare at the empty seat that had recently housed Cyprus.

Sincere...

"Scoot to the end of the chair, April."

Butt ass naked, she obeyed. She sat in a chair, with me on the floor between her spread legs in her kitchen.

I wrapped my arms around her thighs to pull her closer. She didn't budge. My mouth watered.

"Some more."

"You tryin' to break my damn back?"

"Get yo ass up here." Her butt was barely on the chair but she moved her ass further. "Right there." Her pussy was directly in front of my face and my dick jumpin'. I took a finger and played with her clit. I waited patiently.

"Shit. Sincere."

"Be still April."

"I cain't. Shit!"

After a few more strokes, it happens. I watched in amazement as her sweet nectar floated to the surface of her heaven. It looked and smelled so damn good. "Keep your ass still."

She kept moving her legs, like my touch was too much for her.

"Yes. Sincere. Yes." She placed her hands on top of my head, trying to bring my mouth towards her pussy. I was not having it.

Her eyes are on me when we meet gazes. She lets my damn head go. Still playing with her clit, I took another finger and dip some liquid out of her pussy like it was Cool Whip. I pulled on her juices, stretching the string long. It wouldn't break, so I help it along and put my finger in my mouth. Her juices taste so good that I dove head first.

"Oh! Sincere! Oh, shit!" She grabbed my head and wrapped her legs around my neck.

Licking from one hole to the other, I unzipped my pants and pulled out my dick. I took my head from between her thighs, playing with her clit. I waited.

When I see what I think is a decent amount of wetness I gather as much of it as I can off her pussy and spread it on my dick. April pushed my face into her peach.

"Suck this shit Sincere. Oh shit. Oh shit."

As she rotated her hips, I jacked off with her juices as my lubricant.

"Oh! Oh! Oh!"

With every noise she makes she pumped her hips.

"I want you to cuuuum Sincere. The vibrations feel sooo good on my puuuuuussy!"

I stood, picked her big behind up and damn near broke our necks as I carried her into the living room. I threw her onto the couch and spread her legs wide open. When I blew on her kitty-cat I watched as her clit jumped.

"Stop playin' Sincere damn!" I laughed at her. "Aint shit funny now come on!" I peeled her flower open, and gently floated my tongue over its surface. "Ooooooh, yes, yes, yes. That's it. That's it. That's it." Her noises and words were running together. "Yes! Sincere, baby. Yes! Oh shit! Oh shit!"

I was coasting over the pussy and didn't want to come up for air. She wanted it rough, tried to push my head down but I stopped her. "Not yet sweetness. Not yet." After playing with her, getting her sopping wet, I put more of her juices on my dick.

"Gimme suma dat dick."

I wanted badly to stuff my dick in her mouth but this was my feasting hour not hers. Besides, I knew something she didn't. This was my last supper.

My head between her legs, and one hand jacking off, I used the other to play with her big titties. She placed her hand on top of mine and threw her head back.

"Ooooooh Sincere." She was driving me crazy. "Ooooooooh shit!" I applied more pressure to her clit and she tried to close her legs. I stopped sucking long enough to tell her to open back up and then dived back in. She rolled her hips. "Mmmmmmmm Sincere. Mmmmmmmm!"

Her moaning and squirming had a whole lotta precum seeping out the tip of my dick.

"Now April."

She knew what that meant and as soon as I took my suction off her twat, I lay on the floor flat on my back. She immediately sat on my face and rolled her hips. With an arm wrapped around a thigh I pushed her down harder onto my face, with the other I played with myself again. I looked up at her and could tell she was almost there. I couldn't wait to drink in her climax.

With her head thrown back she started to sing. "Yessss. Yes. Ohhh.Mmm. Mmmmmm. Sinceeeere. Yes baaabe."

Then it happened. She pressed her sprout down on my face and I drank.

"Oooooh shit! Shit! Shit! Mmmmmmmmm!"

As she came I did too, and made sure my moans of excitement did what she wanted; Vibrate. April squeezed her legs into my head and then fell forward. With her fat covering my nose I could barely breathe. I was still swimming in the sea of ecstasy.

I growled while she screamed. Then, we waited for a sense of normalcy to return to our bodies. As she climbed off my face to lay on her back, I smelled her mouthwatering scent and my dick got hard again. I knew we were both worn out, but I didn't give a damn.

"Go take a shower so we can get ready for round two." I told her.

Twenty minutes later she came out, and I went in.

After thirty minutes, we started our second round.

Later, after we were finished we took a shower together. Once we were dressed I sat April down and had a talk with my delectable temptation. She didn't take it well.

April...

Sincere was outta his damned mind if he thought I was gonna just walk away from what we had.

We'd been doing this shit for years, and his tongue game is fierce. Just like he was addicted to my scent, I was addicted to his attention. I wasn't letting him snatch that away from me.

We complimented each other. There's no way he could just drop me as if I never existed.

Sincere...

After leaving April's, I went home, took another shower, and took my behind to class.

I tried my best to concentrate on my instructor, but the memory of April's scent and taste had my brain like Jello. It was going to be a long night.

I was in my last prerequisite classes before applying for nursing school. Rumor had it, they only accepted those with the highest GPA. If that was the case, then I was in like Flynn.

Gotta admit, I surprised myself with my academic abilities. Didn't even know I had it in me. Mom was proud too. When I called and told her that I'd made the Dean's list she had nothing but positive things to say.

"Sincere, I don't know why you're so shocked. You were a good student and always excelled. I'm sure you'll be making the Dean's list your entire college years."

She was right.

But it was her next words that made my heart swell. "You've been truly blessed." Mama said, "Sabrina has enhanced your life son. She's not brought nothing but good out of you and I honor her for that."

Years after my breakup with Ramona, my mother would periodically ask if I was dating. I always told her no, which wasn't a lie. The beautiful Mrs. Fleming would grow silent, taking in the shadow of sadness that crossed my face. She never encouraged me to date, allowing me to heal from heartache in my own time.

When I brought Sabrina to the store and gave the introductions she knew it was something special. Whether she knew it or not, her opinion was a valued one. My mother continued to congratulate me on my achievement, but stopped with the praise and spoke with caution.

Something she always did when speaking on a certain topic.

"I know Sabrina chose nursing, but I'm curious as to why you jumped on board. Does it have anything to do with your father's autopsy?"

I was silent.

When she realized I wasn't going to answer she retreated, and again uplifted me for my accomplishments.

Sabrina...

I'd just come in from bailing one of my siblings out of jail when Cyprus met me at the door.

"Hello Sabrina."

"Hey Boss." Boss was his last name and what they called him at his job.

"Thanks for your help today. I really do appreciate it. Where is everybody?"

"Who knows."

I turned and looked at Cyprus. For the first time in years I was scared to be in my own home. All of my roommates knew that, because of my fear of being alone, I asked that we always know where each other was at all times.

Knowing gave me a sense of security. I knew I had easy access to one of the guys at all times, no matter the hour.

If one was on a date, I knew to filter him out of my equation and tap into another resource.

Angela Moore

Even when one moved out of the house he'd tell me to call if need be. I never invaded their private time, because I didn't want them invading mine.

I needed them to rescue me from myself.

So Cyprus telling me that he didn't know where the other fellas were did not sit well with me. It didn't sit well with me at all.

Cyprus had been in my life the longest. He'd tried, on numerous occasions, coaxing me out of the grips of my demons.

We were in a janitors closet at school. I'd had another accident and tinkled my pants. It was no fault of my own. My father had really messed my insides up while molesting me.

"It's okay, Sabrina. You can stay at my house."

The closest was a tight spot, giving both of us limited elbow room.

"I can't. I'm not allowed. You know how he is. And I gotta protect my brothers and sisters."

"How are you going to do that?"

"I don't know. But he's been a tyrant these last few days."

"He's the reason you're the way you are. Come stay at my house, I'll protect you."

"I can't! Your dad was a cop and he'll ask too many questions. Besides, who's going to protect everybody else?"

"You can't even protect yourself so how are you going to protect them!?"

I slapped his face. "You asshole! That was so cruel of you to say! You know what we go through at home you insensitive bastard!" I burst into tears.

Since meeting me, Cyprus has been my shadow, making sure he enrolled in every class I enrolled in.

We were in the ninth grade walking to algebra when I pissed on myself. He immediately pulled me into the closet.

"I'm sorry Sabrina." He held me close as I cried.

Butter Pecan

"He wouldn't let them out of the house today. I think my worrying caused my bladder to let loose."

He knew that was a lie. My bladder let loose whenever it wanted. I barely drank fluids and never ate cereal before leaving for school.

I pulled back from Cyprus, wiped my face with my sleeve and held out my hand. "Give me my clothes, please."

He always carried wipes and an extra set of my clothes in his book bag for me. He had more room in his bag than I had in mine.

I took off my soiled clothes in front of him. When the stench if my urine assaulted his nose he wasn't fazed. He held open the empty bag he'd carried my clean clothes in. I placed my soiled ones inside, naked from the waist down.

"Where are my panties?"

He was staring at my little bush.

"Oh." After digging in his bag he found them and handed them to me.

As I cleaned off my privates and I put my panties on I asked a question. "Why weren't they with my other clothes?"

"They must have fallen out when I handed your pants to you." Cyrus had seen me naked plenty of times and it hadn't been a big deal. He was behaving differently this time. I recognized my father in his eyes. Lust. After putting on my panties I told him to turn around.

"Why?"

"Because I said so that's why."

He obeyed and I finished cleaning the inside of my thighs before putting on my pants. "Okay, I'm ready."

He turned, a disappointed look on his face.

"I'm about to go home Cyprus. Thanks for your help. I really do appreciate it."

"Sabrina, I'm in love with you."

He wasn't telling me anything I didn't already know. Cyprus was the popular kid at school and everything that boy touched turned to gold. He was active in numerous clubs and was the star on the football team. Even as a ninth grader.

Academically astute, he got bored quick. That's where I came in.

I became his 'something to do' project when he saw an upper classman bullying me. He stepped in and saved the day. From then on he was my security.

By choice, I didn't have many friends. Didn't want everyone in my business. Once I felt comfortable I told Cyprus my secrets and we drew close. The closer we got, the more time we spent together.

He never verbalized it, but I knew he felt sorry for me. Not saying so allowed me some dignity. Instead, he told me how beautiful I was.

"Your skin is like a sea of chocolate Sabrina. So rich and milky. I could look at it forever." Even felt that way about my hair. "Can I touch it?"

"I don't see why not."

He did and was enthralled. "It's crisp like leaves on a fall day." He smelled it. "And has the scent of morning dew. Simply breathtaking." At times I'd catch him staring. "Your face is like a wishing well - It has such depth you never get to the bottom of it. Endless beauty, Sabrina. Endless." And my well-proportioned butt. "Like two half-moons. They shine bright to lead us on the road to heaven."

He took my dark hands into his, moving them in every direction, voicing his approval. "What have your hands encountered in this life Sabrina? I wish that they'd not do anything so that they can always remain pillars of perfection."

The contrast of my black hand in his white one made his mouth water.

Boss loved everything about me, but I loved him too. He protected me, something my father should have done. He shielded me from the taunts, something my father should have done. He was my comforter when home life became too much to bear, something my father should have been. He wanted to be my lover, something I never allowed him to be.

That's something my father had already been.

He encouraged me to move in with the college professor. "You're a smart girl Sabrina. It'll be best." So I did and it was best, until the professor intentionally drove into the side of a bridge and killed himself and his wife.

A murder-suicide with no kids or family to leave anything too, except for me. They even left me the responsibility to bury them. That was a closed casket mess. After the estate was settled I inherited their mansion and money. That's when the nightmares started.

"I'll stay there with you Sabrina." Cyprus ventured.

"But what about your scholarship money?"

"I can always go back to school."

He never went back instead he became my live-in protector. We dated separately throughout the years but never anything overly serious. By then we were comfortable with each other. But all hell broke loose when I told him Walter would be moving in with us.

Cyprus had just walked in from an overtime work shift. After placing his gun and badge on the kitchen counter he sat on the couch in the den. I was a career college student on summer break and had dinner prepared with the table set to eat.

"You remember Walter?"

"How could I not?"

I ignored his sarcastic demeanor.

"I've ask him to move in…"

He cut me off. "What the hell is that about?"

"It's not about anything. Walter helps me…"

"How is he helping you? Didn't you catch him cheating? Weren't you just crying to me about how you saw him with another woman?"

"That was last damn year. He's still my friend."

"Just because he's your friend doesn't mean he has to live with you."

"I could say the same for you. You're my friend and you live with me."

"I'm different Sabrina."

"Says who?"

He didn't like that. "Things are fine just the way they are. Why mess it up?"

"He's good for me Cyprus. He offers me something you can't, and I need it in my life. I need him close. Yes, our breakup was ugly but aren't most breakups?"

Thoughts of my past relationships hit a nerve.

"I would love to think that someone would find me worthy of waiting for marriage to have sex with me, but I'm not giving up the goods. No matter how hard they try I'm not going to give in. He did what he felt he had to do and cheated on me. So what. I'd still like to have him in my life."

"He'd be in 'our' life".

My head was starting to hurt. "Our relationship wasn't all bad Cyprus. That man has great qualities that compliment and comfort me. I would like to have them around me continually."

He walked into the dining area, leaned his back against the counter and crossed his arms and legs. "So, who broached the subject?"

"He did but it was only after…"

"Figures. Sounds like an opportunist to me."

"Would you please stop cutting me…?"

"His ass probably thinks he can sweet talk the panties off you."

"WILL YOU SHUT THE FUCK UP!?" While speaking his rhetoric, his selfish butt hadn't even been looking at me and hadn't seen my tears. "JUST SHUT UP!" I ran to my room, slammed the door and fell onto my bed. He was on my heels.

"Sabrina?" He sat on the edge of my bed, tried pulling me into his arms. I fought him off me.

"Don't you see?" I sobbed, "Can you please just look past what you find comfortable and see that I'm dying? You freakin' work the third shift Cyprus. I'm here alone. In this big scary ass house that reminds me of when I was a kid. I'm all alone with nobody to hold me when I wake up screaming, or when I'm paralyzed with fear and scared to move. Could you please see past you and look at me? I've lost twenty pounds in the last three months because it's gotten so bad and it's not getting any better. Can't you see?"

He placed his hand on my shoulder.

"Don't touch me." He knew I was beyond angry. "He'll be here next week Cyprus. Now could you please leave me alone?"

I could tell he felt bad but I didn't care. I needed Walter in my life and I needed him in the worst way.

I didn't hear squat out of Cyprus when Malcolm and Rusty moved in. But, the more men who crossed over my home's threshold, the more distant Cyprus became.

"What do you mean 'who knows?' We're supposed to know where each other are at all times."

"Correction. You are supposed to know where everyone is at all times. They are grown men and don't need me babysitting their every move."

His words hurt. "Why would you say that?"

"Because it's true."

"How long have you felt this way?"

He looked at me as if I was crazy. "Did you really just ask me that?"

"I'm serious, Cyprus, how long?"

He secured the front door and walked towards me. As he drew closer my fear was replaced with sadness. His eyes told it all. Cyprus stood in front of me, put his finger under my chin and lifted my head so that our eyes met.

"Always Sabrina. I've always felt that way."

He kissed my forehead and went to the kitchen to fix his dinner. I went into my bedroom and started packing.

Sincere...

Sabrina was moved in and it felt right.

She had her room on one end of the house, and I had mine. It wasn't long before that didn't exist because of the nightmares.

"Sabrina wake up! Wake up baby!"

"No! No! No! Leave me alone! Get off me!" She was having a bad dream and that shit had my heart beating a mile a minute.

"Leave me alone! Stop!" She was screaming at the top of her lungs.

I ran to my room and got my cellphone. Walter didn't let me get a word out.

"Just hold her man. Hold her, kiss her sweaty forehead and tell her that everything is going to be alright."

He hung up before I could thank him. I ran into the bathroom and got a cold face towel and then hightailed it into her bedroom, I pulled back her blankets and lay next to her.

Although she resisted, I got her into my arms and rocked her back and forth while she cried and moaned. With one hand around her waist I used the other to wipe her sweaty, tear-covered face.

"It's okay Sabrina. I'm here baby girl. I'm here."

It took an hour for her to fall asleep. I made sure I was right there when she woke up.

That was the first night Sabrina stayed at my house. It scared the hell outta me. I knew that baby girl had some issues but damn!

The following morning I had some errands to run. After getting cleaned up and eating breakfast in silence with Sabrina, I headed for the door. When I opened it she about flipped.

"Where are you going?"

I turned and looked at her. "To go take care of some business."

"Well, how long are you going to be gone?"

"I don't know. Maybe about a couple of hours."

"Do you mind me asking exactly 'where' this business is?"

I raised an eyebrow, she raised two. I stood there and looked at her for a minute and then closed the door. I walked back in, took her by the hand, walked her from the dining room table to the couch and sat her down.

"I didn't sleep at all last night." I said.

"Why? Because of me?"

I didn't even answer. "So, since I didn't have nothin' but time on my hands it gave me an opportunity to think. I've decided to quit my job and become a fulltime student."

She couldn't believe what I'd said and expelled a quiet 'what?'

"I'm also going to the bank so that I can give you your money back for these semesters' classes."

"No, no, no, no, no. You can't do that Sincere you have a child to take care of and responsibilities. I knew this was a bad idea when you asked me to move in but you wouldn't listen. I'll just move back into my house."

She'd been around me long enough to know that when I got that real calm look on my face I meant business. She got quiet.

"We not gonna have that kinda talk Sabrina. You are right where you need to be and I'm okay with it. It's going to take some getting used to but I'm up for the task baby girl. No more of that foolish talk, ya hear?"

She nodded in response.

"Good, now would you like to ride with me while I take care of this business?"

She smiled, "Don't ask questions you already know the answers too Sincere."

I smiled back, "Alright then. I'll be waiting right here."

She got up off the couch and started heading for her room. Before she made it there she started crying.

I rose, walked to her and wrapped her in my arms.

"I'm sorry Sincere. You just don't know what's been going through my head. I just knew you were going to freak out about last night and try to figure out a way to ask me to leave. It wouldn't have been the first time. Most men can't handle me. I mean, I know I've got some serious issues, so when they decide that I'm too much for them I have no problem letting them go because I know I'm a handful. But you Sincere. I wanted so badly for you to not be like the others and you're not. You're not."

Her ass was real emotional that morning and I welcomed knowing she needed me as much as I needed her. All her peculiarities served as an antidote for April.

For months we'd been in each other's personal space, but not on the roommate level. I mean, from the day she'd moved in I'd be going into the bathroom after she'd taken a shit. I hadn't done that since Ramona. The reality of our living situation hit me like a truck. Whether I was up for the task or not remained to be seen.

One thing was for sure, the incident of the previous night gave me a glimpse of what was to come, and it was eye-opening.

Now, I gotta admit, it was pretty weird taking Sabrina to my job. I didn't know how she'd react. Yeah we'd been to numerous places together in the past but after last night, I didn't know what she did after those encounters when she left my presence. I didn't know if she went home and one of the boys comforted her or what. After one night of staying with me I realized that I didn't know a lot of things.

The situation with my job took a lot longer than I had expected, but Sabrina was a trooper. It wasn't as if she had a choice.

One thing that concerned me were her fits of fear. It wasn't until after I parked, I wondered how often she had them and if they were during the day or only at night. That was one thing the fellas forgot to tell me.

You see, while packing Sabrina's things into the U Haul, The Dicks gave me a rundown on what to expect. Everybody except Cyprus. His ass was ghost the entire time I was there. Even before moving day, when I went to the house to help her organize a few of her things, he was nowhere to be found.

The other dicks were there though and I had to admit, I'd read them wrong.

I wasn't stupid and knew that at the drop of a hat all four of them would sleep with Sabrina. But, the way they lent a hand at helping her pack all of her things made me think otherwise about their earnest concern for her.

I was impressed with how they made sure I was on top of all her psychological needs. They genuinely cared about Sabrina's welfare.

Since they told me nothing about incidents happening during the day, while at my soon-to-be previous place of employment, I took my chances on taking her inside. I hopped out of my truck, ran around to her side, opened her door and grabbed her hand.

A huge smile spread across her beautiful face. I knew that even if she had an episode, we were going to be alright.

Sabrina...

When I made the decision to move, I thought Rusty would be the one to act a nut, but I was wrong. It was the one I'd wanted the most support from, Cyprus. Since my transition Cyprus had become a real butthole.

He called daily and asked the same stale questions. "How are things going?"

"Things are great"

"Just checking."

"No matter how many times you ask the answer is going to be the same."

"We'll see."

I never questioned his last remark but then one day I did and it wasn't pretty. "What's that mean?"

"Just what I said. We'll see."

I didn't respond.

"He's no different from the others Sabrina."

"How would you know?"

"Because we're all the same and want the same thing."

"He's like no one I've ever met before."

"It'll come out. It always does."

"You say that like you want this to fail."

"Maybe I do."

I was at the mall taking one of my siblings school shopping. When I found myself getting loud I excused myself and went outside. "And why is that Cyprus?"

"He's no good for you."

"You're a cop, not a psychologist Cyprus."

"You know he's going to hurt you."

I was getting pissed but kept my composure. "No, I don't. But if he does I hope that you guys are there for me, the way you were before Sincere." It was like he was trying to give me a reason to doubt Sincere and his ability to be a trustworthy man.

"Just like Walter, he won't be able to wait."

"The same way you couldn't."

"We weren't together."

"Doesn't matter. You still hurt me." Silence. " Don't you want to see me happy?"

"I thought you were."

"Of course I was. But now I'm happier."

"So over here you needed four, and now you only need one?"

"You guys didn't have what it took to complete me."

"It's barely been a year, and you're telling me that he has everything you need in a man to be fulfilled? It must be a miracle."

"No miracle Cyprus, just love."

He sounded offended, "Oh, so you're in love now?"

"For the first time in my life I think I am."

"I've heard that before."

"This is different. Whatever happened before Sincere were just moments in time preparing me for this time."

"So what we had was nothing?"

"What we had and have, was and will always be something, but it wasn't and isn't this. It's different this time." I let that sink in and then continued. "We were young Cyrus. You told me you loved me in highschool. I knew it wasn't me that you loved but the idea of me. I was your delectable chocolate delight. Your trespass. A pastime you got used to. I'm not saying your feelings haven't intensified since then, but I don't think they're the feelings you have when it's true love. Maybe more like a caring big brother."

"You can't tell me how I feel."

"I'm not."

"I'm throwing your words back at you. Stay in your place, you're not a doctor."

"Why don't you want me to be happy Cyprus? Don't you think I deserve that? Don't I deserve a fulfilling relationship? He's different, Cyprus. Do you know why? Because after he found out about my shortcomings he continued to stick around. He didn't flee. Do you know how many guys have walked away from me because I lived with four men who balanced me out?"

"And we still balance you out."

"Yes you do, but so does he."

"What if one day he's not around?"

"Well, Cyprus. If I ever have to cross that bridge, I would like to think that as you guys have supported me in the past, you'll be there to support-"

He didn't let me finish.

"Whatever." He hung up.

I got my number changed and gave it to the remaining three.

Sincere...

An adult relationship was new to me. Ramona was truly the only person I'd been in committed relationship with. Being with Sabrina took some getting used to. But she was worth it.

"Sincere, you didn't have to quit your job for me. I could have easily hung with the fellas until you got off."

"No the hell you couldn't. That would have defeated the purpose Sabrina. Besides, I enjoy your company."

"What if I start to bore you, or you get tired of me?"

"Never that. Even if you get on my last nerve I won't get tired of you. And if I do, I'mma put you in timeout."

We were in the kitchen making dinner. When I'd made that last statement she hit me upside my head. What I'd said was true. Other than the fact that she wasn't givin' up the pussy, we got along great. And don't think I didn't try.

We decided that she'd sleep in the bedroom closest to mine. I suggested getting a baby monitor so I could hear when she had an episode, but she was totally against that. We put our minds together and decided to just move her closer to the master bedroom.

After one particular nightmare I decided to stay in bed with her. The nightmare had been so bad that she started fighting me in her sleep. When I was finally able to calm her ass down I held her close and listened until her muffled moans were reduced to nothing. As I rose to leave she unconsciously held on tight. After waiting about fifteen minutes I tried again with the same result. I stayed.

As I lay there holding her tight, I thought of the trauma she'd endured as a child, the instances that stimulated the nightmares. Then everything shifted. Almost instantly my nose tickled and took in her fresh scent. My thought process immediately went to sex.

As soon as it had, my brain registered her soft skin and the fact that she wasn't wearing a bra.

My dick stood at attention poking her in her belly. When she agreed to move in I assured her that I'd be a good boy and keep my hands to myself. At that moment I knew I'd told her a lie.

She lay on top of my right arm which meant my left was free.
Shit!

I looked down and despite the dark I knew her mouth was slightly opened. She'd fallen asleep in my arms that way many a night while watching a movie.

Since the theater incident I hadn't touched Sabrina's lips. I bent down and missed them. My lips touched her nose instead of her mouth.

That mistake caused her to stir. I froze.

After she relaxed I abandoned the lip action and started rubbing on her thigh. I realized she wasn't wearing any panties under her sleep shorts.

Oh shit!

Thought I was gonna nut on myself. The moment was too intense so I tried once again to get up. Just as before, she started moving. The situation was so messed up that my dick started hurting. It needed relief and needed it bad. When I could no longer take it I quickly removed my arm, made sure she hadn't woke, then went to the bathroom to jack off.

The next day I kept looking at her ass to see if she had on any panties under the tight jeans she was wearing. When my eyes got tired of straining I threw caution over my shoulder and asked plainly, "Can I ask you a personal question?"

She walked into the living room with a bowl of popcorn. We were about to watch the presidential debate.

"Shoot."

"Do you have on any panties?"

I made the question sound generic but deep down my heart was beating extra hard in anticipation of her answer.

She threw some popcorn into her mouth and muffled out her response.

"No. I've not worn them since high school. They cause me too many female problems."

She turned up the volume on the TV as if I'd asked her the weather.

Hell naw she wasn't going back to that house! Not in this lifetime anyway!

April...

So this brotha dun quit his job for this chick? He's gonna regret that shit.

Chapter Five

Ramona...

Sincere's ass had really found someone to settle down with. I knew it was serious when he brought her over to meet our son.

"Hey little man!"

As he greeted Brice, I accomplished my 'woman scan' of Sabrina in two seconds flat.

Sincere lied. That woman wasn't beautiful, she was drop dead gorgeous. She was a chocolate little lady with an Afrocentric look. Her hair was in a nice Afro that screamed 'Fight the power'. Her lips were medium-sized and greasy as hell. It looked like she'd been eating chicken all day. The color was cute tho.

When I looked at her eyes I knew they were going to have his toes curling in the bedroom. The way she dressed was simple, and the cowgirl boots she wore were hella tight and I told her so.

"Since Sinceres rude butt hasn't done any introductions, my name is Ramona." I extended my hand in greeting which she gladly accepted.

"My name is Sabrina. Nice to meet ya."

Her hands were soft as hell. As if she hadn't worked a day in her life. Upon better examination I realized her outfit wasn't simple at all. Although she wore jeans and tee-shirt they were rich in quality and had to have cost a grip.

"The pleasure is all mine." I looked over at Sincere who was looking at me. The joy I saw on his face let me know that he was glad that I was being good. When I looked back at Sabrina, a seed of jealousy entered my heart. It was the first time I'd actually seen Sincere happy.

Sincere...

Sabrina and I were at the mall doing some last minute holiday shopping when all kinds of craziness popped off.

"Sup Sincere?"

I'd know that sexy-ass voice anywhere. It was April, and the moment she made her grand appearance my mouth started watering.

"Hey April how have you been?"

"Good. How about you?"

As soon as she asked the question she looked over at Sabrina. I stepped closer to my woman. "I've been great. Sabrina this is April, April this is Sabrina."

Neither woman extended their hand for a shake but simultaneously said hello. I took ahold of Sabrina's elbow and was about to tell April goodbye, but her nasty ass beat me to the punch.

While making her exit she waved her fingers in front of my face and sang "Y'all have a pussylicious holiday."

As she sashayed her fat ass away, all I could do was drop my head, and it wasn't because of embarrassment.

Hell nah!

It was because before April had walked up to us, she'd dipped her finger into her pussy, and after she'd waved it in front of my face, I'd actually wanted to take her into the bathroom and have her hover over my face. At that moment I was more than glad that Sabrina and April hadn't shaken hands.

"Are you okay Sincere?"

I had to get my shit under control. "Yeah, that was just embarrassing as hell."

Sabrina cleared her throat, "More embarrassing than your dick being hard?"

What kinda shit is this?

I looked down expecting my yardage to be sticking out but it wasn't. I looked over at Sabrina and she started cracking up.

I'd made a mental note to get on April about the petty ass move she'd made. But then I thought better of it. I didn't wanna hear her sultry voice and give myself a reason to fall off and back between her thick thighs. I'd been doing good thus far and I wanted to keep it that way.

Now, concerning the remainder of our nice day out together, I didn't know what to expect. Sabrina continued shopping in silence. I could only imagine what was going through her mind. To keep the peace I took ahold of Sabrina's hand, and as we went from store to store, held it tight.

We were in Dicks getting Brice a bike when we came across one of her previous dicks.

"Hello Sabrina."

It was Cyprus and I must admit the ebony beauty he had draping his arm was kinda cute.

Before Sabrina could speak, I spoke, "Good seeing you again Cyprus."

He had to be out his damned mind if he thought he was going to disrespect us like that. And that included the young lady with him.

When Cyprus looked at me silently, I kissed Sabrina on the cheek. I told the young lady it was nice meeting her and the gently pulled Sabrina along. Two encounters from crazy exes?

"That was weird."

"Hmhmm." Was all Sabrina said for the duration of our shopping excursion.

The drive home was intense.

"Could you turn that off, please?"

I turned off my Eric Benet CD. We rode in silence. When we were halfway home she spoke.

"Who's April?"

Awww shit!

When I looked her way she was looking out of the window as if in deep thought, "Nobody worth talking about."

She waited until we got into the driveway to respond. As I opened my door to get out of my truck I noticed that she was still sitting, looking out of the window.

"Well, considering she had the scent of her pussy on her fingers for 'us' to smell I think she's worthy of a conversation." I sat back in my seat, shut my door and exhaled. "Sincere, before I moved in here we were to come clean about our past. I don't recall an April ever being mentioned."

That's because I never mentioned her!

She turned and looked at me. "I thought you told me about everyone you've slept with."

"I did Sabrina."

"Well it seems as if you forgot one Sincere. Have you been sleeping around on me?" She looked as if she was about to cry. "And to think I told Cyprus that you were different." She grabbed for the door but I locked it. *Click!*

"What the hell you mean you told Cyprus that I was different? What y'all doin' discussing me?"

I was using anything I could to get the topic of the discussion off April. It didn't work.

"I thought you said you wouldn't hurt me." A tear fell down her cheek. That shit broke my heart. I tried scooting closer to her but she wasn't having it. "Please don't. Will you unlock the door?"

I sat back.

"Look at me Sabrina." She'd turned her back towards me. "Please."

She didn't.

"I didn't lie to you. You asked me to tell you who I'd slept with and I did. April and I have never slept together." I paused for a long time and just as I was about to tell her about our relationship she spoke.

"Sincere, I'mma tell you this." She turned toward me and broke my heart again with her stream of tears. "That woman blatantly disrespected me and you're hesitating to tell me the depth of your relationship, which I know was an intimate one. If your tongue doesn't come down from the roof your mouth, I'll be back with 'The Dicks' so fast you'll think I never left."

"I just smelled and ate out her pussy."

She got a confused look on her face. "What did you just say?"

"That's why I didn't mention her. I've never had sex with April. Our intimate moments were strictly oral. No penetration."

She got quiet and looked out of her window again. All kinds of shit was going through my head. "It's okay, I understand."

What in the hell did that mean? "Understand what?"

She turned and took my hand into hers. As she spoke, she looked at my mouth, "That for her to behave like, that your pussy eating game must be fierce."

I wanted so bad to kiss her!

Sabrina...

As I sat in that truck I wanted to break down, but I didn't. We'd been going strong for almost a year and all seemed to be going well. One thing I'd told Sincere before moving in was that cheating was non-negotiable. I wouldn't tolerate it. I guess he didn't believe fat meat was greasy.

Although I wasn't giving up the goods, I knew I was worth the wait. If my man didn't think that was the case then that was his problem; I refused to compromise.

I wanted so bad to give Sincere my all, but something told me to hold back. Not just the physical, but my heart.

I already knew he was going to try to justify not telling me about April by saying that they hadn't had sex, but the fact that he hadn't mentioned her confirmed what I'd suspected. What's done in the dark always comes to the light.

Although Sincere and I weren't having sex, before we'd moved in together, we were around each other enough for me to predict his routine.

On the nights that I'd be chilling with my roommates and couldn't get in touch with Sincere I knew he was most likely having sex with someone. He wasn't my man, and I wasn't his woman. He could do whatever he wanted. I still felt a sting of jealousy knowing that he was touching and caressing another female. That's why before we decided to take our friendship to the next level I asked him vital questions about his past relationships. Sexual or otherwise.

The way April's eyes bore into him let me know that that was not the last time we'd be hearing from her. I wasn't about drama, so that'd be an issue he'd have to deal with alone.

Why couldn't he have just told me everything?

Sincere...

When we finally made it into the house Sabrina put our packages away, then went to her bedroom. That wasn't good, so I tapped on her door and called her name. She didn't answer.

When I went to open it and I found it locked my thoughts were confirmed. There wasn't shit I could do or say.

Two hours later there was a knock at my front door. I opened it and saw those four dicks on my porch and one of them was dressed in blue. Now I had plenty to say.

I slammed my door in their faces and then tapped on Sabrina's door, "You've got company." I stood right there until she opened it. As soon as she did I was on that ass. "Why didn't you tell me Cyprus was a cop?"

Her eyes were all puffy and shit from crying but I didn't give a damn. "What?"

"Why didn't you tell me that asshole was a policeman?"

She tried walking around me but I wouldn't let her. She glared at me with puffy eyes. "Why didn't you tell me you were eating April's pussy?"

"That's trivial compared to my question."

"Excuse me?"

"Yeah, that's right, trivial."

I walked into my living room and looked out my window. They were sitting on my front porch chatting it up like old chums. I turned and looked at Sabrina, "When will you be back to get your things?"

"Soon."

"You need to come and get them like yesterday."

She put her hand on her hip, "Really Sincere? So, you say nothing to me about a whole sexual relationship and you consider it trivial. I say nothing to you about my roommate being a policeman and all of a sudden it's a great betrayal on my part? What Cyprus does for a living is none of your business."

"And where the hell I put my tongue is none of yours."

Tears welled in her eyes. "You selfish bastard. Fuck you Sincere!"

That got my attention. Sabrina never cursed. "What did you just say?" I asked more from shock than anything.

She walked her little ass up to me and with her petite finger pointed it on my chest. "You selfish piece of shit! Fuck! You!"

I was close to the door so when she went to open it I blocked her. "Don't leave. I'm sorry. There's just a lot you don't know."

"Sincere I'mma need for you to move."

"April!"

Shit!

I tried to cover that up. "Sabrina."

I cain't believe I just said that! Shiiiiit! April's ass is grass!

Sabrina held up her hand and closed her crying eyes. Nothing else needed to be said.

Sabrina...

Silence was the sound on the drive home. As I replayed the last few hours in my head nobody said a word and let me have my moment. It was a long ride.

When we got to the house I went into my room and stayed in there for days. The only time I came out was at night, and it was to go to Walters's room. I think he knew that I wasn't going in there just about my nightmares.

I was glad that the mall incident happened during school's winter break.

Sincere and I had scheduled our classes to coincide. If classes were in session I was guaranteed to run into him, which would be heartbreaking.

I knew how aggressive he could be. If I tried to dodge running into Sincere on campus he wouldn't hesitate to boldly walk into my classroom, forcing me to talk to him. School break saved me from that fiasco.

All I could do was keep asking myself: How could I have been so stupid?

I should have known better. History always repeats itself when it came to me and men. No matter how many guys I'd met and dated none found me worth of waiting for.

Cyprus had been right. It irritated me to admit it.

I concluded that I'd have to resign myself to possibly never coming across a man who loved me enough to make that sexual sacrifice. I would have to be content with being alone.

I wished Sincere was different. I wished that from the bottom of my heart. Then I remembered that he'd called me by another woman's name. That alone pushed him into the Do Not Return slot.

Sincere...

How could I have been so stupid?

I knew I should've told Sabrina about April but I couldn't bring myself to do it. I was afraid that telling would completely sever all ties with easy access to April's ever-ready, ripe fruit. I should have done it anyway.

I wanted to keep April a secret so I'd have admittance to drink from her fountain without Sabrina knowing.

Yes, I'd cut off most ties to April and had planned to keep it that way. But a brotha was young, fine and always horny. I took care of my needs, but if the urge for sex became too overwhelming I knew someone was a phone call away.

Damn! Did I really call Sabrina, April?

Shit!

And, she knows absolutely nothing about why I feel the way I do about the police. I totally lost my mind and clicked on her.

I had to make this right.

Somehow, someway, I had to get my woman back. Before I did that I needed to catch up with April's dirty butt.

What kinda shit is this?

I drove like a bat outta hell to April's house only to find her ass had moved.

Shit!

A month passed and I didn't see or talk to Sabrina, not even to pick up her things. I think she had no problem leaving her belongings at my house, even if it meant forever.

What really messed me up was when classes resumed and she didn't show up for any of them. I'd been looking forward to seeing her too. Actually, I needed to see her.

On the low, I stalked her classes to see if I could get a glimpse of her and was disappointed every time.

Shit!

While at the crib, it was hell walking past her bedroom every day, looking at the essence of who she was and she wasn't there. It was eerie, like she'd vanished from thin air.

Walking past her room also reminded me of what a complete jerk I'd been.

Sabrina...

It was time to start clinical. To make sure I wouldn't run into Sincere after winter break, I dropped out of culinary school and hit the nursing books hard.

I picked up where I left off, having previously held off taking my nursing classes to wait for Sincere to catch up. By the time Sincere made it into his clinical I'd have already surpassed him with most of my clinical being completed.

Because I'd lived with the professor I was able to connect with his colleagues and expedited a lot of my lessons. It wasn't easy to maneuver, especially when it came to the clinical portion, but I was able to dodge the Sincere bullet.

The fellas never asked me one thing about the Sincere situation, even months after getting my butt outta bed and back into a routine. It was as if they had been expecting it.

I didn't care what they thought or expected. I pushed Sincere to a place in my mind where he didn't exist and lived my life as if he didn't.

Sincere...

Every time I walked into my house Sabrina's absence was palpable. So was my immaturity.

I finally found a woman who wasn't out for my money or dick and I messed it up.

And when Mom, Ramona or even Brice asked about Sabrina, as best I could, I blew them off.

Shit, my heart was hurting and I really didn't want to tell anybody about what had happened. I guess I didn't have to; It was written all over my face, and showed in my foolish decisions.

"Come on Ramona. I ain't had no pussy in damn near two years."

"You ain't gettin' me caught up in yo mess." Ramona pushed me off herself and curled up on the other side of the couch, "I like Sabrina, and nine times outta ten y'all gonna be back together. Besides, when you broke it off with me I got serious with my man and we've been good."

"Who you tryin' to convince? Me or yourself?"

"I'm serious. I'm not saying it's been easy but I have really been trying to stick to my guns and be faithful."

As soon as she said those words she looked at my crotch.

I wanted to believe Ramona but knew otherwise. I got off her couch and went into our sleeping son's bedroom. I gave him a kiss on his forehead, walked into the living room, gave Ramona a kiss on hers, then bounced.

I got into the nursing program and started getting into the heat of things. The whole ordeal required total commitment. Returning to my old job part time crossed my mind, but I was glad I didn't. With clinical twice a week during the day I also had a class at night that divided my days into chaos.

While in school I hoped to run into Sabrina. It never happened.

I did run into a few new honeys. Before you know it I was back to my boyish, hoeing ways. The chicks were fine and smart, but brought drama with those brains and beauty. While speaking with one of my regulars on the phone, shit got heated.

"Why not Sincere?"

"Because I'm not ready for all that."

"We been fuckin' for six damn months and you tellin' me that you're not ready for commitment?"

"I already told you that the only woman I'm committed to is lady education. I don't have room in my life for anything else."

"But you got room to slide up in my pussy? You full of shit Sincere!"

Click!

Two weeks after me not calling her drama-filled ass, she was at my crib.

"Oh Sincere! Yes baby! Fuck this shit!"

They always came back. Even Ramona. Everybody but Sabrina.

Sabrina...

It was summer break and Sincere was almost a forgotten thought.

I'd given myself a hiatus from heartache and dived into my books during the winter and spring session. I decided to give my brain a well-needed break and passed on taking summer classes.

"So what's the plan for today?" Asked Malcolm.

As an elementary school teacher he was also on break. From the start of summer we'd done activities together. He too was in heartbreak hotel and tried staying busy.

"Haven't decided. It's too hot to ride so I'll probably do some online shopping." It was midday and we'd just finished watching a movie in the livingroom.

"Wanna go swimming? I think I'm good for a few laps." He flexed his muscles.

Poor thing. He dated his lady for two solid years. From what I heard, she'd broken it off with him because, according to her, his dick was too small. His ego was crushed. Since then all he's wanted to do was manly stuff, even if it killed him.

"Maybe later. It's really too hot to do that Malcolm. You're gonna give yourself heatstroke."

He took everything I said as offensive, as if testing his manhood. "You would say that. I'm out."

I was going to check him on his smart, unwarranted comments, but not that day. "Which are you going to do?"

He said 'neither' and stormed out the door. "Jerk!" I yelled at his moody butt.

"Who are you calling a jerk?" Cyprus asked as he entered the room. The topic of Sincere never popped up, but on a daily I saw it in his eyes that he was ecstatic that it hadn't worked.

He'd also become extra touchy feely which really creeped me out. Before he could start rubbing my shoulders, I got out of my recliner. While making my exit, I answered his question. Then I went into my bedroom and locked my door.

After getting comfortable, I pulled out my laptop and did what I told Malcolm I was going to do: Online shopping.

Two days later Sincere was at my front door.

Sincere...

It was summer break and my brain was fried. Clinicals and classes were time-consuming and strenuous. This brothaman needed his brain to rest.

Because I wasn't lazy, I called my previous employer and asked them if they needed any part-time help. I'd been gone awhile, but they gladly welcomed me back. Mom had plenty of help, but every now and then I lent a hand at her store. My workweeks were in full swing and I welcomed them.

All was well in Sincere's world, until life happened.

One day, after all the packages that were to be delivered were secure in my FedEx truck, I skimmed over my route and hit the streets. It was hot as hell, and the truck door being open for easy delivery of packages didn't help.

By my third delivery I was dripping in sweat, working on my second bottle of chilled ice water.

I was in a zone when I realized what street I was on and whipped my truck to the side of the road. I had to do a doubletake of the address.

Shit!

All I could do was shake my head. I wanted to kick myself in the ass, instead, I took out my handkerchief, wiped off my face, and drank some more water.

After a few minutes of idling in my truck, trying to come up with a different plan of action, I looked at my watch, put my truck into drive and drove up the street.

The packages had to be delivered. I just wished I'd paid more attention to my routes before I left the station. I surely would've given my assignment to someone else.

I shook my trepidation off, pulled up into the driveway and made my delivery.

Sabrina...

I was in the kitchen when the doorbell rang.

I got excited, "It could be my packages!" I stopped making dinner and hopped my happy butt to the front door.

Cyprus blocked my view when I got close. "I'll sign for them."

"No big deal, they're my things. I can sign." I playfully elbowed him out of my way and then I froze. "Sincere?"

He looked as if he'd prepared himself to see me. "Hey Sabrina. How you doin'?"

With education always on the brain I ignored his question and anxiously asked mine. "You still in school?"

He smiled showing off what I learned in school were considered a birth defect: His sexy dimples.

"Yah, I'm still in school. Just taking a break. How about you?" I took the small tablet out of his hand and signed for my items. "I needed a break too. Are those my things? Oh. I'm sorry, I'm good Sincere. And you?" He looked sexy as hell in his uniform!

"I'm good. And, glad to hear it." His eye shifted to behind me so I looked over my shoulder. Cyprus hadn't moved from where I'd shoved him. "You need me to bring those in for you?"

Cyprus answered for me, "She doesn't need any help. I got it." He gently pushed me out of the way, picked up my boxes and then tried shutting the door.

Sincere stopped it with his foot. "Can I talk to you Sabrina? Privately."

Without giving Cyprus a second thought I walked out onto the porch and closed the door behind me. This was the closest I'd been to Sincere since I'd moved out. What I saw was absolutely delicious.

For a few seconds, we did nothing but look at each other. He finally cleared his throat, "I was a stupid ass Sabrina. I should never have spoken to you like that nor disrespected you. I want to apologize. I tried calling but you'd gotten your number changed." He paused as if waiting for an explanation. None was given so he carried on. "I've missed you tremendously. More than I thought I would." He looked at his watch. "I'm on a tight schedule today, but was wondering if when I got off we could meet somewhere to talk."

I was at a crossroad. I could tell he was earnest, but I also saw his betrayal. "Let me think about it."

"Fair enough. My number is still the same. You got it?"

"Nope."

He pulled out his phone. "Give me your number that way when I call it you'll have mine."

He thought he was slick.

"In your dreams."

He took a step closer. "Girl, I've been dreaming about you since the day you walked outta my house."

I smile and went into my house. When I walked in Cyprus was still in the same spot, with my packages around his ankles.

Sincere...

When I saw that beautiful queen make her grand appearance into the doorway, my heart skipped a thousand beats. She was just as astonishing as the last time I'd seen her.

After laying eyes on my beautiful Sabrina, my workday became less hectic. Once off work I rushed home, took a shower and kept my phone on my hip waiting for her call. When she didn't, I was cool with it. I knew it was going to take her a minute to digest seeing me and unexpectedly at that, so the next day I did the same thing.

Got off work, rushed home, took a shower and then waited. Come day three the rush was gone but I did wait around to see if she would call. She didn't, and I was pissed.

Her ass made me wait four long weeks. In-between, whenever my phone would ring I'd break my neck to answer it, only to be disappointed. When I got tired of her petty games, she called, when I was least expecting it.

"Hello?"

When she said nothing I looked at my caller ID. A private call. I knew it was her. I put the phone back up to my ear. "Sabrina?"

I said that with caution. Since she'd moved back in with The Dicks I didn't know if one of them were being childish by calling me via her phone. More specifically, Cyprus.

I heard her exhale, "Yes Sincere it's me."

Her voice was music to my ears. "You been okay?"

"I've been good. Look, are you available? I'd like to talk to you face to face. But not at your place. A neutral area."

I had plans with a sweet piece of caramel but threw her and our plans out the window. "Sure. You had dinner yet?"

"Yes I have. Just finished eating with the boys."

I didn't like that answer so I moved on. "How about we meet at The Boatyard for a drink. That way we can sit out on the deck and listen to some live music. Cool?"

"That'll work. Give me a minute to clean up. I'll meet you there in an hour."

Her response was a barely audible whisper, "See you soon."

"See ya."

I hopped off the couch and took a quick shower. This was my second, last and only chance. If I blew this opportunity I'd never get another.

After getting fresh and splashing on some cologne, I snatched up my keys. Just as I placed my hand on the doorknob, I wondered what she wanted to meet about. I figured it couldn't be all bad. If she wanted nothing more to do with me, she'd have never called.

I optimistically left my house, praying my dreams of a happily-ever-after were about to come true.

Sabrina...

Seeing Sincere after four months stirred up a lot of buried emotions. It wasn't like my previous boyfriends, this was something different. And, after I'd closed the door, seeing Cyprus standing in the entryway didn't help. Cyprus brought those buried emotions regarding Sincere to the surface.

"Did you give him your number?"

I gave him a perturbed look. "And if I did?" For the most part I was a passive woman, but Cyprus and his obsession with Sincere was rubbing me the wrong way.

"If you did, then you're stupid."

"What did you just say to me?"

"You heard me the first time." He bent down to pick up my packages.

"Leave them right there." He slowly stood from his stoop and looked at me expectantly. Just like I wanted. "Cyprus," I said, "I am so tired of you trying to dictate my life. If I want to give out my number, I will. It's none of your business."

"I don't care who you give your number to, just not to him."

I had it. "What is this beef you have with Sincere?! From the very beginning you've had an issue with me dating this man! What! Is! It?!"

I'd gotten so loud that Rusty came running out of his room. "What in the hell is going on out here?"

We paid him no attention. "What is it Cyprus? Huh?" I stopped and squinted my eyes. "Are you jealous of him Cyprus? Of us?"

He said nothing but Rusty did. "Jealous of who? What in the hell's going on?" I walked closer and looked into his eyes. "There's something you're not telling me."

Anytime I met a man, I'd give as much information about him as I could to Cyprus. He'd run a criminal background check. Surprisingly, a lot came back as clean as a whistle with not so much as a traffic ticket. Sincere was one of them.

He finally spoke. "All things aren't as they seem Sabrina. Everybody, before you meet them, has a past little lady, and I suggest you start paying attention."

"Isn't that what you're for? You said his record was clean. Stop talking in riddles and tell me what I need to know."

He smiled. "No my dear. What he's hiding should have been told to you from the start. Those files are sealed. I will tell you this. He is my public enemy number one. There's a reason he don't like the police. So with that being said, good luck."

He walked away and left Rusty and me hangin'.

Because of that conversation I held off calling Sincere. I deeply wanted to call him sooner, but fear of the unknown halted me.

What was Sincere hiding from me? Should I be afraid? And what was up with "public enemy number one" statement?

I needed answers. With Cyprus withholding information, I did the next best thing and Googled Sincere. To my disappointment, nothing came up. I Googled him over and over again, with the same results.

It was like Sincere didn't exist. Getting his current information was also null and void.

According to Cyprus, Sincere had secrets and I wanted to know what they were . After my search turned up empty I waited a few more weeks, then picked up the phone and told Sincere that we needed to talk. Sadly, his number was still in my contacts.

As I drove to the Boatyard I became mad at myself. I knew, without a doubt, that I was using my curiosity of the unknown as an excuse to see him.

Sincere...

I purposefully made it to the restaurant ahead of Sabrina. Because I didn't know the nature of our meeting, I wanted to look at her uniqueness before she sat down. As expected, she took my breath away.

As she searched for me, her sexy-ass glossy lips glistened like the sun shining on the sea. She took a slow stroll around the deck, trying find me and an empty table. Some fellas offered their seats, and I beamed when she kindly declined.

Vultures!

The closer she got the better I was able to see her outfit. She wore a sexy tunic shirt, some jeans and some expensive cowgirl boots. She felt me staring, turning her head to look straight at me.

Instantly I stood and placed a big fat smile on my face as she made her way toward me. Although she didn't have one on hers, I wasn't fazed. I wanted to give her a nice tight hug, but thought better of it. Instead I pulled out her chair. After she was seated I took mine, and waited.

"Hello Sincere."

"Hello baby girl."

She picked up her menu and stared at it for a long time. I knew she was stalling 'cause she told me that she'd just had dinner with The Dicks. The waiter approached and she ordered a water and a glass of Chardonnay. She put her menu down and looked around. "The band's good tonight."

That wasn't our first time there together.

On those hard strenuous days of class, periodically we'd treat ourselves to a moment of cool jazz and memory making moments. I was just sad we weren't making any good memory moments at that moment.

"Yeah it is." I said to fill the silence.

Since she acted like she was in no rush to talk, I sat back and enjoyed the ambience. It wouldn't be until the band was taking a break and she was ordering another drink that she'd speak.

"How'd you do with your clinical?" She asked.

I was glad she started off with something simple. "They were cool. Met a lot of new people and find medicine quite interesting."

"Is that riiiight?"

"Yep. How about you? You started clinical yet?"

"Started and almost finished."

"No shit?! How the hell you pass me up?"

"I gots connects my man. I gots connects."

We laughed. Her reply broke the ice and I relaxed. We started talking at the same time, beginning the 'no you go ahead' game. "Ladies first Sabrina, so you go ahead."

"It's no big deal. You're fine. You can go."

After the fifth go around I relented. Her hands were on the table so I took a chance and reached over and grabbed them. "I'mma keep it real with you." She took her hands back. I inhaled deep and loud and then leaned back in my chair. "I deserve that." I looked down on the table, leaned back in and took her hands back into mine. She smiled. "I am truly sorry for being such an ass Sabrina. It wasn't right nor fair."

She cut me off. "Where are you from Sincere?"

I dropped her hands as if scorched. "What?"

"Where are you from and why can't I find anything about you on the Internet."

"Why are you trying to find something about me is the question."

"Are you going back on what you said about being real with me?"

"Never that. But I do want to know why you have inquiries about my past."

"I just do." She looked away which gave me my answer.

"Sabrina?" She turned back towards me. "I will tell you anything you want to know, except what went on with me before my mom and I moved here. I want you to know that I was a kid when we moved which means there was nothing illegal going on in my life. I'm not trying to rehash any memories. It takes me to a bad place but trust me Sabrina. It's nothing that would endanger myself or anyone that I hold dear to my heart." She started biting on her bottom lip. That shit was sexy as hell. "Now back to what I was saying."

She interrupted, "Do you not find me dear enough to share those things with me? Especially the way you behaved after seeing Cyprus in uniform? I mean, you literally clowned on me because of him. I'm just trying to understand."

"How can I make you understand something I don't understand myself? It's in my past for a reason and considering the circumstances, I think Mom and I have adjusted well. Besides, me, my mom and only one other person knows about my past upbringing. That's Ramona."

"Well isn't she lucky."

"I was young when I told her and promised myself that I wouldn't tell anyone else. I guess I stand corrected. It's obvious that dick Cyprus knows what happened so I guess that makes two people." I looked at her real strange, and before I could ask she answered my question.

"He won't tell me."

"Wow. What kinda friend is that?"

"It doesn't matter."

"You're right, it doesn't. And I really don't appreciate him using his badge to find out shit about me." Her eyes got big. "I think we've spent enough time talking about his petty ass. I want to talk about us."

"What about us?"

"Look baby girl. You didn't call my phone to ask me questions about my past. You could have contently lived and died without knowing that bit of information and never called me again." She said nothing. "I ain't apologizing no more because I know that you know how bad I feel about acting so childishly. But what I am going to do is ask you if we can give us one more try.

I've never met a woman like you, Sabrina. You give me purpose and are always in my corner."

"Not always."

I ignored that. "You are one of the most beautiful, intelligent, and sexiest woman I know. I thank God for bringing you into my life because I've flourished since you've been in it. Not to be funny, but since you've been gone, I've realized that with or without you I'm still flourishing, but I'm not trying to take this journey alone. It's because of you I realized my potential Sabrina. I started with you and it's with you that I want to finish it. I've really missed you baby girl. More than you know. Hell I've missed you so much that I left your room exactly the way you left it, dirty clothes and all."

She frowned up her nose.

"You think that's bad? Sometimes, just to smell your scent, I even sniff that shit. If you wore panties I'd probably sleep with those damn thangs."

She leaned in, hit my shoulder and cracked up. She laughed so hard she almost fell out of her seat. I wasn't laughing. I missed her ass bad. She was so damn beautiful.

After she calmed down she took a sip of her wine. As she drank, she looked at me over the rim of her glass. I watched as she swallowed, wanting to jump over the table and lick her damn neck. Just as I was about to speak, she stopped me by holding up a finger.

"Okay! Boy you know you crazy! But seriously Sincere, you absolutely, positively crushed me. I thought you were different."

"I am..."

She closed her eyes and held up a finger. "Please don't. Just don't." I shut my mouth. "I really set you apart from the rest only to be disappointed. You hurt me Sincere."

"Sabrina baby, I'll make it up to you if you just give me a chance. I promise."

"That'll take a lifetime."

"Well, since that's all we got, I'm down. I'm serious baby girl, I don't want you in my life I need you in my life. After you left I went back to the same old emptiness."

"What you mean by that?"

"Don't ask questions you already know the answers."

"Naw brothaman. The last time we talked about your past expenditures, you left some things out. We not having that this time. So again I ask, what do you mean by that?"

I'd walked my ass right into that one. Because I wanted my baby back, I let the chips fall where they may. "I've been endlessly sleeping around, Sabrina, and no that does not include orally." I had to put that out there.

She turned her head and started people watching. I could only imagine what was going through that pretty head of hers and soon found out. With her head still turned she started with the questions. "Your answer means no April."

"No April, or anyone else I've told you about." She looked at me out of the corner of her eyes.

I held up my hand. "Scouts honor."

She smiled. "You wish you had the honor of a scout."

I said nothing.

"Sincere?" She looked at me.

"Yes, baby girl?"

"In all my dating days, I've never given a man a second chance."

"Not even The Dicks?"

"Not even The Dicks."

"I see why they're so possessive. So you didn't give head dick another chance either?" She shook her head no. "Explains why he's so damn bitter and envious."

"I wasn't finished."

"Sorry 'bout that."

" I want so bad to trust you. I want that so bad."

"I'm through. Although you ain't givin' up no pussy I'll beat the meat till you ready."

"Do you have to be so vulgar?"

"Hey, it is what it is."

She looked at me for a long time, shook her head and then started crying.

Damn!

I hopped out of my chair and made my way to her side. After pulling her into my arms I comforted her as best as I could. "Don't cry baby girl. I am so sorry I brought you to this. Please forgive me. I'm through Sabrina. I'm through. I promise you I am."

I got some snooty looking sneers from the other patrons but I didn't give a damn. The only person I was concerned about was Sabrina.

Sabrina...

I was scared of the freedom to make the choice of going back to Sincere. I'd never made it before. I'd watched as my mother took my father back repeatedly. Promised myself that I'd never be that desperate.

Am I desperate?

On my drive home from the restaurant I asked myself that question numerous times.

Hating myself for doing what I said I'd never do and giving him my number, I turned my radio all the way up. At times I was my own worst enemy. But I loved him. I absolutely loved Sincere Fleming! At that moment I realized that, besides my father, Sincere was truly the second man I'd ever loved. Everyone before for him was child's play.

When I got home I had an audience. All four of my roommates were waiting on me. When I looked at Walter's smile, I dropped my purse and ran into his arms, glad to know that he understood.

It wasn't until I'd stepped out of his embrace that I notice that one of my friends had dismissed himself. I wasn't surprised. Ignoring his temper tantrum, I sat and talked to the remaining three. I let them know Sincere and I were taking it slow. That he'd wanted me to immediately move back in with him, but I'd declined. My roommates were grateful for my decision.

"You looked physically ill when you moved back here," said Rusty, "I just don't want to see you go through that again. Actually made me wanna go over to his crib and kick his ass."

I started laughing. "Rusty, now you know that's not nice."

"I don't play nice when it come to you."

"Is that riiiiight?"

"Damn skippy! I'll catch a case 'bout my cupcake. And that's on any given day young lady."

Cupcake was a name Rusty'd given me when we dated. He said I smelled fresh, like I'd just come out of the oven. I knew Rusty loved me with all of his heart, but he was a bit over the edge for me.

"I don't think I'll need you doing that my friend." I looked at my guys and started crying again.

I was truly blessed. My friends would climb a thousand mountains to get me back, yet there was nothing they could do for a second chance. But in spite of that, they were there for me.

I had actual friends who cared about my wellbeing. They were stuck under a roof where they regretted messing up with a woman who genuinely loved them. Their pure love for me pushed me forward every single day.

"I am so happy you guys are here. You just don't know how much this means to me. You just don't know." As I cried, they held me close, all three.

Rusty, Malcolm and Walter knew I was embarking on a journey they'd wished I'd taken with them. They also knew I was afraid. I'd taken a leap of faith to walk on uncharted terrain, and they vowed to be with me every step.

I felt the presence of another: Cyprus. He added himself to our hug, and I bawled tears of joy.

My circle was complete.

Sincere...

After our dinner I rushed home and cleaned up the crib. Cain't even lie, a brotha has been down in the dumps since Sabrina left. It showed in my housekeeping.

With purpose back in my life, I purposefully went about being productive and put my house in order. After finishing I called Sabrina. I intentionally held off calling, giving her time to process our talk. After two hours I started missing her ass so I picked up my phone.

"Hello?"

"Girl, don't act like you don't know who this is."

I could feel her smiling through the phone. "Hey Sincere."

"Hey baby girl. You don't know how refreshing it is to hear your voice."

"Same here."

"You sound like you were crying. You alright?" I regretted asking that question.

"Yeah. I just got through with a heart to heart with the boys."

"Sorry I asked."

She laughed. "Don't be. You'll be surprised to know that they were actually glad to hear that we were working on getting back together."

"Working on it? I thought we were together." I knew she wasn't telling me the whole truth. "So, are you trying to tell me that the main dick was happy 'bout us?"

"Well, almost everybody. And yes, we are working on getting back together. I gotta take it slow with you. You like to move too fast."

"Yeah, I didn't think he would be fond of your announcement." And I really didn't give a damn. "And what do you mean I move too fast? When a man knows what he wants he goes after it. And I want you." Shit, Sabrina needed to know how deeply I loved and needed her. "I hope you don't think my feelings have changed. I still don't like the idea of you being over there with those four dicks swinging in your face. And the fact that they all probably know that you don't wear panties don't sit well with me."

"You don't forget anything do you?"

"That's vital information girl. Shit, no panties allows for easy access."

She laughed. "You so nasty."

"Nope, just a man who's falling in love."

"Say that again."

"Just a man who's falling in love."

"One more time."

I said it super slow, "Just...a...man...who's...falling...in...love."

"How do you know?"

"How do I know what?"

"That you're falling in love."

"One of the main reasons is because I miss yo ass already, but secondly because I just know. Never felt like this about a woman before."

"Mmm hmm."

"Hmmm what? You don't believe me? Baby girl I miss seeing your lopsided afro in the morning."

She sounded shocked. "You noticed that?"

"I sure did. Along with the fact that you never put the damn cap on the toothpaste."

"Did that bother you?"

"Like nails on a chalkboard."

"Why didn't you ever say anything?"

"Gotta pick my battles. I'd rather just put the top back on and hope you're around to do it the next day. I miss taking a shower after you and smelling that sweet body wash stuff you put on."

"Which one?"

"Every last one of them. I do wish you'd wash out the tub when you get out of the shower though."

"I'll work on it. The boys usually do that for me."

Didn't want to hear that!

"I miss watching your pretty little hands peel off the edges of your bread. I loved looking at your throat as you drank the milk out of the carton. Never seen a woman do that."

"And probably never will. What else?"

"Oh, you lovin' this aint you?"

"Yep. Continue."

"I miss you Sabrina. Every. Single. Thing." Her other line started ringing, "You going to answer that?"

I could hear her remove the phone from her ear, then I heard the dial tone.

Sabrina...

I scrambled out of the bed, ran into the living room and screamed. "He's dead! That muthafuckas dead!"

They all knew I was talking about my daddy.

Chapter Six

We sat in silence as Cyprus drove us to the hospital. They knew my story. I kept nothing from the men I dated. To understand me they needed to know where I came from.

Grown men couldn't comprehend how a grown man could find a child attractive, let alone his own daughter. But that was my daddy. Whether they understood or not, that evil man's blood swam through my veins.

When we got to the hospital they stood to the side as I made inquiries. After finding out where my father was we went to his room.

They walked inside with me. I wouldn't have had it any other way.

Within his temporary tomb were my mother and two of my sisters, identical twins Priscilla and Pamela. As soon as I walked in my sisters, in unison, said my name and ran crying into my arms. They were eighteen; smoked weed like it was oxygen and chronic pill poppers.

"He's gone Sabrina. He's gone for good." I held them close, rocking them back and forth.

"We're free," Priscilla sobbed, "The devil has died."

I burst into tears. Evil lay motionless, but I knew he still reigned supreme in my siblings.

We eventually got ourselves together.

The twins held each other close as I made my way to the opposite side of the bed. I did not want to be next to Carmen, our mother.

I looked at a very handsome man who looked like he was sleeping and placed my hand on his chest. I had to be certain that it didn't rise and fall. An indication that I'd been lied to.

After confirming that there was no life left in him I balled my hand and angrily hit his chest.

Everyone in the room gasped.

I hit him again, and again and again. As I did, the memories came. Memories of him telling me to open my legs. His big hands on my small body.

"Come on Sabrina. Open those legs for daddy."

My chest heaved as I hit his. I wanted to punish him. Cause him pain the way he'd caused me pain. After the first few punches I couldn't, anymore.

"Shhh, if you make a sound I won't feed you tomorrow. Now put yo mouth on it."

His voice was in my head and I want to scream!

"Sabrina can't come out to play today. She's gotta take care of house duties."

"Oh yes Sabrina. Just like that."

"Yo little shit is so tight."

"Put ya mama's high heels and wig on for me."

And then there was rejection.

"You getting' too big baby. Tell Carmella to come here."

I guess I'd subconsciously started clawing at his face because I was suddenly being lifted by the waist away from my father.

I clicked. "You fuckun bastard! You ruined us! You perverted child molester." Screaming and yelling I scratched at the hands that held me. "Put me down! Put! Me! The! Fuck! Down!"

The twins were holding each other, crying. Then I saw Carmen. "You let him do this to us! You bitch! You heard us and didn't do shit! You bitch! You fuckin' bitch!"

Sincere...

When the lady at the information desk asked me if I was family, I lied.

She told me Sabrina's dad's room number. As I made my way to the elevator I felt real bad for Sabrina. She'd told me the things her dad did to her and her siblings. Things I tried understanding but couldn't.

One night while watching a movie she blurted out a comment that left me speechless.

"Because I started developing breasts he stopped touching me. I had just turned eight. My little body was too adult for him. But he'd already stimulated me. I wanted that feeling to continue. One day I walked up to him and put my hand on his dick. He damn near broke my arm. 'Don't you ever fuckun' touch me again! Do you hear me?! Ever!' Crying, I shook my head yes."

After finishing her statement she took the remote from me and turned up the volume as if trying to drown out her own memories.

I didn't know how she felt about his passing, but from her bland text, I knew it wasn't good.

Walking towards her dad's hospital room I heard all kinds of commotion coming from behind his door. I didn't make it inside because as I reached for the doorknob the door flew open. Malcolm had his arms around Sabrina's waist, hauling her into the hallway.

She clawed at his bloody hands, trying to get out of her arms of bondage. I was shocked shitless.

"You stupid weak biiiiiiitch!" She screamed.

Followed by them were the rest of her bodyguards. They had their heads down and their hands in their pockets. I could tell that they were hurting for Sabrina.

"I hate you! I fuckin' hate yooooooou!"

Malcolm placed her on her feet and turned her towards him in an embrace. She held onto him tight and wept.

"Why did she let him do that to us? Whyyyyy?"

He rubbed her head and tried giving her words of comfort. When he looked up and saw me he nodded, as if giving me permission to take his place. I didn't know if she wanted me, so I played it safe.

"Sabrina?"

She turned in Malcolm's arms.

"Sincere?" She extended her weak limbs. "Oh Sincere." She was so broken and sad. All her barriers were down and I saw an eight year old child.

We walked towards each other at the same time.

"Oh Sincere. He hurt me. He hurt me bad."

I lifted her into my arms and held her tight. "I know he did baby girl. I know he did."

And I held her tight. "I got you sweetie. Get it all out. I ain't goin' nowhere."

And I held her tight. "I know it hurts. I'm so sorry Sabrina."

And I held her tight. "It's okay. We're here for you. All of us are going to see you through this."

As I held her tight, my eyes met with her men, but remained on the head dick, Cyprus. "I love you Sabrina. From this day forward baby girl it's me and you."

I meant every word I said.

We stood in the hallway a good thirty minutes. Once she calmed down a bit, I led her to a chair that was outside of her dad's hospital room door. I sat and placed her on my lap.

With my arms around her waist and her hands wrapped around my neck she mumbled, cried and mumbled some more. People came and went, including her roommates. By the time they wheeled her father's body to the morgue, she'd fallen asleep.

I drove Sabrina to my place, parked the truck with my sleeping beauty inside. After opening my front door I went back and carried her to her bedroom.

I then locked up the crib, took off her boots and socks and covered her, still dressed in her day clothes, under the blankets.

I took a much-needed shower, tidied the house and fell asleep on the couch. Two hours later I heard Sabrina's smothered cries. I found her weeping with her face in a pillow. I didn't know if she wanted me at that moment, so with caution I approached.

Her shoulders shook like tiny earthquakes had rocked her body. Her pain caused me pain. I decided to pulled back the covers. As soon as I did she lifted her head, turned towards me and gave me a look that said I wasn't moving fast enough.

She didn't need to say another thing.

I plopped into bed, letting her place her head on my chest. I pulled the blanket over us. The only thing between us tonight was unspeakable love. Love that lasted a lifetime.

When she climbed out of bed the next morning, I had her toothbrush with the toothpaste cap off and waiting for her.

I'd slipped out and went to the store. I hadn't wanted to leave her alone, but a brotha didn't have a crumb in the crib.

After she finished freshening up, I had some juice and fruit waiting. She walked into the kitchen looking like a breath of fresh air. After giving me a faint smile she sat at the table. Before she could get a morsel to her mouth, her bottom lip started shaking and she started crying. Before she could blink I was by her side holding her.

"I'm sorry." She sobbed. She held onto my waist as if her life depended on it.

"Shhhh. Just let it out."
And she did.

The rest of the day, her phone surprisingly didn't ring. Not even her siblings called.

"I think it's time for me to go home."

I did not want her to leave. "Why do you have to go Sabrina? You have everything you need right here."

"I got to. It seems like the right thing to do. Besides that, I've got to get things ready for his funeral."

"Your mom's not taking care of that?"

"How can she? I've been supporting them for the past few years."

I was confused. "What?"

"Sincere, my father abused and drank my family's way into poverty. If it wasn't for my second family leaving me their trust, I'd be in the same boat. There is no way I could leave my brothers and sisters destitute because of them. No way."

The creature in front of me was phenomenal. Her words made my heart swell. "I understand, and I'm sorry for being greedy," I said, "But can't you take care of that while here? I'll help you and what I don't know, my mom can help. She's been through burying someone before. I mean, I just got you back." I may have sounded desperate but I didn't care. I wanted her with me.

Without hesitation she replied. "Wish I could Sincere. Can you take me home now?"

You are home! I thought. She was tired and that's the only reason I didn't press any further. "Alright baby girl. Get your stuff together."

As she rose to stand she broke into tears. I rushed to embrace her, but she brushed me off and got her boots from her bedroom. She cried the whole way to her house.

Sabrina...

The days following his death were a blur.

My team of four helped me make the arrangements for my father. They asked no questions and did whatever I asked. All four knew that I was barely functioning and didn't want to be the reason that I cracked.

During the ordeal, I never communicated with my mother. I had them do that. As far as she was concerned I was free to make all the decisions. With that being the case, I had Malcolm pick the color of the suit that man would be buried in. Cyprus got the funeral procession escorts taken care of, and Malcolm and Rusty put the obituary together.

On the day of the services seven of my eleven siblings showed up. I was surprised that many came. What really blew my skirt up was that in spite of the relationship our father had with us, my dad was very popular and well-liked in the community.

Before drugs and alcohol totally consumed him, he was a functioning alcoholic. He worked at the local transmission company, and was the man to go to if you had work-related problems. He usually got them solved. Because of that, he accumulated a slew of professional groupies.

My family was polite to all who said nothing but good things about the man who polluted our lives. When the service was over we held each other very, very tight and cried.

Although Sincere witnessed my nightmares, he'd never seen my rawness until the hospital. My father's passing had unleashed a part of me that I'd suppressed. I was angry at the world.

I snapped on him multiple times while making funeral arrangements, and a few times after the services. I learned that Sincere was a very understanding and patient man, something I hadn't always previously seen. I actually thought he was the total opposite.

My previous explanation as to why he sometimes acted like a spoiled brat was 'the only child syndrome'.

Given the right situation, you realize your preconceived notions can make you look pretty foolish.

Sincere...

It wasn't easy being around Sabrina and The Dicks while she mourned. She snapped at all of us like we were damned kids! And our simple asses did whatever the hell she said without a second thought.

But in spite of that, I beheld a strong woman.

How the hell you gonna give the man who violated you such an elegant service? Her ass spent a grip on everything, including his footwear. She had her four servants doing her bidding, and asked me to find shoes for her pops.

"Sincere, they can't be less than two hundred dollars."

I wanted to scream 'two hundred dollars for a dead man?!'

She'd said it with such an edge that all I could squeeze out was a weak "okay."

She was so stressed that I wanted to remove the creases that had taken residence between her eyes.

Two days before the funeral I damn near had to drag her out of the house. In my opinion, Sabrina needed a different scenic view, so I took her to the fair. It sounded simple but I learned getting Sabrina out was not an easy task. I also learned that if I'm good at anything, I'm good at putting my foot in my mouth.

"I don't want to go Sincere. Black folk act crazy at stuff like that and I don't like crowds."

"Baby girl, you're gonna have so much fun it's gon' seem like it's just me and you up in that piece. Nobody else will exist. Just me and you." I'd gotten tired of seeing her interact with her dicks and wanted her to myself for a while.

"I've got way too much to do and I'm tired. Emotionally and physically."

I got frustrated, "I need you Sabrina. I need time with you and nobody else. Don't you miss me?" I regretted it as soon as it came out my mouth.

"You selfish bastard."

Oh shit! "I didn't mean it like that."

The creases between her eyes deepened. "Yes the hell you did." She cried and I felt like shit.

"Sabrina baby listen." She tried getting up off of her couch. I pulled her back down. "Just hear me out. I have watched you consume yourself with sadness. I'm not saying it's not warranted, but you're killing me. The woman I knew is gone. You have not laughed, smiled or said one positive thing since your father passed. You hardly eat. You've lost a hell'va lot of weight. I just want to give you a break, get you out of this house, get you into some fresh air. Yes, I want you for myself for a while but I also want you to have time to yourself so that you can get refreshed.

The next two days are going to be crazy. Can we at least spend a few hours away from the madness? Just a few?"

She bit her bottom lip. As her tears dripped, I wiped them from her cheeks. She took the tissue from my hand and blew her nose. The moment was way too tense so I made light of it.

"You gotta booger hangin' on the edge."

She didn't have a booger, but I wanted to see her smile. It worked.

I watched as she stood and went into the bathroom to check. When I heard the water running I knew I'd changed her mind.

The fair was a great idea. We ate like pigs, watched a horse competition, and rode a couple of rides. She saw a lot of people who gave condolences. Although I tried to cut those conversations short, she stood strong but broke down a couple of times. For the most part the excursion was a success, until we saw April's ass.

I saw her first and tried my damndest to go in a different direction. It was too late.

"Sup Sincere?" She was talking to me but looking at Sabrina.

I cut right to the chase. "What was up with that foul move the last time I saw you?" I pulled Sabrina close.

April rolled her eyes at her and looked at me. "I don't know what the hell you're talking about."

"Yes the hell you do…"

I was about to say a mouthful until Sabrina cut me off, "Oh, you talkin' bout that time she fanned her sour pussy scent in our faces baby? That move was more that foul, sweetheart, it was downright…"

"What the fuck you say bitch?"

April was hot so I added some embers to that shit, "Damn how rude of me," I said, "Let me do some re-introductions. Baby girl, this is April, April this is my fiancé' Sabrina…"

"You dirty muthafucka!" April slapped the shit outta me and walked the hell off. When April looked over her shoulder she had a mean mug on her face. I had one on mine too.

Mine said 'I'mma fuck yo ass up the next time I see you!'

Looking like a big grizzly bear she turned around and kept movin'.

"Are you okay?" Sabrina tried to remove my hand from my throbbin' cheek.

"Yeah I'm good. Come on let's get out of here." I grabbed her hand but she didn't budge.

"So you ready to leave?"

"Hell yeah! She just messed up my night." Again, I tried to leave but got no movement.

"So this night is about you?"

I stopped, closed my eyes and dropped my head, "I oughta be ashamed of myself."

"Yeah you oughta be."

I walked close to my baby and with my head still down waited until we were toe to toe. I bent and placed my forehead onto hers. Her eyes were closed. "What do you want to do next baby girl?"

"Nothing, just stay like this."

I placed my hands on her hips. "What if April comes back and does a sneak attack, and pimp smacks me on the back of my head?"

She was quiet for a few seconds, "I'mma just hafta kick her ass."
We bust out laughing.

There was one more downfall to our adventure; All the chicks throwing shade.

I was young, fine, and successful and I had my share of easy pussy. It showed when Sabrina made an obvious statement, "You sure know a lot of women Sincere."

"Not really." The truth was I didn't know half the women who spoke to me. Shit, most I couldn't remember their damned names. Those chicks were one stop shops but I guess my dick game was worth remembering because they sure in the hell didn't forget me.

"Part of my past Sabrina. Part of my past."

"Well, as you can see your past has a way of affecting our future."

We'd been walking hand in hand through the fairgrounds. I stopped under the ferris wheel and looked in her eyes. "I'm not proud of some of the things I've done, but I'm not that man anymore. I'm good. You're more than enough woman for me."

"Even without the pussy?"

"Baby girl, it's because I haven't had the pussy that it's been confirmed."

She smiled.

"Will you do something for me Sabrina?"

"Depends."

"Will you come home with me tonight?"

"Was that part of your plan?"

"Nope. It's just I had this strong desire to hold you through the night."

"You'll say anything to get me over there."

"I'm serious. I just want to hold you tight and never let go. I want to somehow assure you that I'm here for you, and I want to help you get through this. They've had you throughout this whole ordeal and I just want a moment to myself."

She knew I was talking about the four dicks, "I've just got so much to do Sincere."

I got a calm look on my face. Her ass hadn't done a damn thing since her father died.

"Don't look at me like that Sincere." She knew I wasn't for the bullshit. "Okay, okay, okay. I'll come over."

I took her hand into mine and kissed it. "Thank you." I bent down and kissed her cheek. I started walking but Sabrina stayed put. I turned to see what the holdup was and saw she had her head down.

"Sincere?" She was crying. I walked back over, stood in front of her and lifted her head with my finger. Sabrina lifted her eyes and softly spoke. "Thank you."

I was taken aback. "For what?"

"For everything. But especially for April."

I shook my head, kissed her forehead and embraced her. "Anything for you baby girl. Anything for you."

The night ended with me winning her an itty bitty stuffed animal, and us with fat bellies.

When we returned to my crib we kicked off our shoes, went into her room and crashed.

A few hours later she woke up screaming. I was there to calm her down. When the sun came up and I reached for her.

She was gone.

Sabrina...

I was scared of Sincere. The problem was the deep feelings he had for me. I was definitely feeling him and hed confirmed how he felt for me, that's where the problem lay.

Being around him made me want to do things I knew I shouldn't. I'd never had a sexual relationship with anyone besides my father, yet unlike everyone else, Sincere stimulated all my desires.

Even during my emotional breakdown towards my dead dad, the sexiness Sincere expelled dripped into my core. I understood why April and all the other women we encountered at the fair looked at me with envy. Mr. Fleming was everything a girl dreamed. I had to get out of his house before I did something I regreted. Especially with my emotional state.

Needing to pee, I woke to him holding me close and his hard dick poking my back. I immediately became aroused and knew I had to leave.

I took a cab home and took a shower. I hadn't touched myself since I was ten, but found my mind drifting to all the intimate moments Sincere and I had at the fair. My hand drifted down to my place of pleasure but halted when there was a knock at my bathroom door that caused me to jump.

I was frustrated sexually and mentally. "What?!" I hadn't meant to yell.

"Sorry Sabrina," Malcolm said through the slightly ajar door, "Pamela is on the phone. She said that it was an emergency. She couldn't reach you through your cell so she called the house."

I didn't answer. Instead I washed quickly, dried, and got dressed.

A call from one of the twins always meant drama. Time was of essence. I called her back.

"I love you Sabrina."

I exhaled long and hard as she burst into tears. I sat on my bed and looked at Malcolm.

He'd taken the call and knew, just like everyone else in the house, what was to come when one of the twins called. Absolute hell. I gave him the 'everything is cool' look then gave my full attention to my broken sister.

"I love you too sweetie. More than you'll ever know."

For once, we had a nice and civil, non-drug induced conversation.

The boys took time off work to help me with making arrangements for my dad. As soon as the services were over they dived right back into their routine. Summer break was over. Within that time I'd rekindled my romance with Sincere and buried my father. Surprisingly, Sincere helped me get back to being Sabrina. He'd once again resigned from his FedEx job. The torch of education like fire in his bones.

"It's almost time to register for school."

"I'm just so drained Sincere. I don't know if I have it in me. I really don't. I just buried my dad and I just don't think I have the energy for anything else right now."

"I must have the wrong number. Sabrina?"

I smiled. "Yeeees Sincere."

"Today is the last day to register. I'm on my way."

I tried to protest but he hung up on me. With heavy feet I climbed out of bed, took a shower, got dressed and waited.

An hour later he was at my door. "Now don't you look scrumptious?"

I was in a pair of raggedy jeans, tee-shirt and boots. I hadn't even combed my hair yet. "Whatever, come on in."

He spoke to Walter and Rusty, then followed me to my bathroom and watched as I finished getting ready. As I was picking out my fro I shifted my gaze and met his eyes through my vanity mirror. He was one fine man with lips that always looked juicy. Like LL's.

"What are you staring at young man?"

"You." He walked into my space and stood behind me. I kept picking. "The most beautiful woman in the world."

"Is that riiiiight?"

"It surely is." As I patted my hair pick down, he moved in closer placing his semi-hard dick directly above my ass and his hands on the front of my thighs. "The most beautiful and sexiest woman I've ever known." He bent and with his eyes locked on mine, kissed my neck.

I thought I was going to faint. "Don't do that Sincere." It had come out as a whisper and I wasn't sure if he'd heard me.

"Why not?" His voice was thick with desire. With his eyes still on mine he pulled me back into his fully erect dick and licked my neck with his beautiful fat tongue.

When I felt pressure down there I knew I was in trouble. "Don't do that Sincere. Please, please, please don't." He sucked on my neck until it hurt, pressing me from behind with his dick. I couldn't help it. I had to feel a part of him on my hot spot.

I closed my eyes and unzipped my pants. I bent my knees, placed my hand on top of his and put his hands down my pantiless jeans. He applied more pressure from the back, making me insert one of his fingers into my pussy. With his foot he slammed the bathroom door shut.

"Oh shit. Sincere." He took his other hand and started playing with my breast.

"You feel so good girl."

I started moving his finger in and out of me, making sure it hit my clit. "Oh, oh, oh." I started rocking my hips. It felt so good I thought I'd scream."Sincere. Oh Sincere. Oh yes baby yes." It had been so long, way too long. I placed his wet finger on my spot and held it there. I wanted his finger to become one with me. I placed both hands over his and pushed hard. I lost it, moaning loudly. Sincere placed a hand over my mouth. Tingling coursed throughout my body, my knees buckled under me and he kept me afloat at the waist. As I removed my hands and placed them on the sink, he picked up where I left off by applying pressure.

When I made too much noise Sincere used the hand he'd been holding me up with to cover my mouth. With his waist he pushed me against the sink for leverage.

Deep within me I let out a deep groan, and a lone tear glided down my cheek. As the muscles in my pussy contracted my breathing became shallow. Sincere used that moment to turn me around and drown out any cries that may have escaped my throat with his mouth.

With his huge hands he pulled off my pants, lifted me onto the sink and with his jeans still on placed his dick on my clit. I wrapped my legs around his waist as he rolled his hips.

"Yo shit smells so damn good!" I'd never paid attention to my scent, never had a reason or an opportunity too but he was right, the scent of my arousal turned me on even more.

"Oh, it's about to happen again. Oh! Sincere!" I grabbed him around his neck and buried my face in his shoulder. Again a deep moan escaped me, and he stopped moving and went stiff, moaning loudly in my ear. His knees got weak, and with my legs still around his waist, he backed into the bathroom door and slowly slid to the floor. I finally realized he was having an orgasm. The thought made my pussy jump more.

"Oh shit Sabrina. Damn girl!" Sincere rolled his hips, pushing me down on his dick and the friction was a turn on as well.

Once the quivering of my abdomen subsided I took my head off his shoulder and kissed him. "Thank you Sincere."

He pulled back and acted as if I hadn't said a word, "Sit on my face Sabrina."

"Huh?"

He lay back on the bathroom floor. "Just for a second. You don't have to stay there. Come on." I didn't know what the hell he was talking about and the look on my face told him so. "Okay, come here." Sincere yanked me by the arm. He was so damn excited he almost pulled me past his head. "Now squat."

"Squat?"

He wrapped his arms around my thighs and pulled me down onto his face. The feeling was so damned heavenly that I caught my breath. "Oh shit!" I placed my hands on his head and started rolling my hips.

"Yeah, gimme that pussy."

The fact that I was doing something right for the man I loved was such a turn on that I started feeling the pressure again. I placed my hands above his head and started rocking back and forth. "Sincere?"

The grip he had on my thighs was tight. He pressed me further onto his face and I tried helping by letting all of my weight go to my hips. "Oh yes!" My mouth opened and my eyes closed as he hungrily licked me from one hole to the other. My ass started rocking faster and as I did he pulled me down harder on his face. "Yes baby, right there." I broke into a sweat and so did my pussy. I stopped rocking and with his arms holding me in position Sincere rolled his tongue around my clit and sucked hard.

I reached up and pulled down a towel to scream into it.

I tried to get away by he wouldn't let me. As my juices flowed he licked every last drop, basking in the taste of my elixir.

Angela Moore

Sincere...

When I arrived at Sabrina's house to pick her up for school registry, it wasn't my intent to get so caught up. Since it happened, I was more than okay with it. It was bound to happen. That it happened at her crib was alright with me too. It let all the little dicks know who's dick superseded theirs.

While Sabrina lived with me, and when April wasn't available, I masturbated to keep my lustful thoughts in check. Being around all that sexiness without touching was not easy. Neither was risking her moving out by violating her wishes.

I did what I had to do to keep her around, and thoroughly enjoyed catching on to her little habits. Like how she always left the door slightly open when she used the bathroom, or how she had all of her boots color-coded in her bedroom. That she returned whatever shoes she wore to the exact spot she removed them tripped me out. That's how I learned she had some obsessive compulsive ways.

She ate one item at a time during our first date; That's how she ate every meal. I wondered if that habit stemmed from something from her childhood. Those little things drew me in, but what I hadn't expected was for her elixir to taste and smell so damn good. All this time I'd been so caught up with April and her mouthwatering pussy, and I had something better right in my face.

And that I truly cared about baby girl didn't hurt.

Sabrina knew she had a mannerism that drew in men. That she didn't dwell on it made it all the more sexy. I'd seen the way men would look at her when we were out. It caused me to hold her hand a little tighter.

I know I'm an eye catcher. I could blow a kiss at a chick and she'd be ready to drop her panties. But Sabrina? All she has to do was walk into a room and a real man's dick was gonna jump. After being around her I understood why her roommates had no problem moving in with her. They got to keep an eye on the pussy. Little did Sabrina know, she had those fools at her beck while unknowingly playing with their weakness in her innocence.

After our bathroom rendezvous I could tell that she felt ashamed. To give her some dignity I lifted her pussy off my face, put my dick in my pants and went into her bedroom and waited. After thirty minutes I went in search of her.

I tapped on the slightly ajar bathroom door and walked inside. My dick got hard when I saw her silhouette through the shower curtain. I must have moaned or something because she threw back the curtain and while covering herself said in a whisper-scream.

"Sincere! You cain't be in here."

I gave her a crazy look. "After what we just did? Whatever."

"I'm serious. I don't feel comfortable."

"Sabrina, you just had ya vaginia all up in my face."

"My point exactly."

I sat on the toilet. "How long are you going to be? We gotta get up to the school before it closes."

"Well if you leave it'll be about ten minutes."

I looked at my watch. "Naw, you're gonna hafta get a move on. We're already cutting it close."

"Well if you would…"

I showed her some privacy by shifting my gaze elsewhere. With desire in my voice, I spoke my piece, "I ain't goin' nowhere. Now you need to wash ya little shy ass up so we can go." She was so damned pretty I could eat her up.

Sabrina slammed the curtain shut and finished washing her body and you had best believe I looked.

"Stop looking at me Sincere. You're making me nervous."

"You should be." I forced myself to look elsewhere. When my eyes fell on the magazine rack I picked one up. It was a Jet. As I leafed through it I hoped she'd get a move on; We had classes to register for. When I heard the shower being turned off I reached for a towel and handed it to her. She stepped out with it tightly wrapped around her body.

"Will you leave now?"

"Nope. You go to your room. I gotta get myself together. I'll be in there in a few."

When I started taking off my shirt she ran out of the bathroom. I took a quick shower, dried off and went into her bedroom with the towel wrapped around my waist.

She was fully dressed. "You could have gotten dressed in the bathroom."

"I know." I dropped the towel and she damn near fainted. I wanted to laugh but didn't.

Because of the mess I'd made in my underwear, I put on my pants with no draws on and very carefully fastened and zipped my pants. She had her back to me. "You better get used to this."

"To what?"

I didn't answer, just finished getting dressed.

We were ready we made a quick exit out of her crib, as we did, four sets of eyes watched our every move.

After registering for school we were quickly back into the swing of things. The day following registration we got books. Two days later we were in class getting our clinical assignments.

Sabrina was ahead of me but I didn't care. I was just glad that I was able to see her on campus. When we weren't in school we spent as much time together as possible. That usually included Brice, which was something she liked.

"You wanna go to the movies Sabrina? There are a few good ones out."

"Is Brice coming?" I could hear her anxiety through the phone.

"Yes, Brice is coming."

She exhaled,"What do you wanna see?"

Since our bathroom incident Sabrina refused to be alone with me. According to her, "I can't trust myself around you Sincere. I gotta be safe." So she used my son as a cock blocker and I told her as much.

"How dare you say that I'm using that baby."

"Look! I'm just calling it the way I see it. And his little ass does whatever you tell him to do. Even sit in the middle."

"I've never told him to sit between us. That's something he's done on his own."

"Yeah right."

"I'm serious Sincere. There's no way I would use Brice to prohibit me from wanting to touch and kiss all over that sexy body of yours. No way at all."

"That's what the…" My voice was thick with desire and I barely got my statement out. I cleared my throat. "That's what the hell I thought."

She laughed. Sabrina didn't often express her intimate desires. When she did, it was like getting a drop of water on your tongue while in a desert dying.

It was hard to believe that it had been three years, but I finally graduated college. Sabrina already had her degree, and I tried repeatedly to get her to move back in with me while I was in school, but she wouldn't budge.

"I'm trying to get to heaven Sincere."

I let her have her moment because I had a plan.

Graduation day my mom, Sabrina, Brice, Ramona, and Ramona's dude all attended. It was one of the proudest moments of my life.

"If your dad was here he would be beaming with pride, son. I just know he would."

I kissed my mother's forehead, "I know he would be too mama."

After the ceremony, we went to the Eagle's Nest restaurant located downtown for dinner. While there I told everyone that I got hired as a student nurse at the Wiz. My mom looked at me with some reservations. Instead of indulging, I smiled at her with understanding. No one knew about our silent conversation but us.

We ate good and enjoyed hearty conversation. By the end of the festivities Brice was knocked out.

"I'm going to take him home. He's exhausted. I'm proud of you young man, and I'm sure our son is too."

Ramona's eyes started misting over. "Sincere, I'm so glad he got to witness this moment. There aren't a lot of men like you, my friend. And I want to say thank you." We embraced, then she hugged Sabrina. "I never knew he had it in him. I want to thank you for making him a better man for Brice to admire."

After the women hugged I gave Ramona's man some dap, kissed Brice goodbye and watched as they made their exit with Mom in tow.

I turned to Sabrina, "I got a surprise for you."

She smiled, "You dooooo?"

"I surely do. Come on." I took her by the hand and led her out of the restaurant. Outside was the horse and carriage I reserved. I got in.

"Come on baby girl and get yo sexy fine self up here." I held out my hand and helped her up. Before she could sit, I shifted her waist and had her sit on my lap. She wrapped her arms around my neck.

"Mmmmm, you so nasty," she crooned.

My dick was hard as a rock. I placed my mouth close to her ear, "You wearin' that sexy ass dress with the back out and no damn panties. What do you expect?"

She giggled. Yep, I was still jacking off. But not for long.

"Ready folks?"

"As ready as ever."

The carriage took off and she held on tight.

As we were driven throughout downtown we sipped wine and enjoyed the site of Indianapolis at night. At the end of our ride, I generously tipped our four-legged taxi and helped Sabrina down.

"What's this about?"

"You'll see." I placed my hand around her waist and led her inside.

"I'm not dressed for this."

"Whether you were dressed or not it wouldn't matter because ya ass still wouldn't be able to dance."

She tapped me upside my head, "Oh shut up."

We were at Club Sparkle, the place where we first met. As I gave head nods to the bouncers, we cut the line and walked right in. It took a minute for my eyes to adjust to the black interior but once they had, I led Sabrina to our RSVP spot in a dark corner. When she started to sit I stopped her and pulled her into my arms.

Butter Pecan

"Naw baby girl, it's all about you tonight." As I led her to the dance floor she stopped me.

"If I remember correctly you told me 'you were so bad that I promise to never take you out dancing again'. Hmmm, I think those were your exact words. The first words you'd ever spoken that hurt my feelings."

Damn! I'd forgotten I said that. "Well baby girl, that was before I fell in love with you." That put a smile on her pretty face. "Come on," I said.

All eyes were on us as I led her to the dancefloor. The female eyes were on me because I'd had sex with half of them and they beheld why I was off the market. The men looked with envy. The Pharcydes 'Passin' Me By' was bumpin' and I pulled my baby close. She wrapped her arms around my shoulders, and I wrapped mine around her waist. We danced to the music, our heartbeats beating as one.

I placed my forehead on hers and as my dick grew hard against her abdomen we looked into each other's eyes, "I love you Sabrina."

She smiled, "I know Sincere."

I pulled her closer and placed my lips close to her ear and with my eyes closed told her all that was in my heart, "I love everything about you, young lady. Your inner and outer beauty. The way you take care of everybody and don't think twice about it. How, although I can't stand The Dicks, you refuse to abandon them for me. How you never, not once, questioned Brice's blood relation to me. I don't know too many women who would honor a man in death while he destroyed their lives.

Although your family is crazy as hell, I love them all because they're a part of you. You make them look normal, whatever that is. I love you for not asking questions about my dad. Also," I grinned into her ear, "You have tortured a brotha by not giving up the pussy."

She hit me on my shoulder and I felt wetness on the side of my face. "But I admire you for sticking to your morals. I know you ain't got no panties on up under this thin-ass dress, and I want to tear yo ass up but I wanna do it the right way." Her shoulders started shaking. "I want to do it your way, baby girl. That's the only way it'll feel right."

She squeezed her face into my neck and cried. I held her close and patiently waited.

—175—

We stayed like that for five songs and I'd have stayed thirty more if that's what it took.

I finally heard her mumble some words. "I love you Sincere."

That was all the yes I needed. I took her hand and led her off the dance floor, to the bathroom and waited outside until she got herself together. When she emerged we went back to the table.

With playful eyes I asked, "You ready to go?"

She looked insulted, "What? You don't wanna dance with me?"

"You aint about to embarrass me out on that dance floor." She hit my arm and laughed. "Alright, come on baby girl. Let's go bust a move."

She raised her arms above her head, "Let's do this."

I pointed my finger in her face. "Now I said bust a move not bust ya ass."

She cracked up and I watched as she danced like a white girl all the way to the dancefloor. I loved every move she made.

We danced the night away and I dropped her off. The next day I called my mom. "You ready to have a daughter in-law?"

"It's about damn time."

I was a little offended. "Why you say that?"

"Boy from day one I knew that girl was for you but I couldn't say nothin'. You had to find that out on your own."

"Well, I have, and I need to find her a ring. You wanna go?"

"What time you picking me up?"

My mom and I spent hours shopping for the perfect ring. I finally decided on a Vintage Diamond Engagement Ring. That baby set me back seventeen stacks but she was worth every cent. Afterward we sat down for a hearty dinner.

"You sure you ready for this?"

My dad was killed before I was born, and I recognized the anguish that life had brought my mother.

"I'm sure. It's time. I wanna give you some grandbabies before you get too old. Give you something else to babysit besides that store."

"Oh shush." Our waiter arrived so we ordered. When he left, we picked up where we left off. "You decide where you're going to work after your boards?"

"Of course. The Wiz if they'll have me."

"You know they will. Your father left you fine footsteps to follow. It was only periodically but he still made an impact."

"I know he did. That's the very reason I wanna work there."

"How do you think you'll feel knowing that's where he died?"

"It felt kinda weird when I was there for my clinical. At times it felt like I was walking down hallways filled with ghosts and secrets. I shook it off, so I think I'll be alright."

"And working with your soon-to-be wife. You don't think that'll be a conflict of interest?"

"For who?"

Mom laughed.

"Sabrina has never worked a day in her life and I don't count clinical as work. That's free labor. I think we'll be fine. Besides, I'll only be working a couple of nights a week."

She got serious and reached across the table and took my hands. "Sincere, you do know that when public servants are hurt on the job, they go to that hospital? If something happened, do you think you'll be able to take care of the people in blue?"

Our appetizers arrived and I was glad for the distraction.

While Sabrina was doing free labor at one of the local hospitals, I asked The Dicks if I could meet with them. They all agreed. Two weeks after purchasing her ring I was seated in their living room.

"I'd like to thank you guys for agreeing to meet me. I'm doing this because I love Sabrina, and because I know that she loves you guys."

Before I could finish Walter walked up to me, hand extended.

"I know where this is going my man and I'd like to be the first to congratulate you."

A little surprised, I stood and shook the mans hand , "I appreciate that Walt. I appreciate that a lot."

I looked at the remaining three, and concluded that they needed to hear it out of the horse's mouth.

"For the rest of you, as a courtesy to the woman I love, I want you to know that I will be asking her for her hand in marriage. I know it would tickle her pink if you guys were happy for her. But if not, then that's fine too." I looked at Cyprus. "With or without your blessings we're jumping that broom. I just wanted to give y'all the heads up." With no more words of encouragement coming my way, I made my exit, not giving a damn.

Sabrina...

Tensions were high at the house and just as Sincere talked with the boys, I did the same two days later.

"I'm sure you guys know why I wanted to talk."

Walter was the only one with sense. "I'mma tell you like I told him." Walter said, "I'm happy for you guys. It's been a long time coming and you deserve it."

"So what are we supposed to do without you?" Rusty's needy butt complained.

"The same things you've been doing when I'm not here. Living. I'm getting married fellas, not dying." I looked at them individually. "I'll be back to visit the same way I did when I lived with him. Nothing's really going to change."

"Everything is going to change. You'll get with him and forget we exist." Rusty whined.

I rolled my eyes. Men could be such babies. I ignored that last comment but sprung a proposition on them. "Guys? I need you all to look at me." Walter was the only one who had eye contact with me the whole time. The others acted like they didn't want to comply. "Please."

They slowly looked up, one at a time. Their pouting was starting to get on my nerves. "I need to ask you all a favor." I swallowed because what I was about to ask them would throw their lives into total chaos but it would take the focus off me.

"Anything for you Sabrina."

You say that now.

I took a deep breath and then blurted it out. "I need for you guys to look out for the twins for me."

"Hellllllll no!"

"Come on Walter." I thought he'd be the main one on board. "This house is big enough for all of you. And y'all won't even know they're here." I knew that was a lie. My sisters were like two Tasmanian Devils.

"Says who? Those girls are like two Tasmanian devils."

Dangit!

"I'm out! I cain't do it Sabrina. I just cain't. They'll have me catching a case up in this piece. I'll get a damn apartment before I agree to that."

I was a little offended. "There are four of you guys here." Before I could finish, Walter yelled out "three". I rolled my eyes. "There are four of you guys here. Y'all can handle them. They're kids."

"They're adults with no boundaries, Sabrina." Cyprus corrected, "I'm with Walter on this one. They are a bit on the crazy side but you know what, so was I at one time."

I looked at Cyprus in shock. He was the one I thought would be protesting. "Really?"

There was total silence.

"I got you Sabrina," Cyprus eventually said, "Even if these three don't stay, I'm in."

I was so happy to hear those words float out of his mouth that I ran to him and threw my arms around his neck. "Thank you so much Cyprus!" I was like a kid and started jumping up and down when I let him go.

With a big cheesy smile on my face I looked at the remaining two. I say two, because Walter was like putty and I knew I'd be able to get him to change his mind.

When neither budged, with my hands in a praying position I went to each one individually, poked out my bottom lip and begged,

"Please, please, please do this for me. It's not like they're strangers. Y'all already know them. Please."

Rusty spoke, "So we get the two of them while losing you? That don't seem like an even trade. But I'll do it cupcake. When I said anything for you I meant it."

I jumped up and down clapping my hands.

"So I don't get a hug?"

I laughed, "Of course you do." I gave my friend a big bear hug and kissed him on the cheek.

"Oh, so you givin' out kisses? If that's the case I'm in." When I turned to look at Malcolm he had his eyes closed and lips puckered. I laughed like a teenager, skipped over to him, and with the innocence of a child, maneuvered my head to kiss him on the cheek.

He opened his eyes. "Aww yes, just the way I imagined it."

I sang "whaaaat eeeever" then stood in front of Walter.

"I ain't budging Sabrina." Walter said stubbornly, "You may as well stop blinking those pretty brown eyes of yours cause it ain't happenin'"

I lay it on thick. "You know you're their favorite. When they asked me if they could move in you were one of the men they talked about the most. And you know they absolutely adore Walt Jr. and he adores them. They're just as smart as I am and will be able to help out with his studies. They just need a little direction, Walter, and just as you guys have helped me I know that you can help them," I stood closer and whispered, "You're the key Walter. Help my sisters, please. I'm begging you." Although I'd been joking, I wasn't exaggerating and got teary-eyed.

"Please."

When a tear slid down my cheek he pulled me into an embrace, "Shhhhh now. You know I hate to see you cry."

"I just don't want to see them end up like the rest."

"I know Sabrina. I know." He let me cry. When I finished he gave me a little hope. "Let me think about it Sabrina. Those are some bad ass little girls but with the four of us, we should be able to help them. Just give me a few days."

I wrapped my arms around his waist, "Thank you Walter."

He kissed the top of my head, "No problem little lady."

That night I lay in my bed and cried tears of joy.

My father had done things to his children that had thrown us into a cycle of self destruction. He had deeded us a life of doom, but I'd beat him at his own game. Most of his destructive principles had crippled the majority of his children, but not all.

That's why I cried.

I had been snatched out of his abyss of darkness and was given a second chance. Because of my recovery, it was possible to give two more children a glimmer of hope.

Three out of eleven wasn't bad. It wasn't bad at all.

As I drifted to sleep, I played and replayed the whole day's scenario. It dawned on me as I pondered Cyprus's quick response to take on my hostile sisters, that he had an ulterior motive. Having them around meant access he wouldn't otherwise have to me. I would be a married woman, and we knew Sincere was not into sharing. Oh well.

If that meant my sisters would be taken care of, then so be it. If Cyprus's selfish motives were the key to a peaceful realm where my sisters were concerned, I was okay with that.

Sincere asked me to come to his house for dinner. Since the oral sex bathroom incident I promised myself I wouldn't be alone with him. He'd tried numerous times to get me over to his house. It was hard, but I stuck to my guns. Sincere said that this dinner would be different even though he wanted to, "spread my legs like peanut butter and jelly on two slices of bread" he planned to adhere to my wishes and wait for our wedding night.

I was a little hesitant until he said I had more than dinner to look forward to. When he told me to dress up, he'd sealed the deal. After dressing, I stood in front of Malcolm and Rusty, did a little spin and asked them how I looked. They were just about speechless.

"Guess that means I look great. See y'all later." I giggled as I walked out of the door.

When I got to Sincere's he opened his front door, then slammed it in my face. I heard him mumble "shit". I cracked up.

I knocked again and had to wait a few moments before he opened. He stood and blocked my entrance.

"You tryin' to give a brotha a heart attack?" I tilted my head to the side, looked up into his handsome face and wondered how I'd been so blessed. "I didn't masturbate today and with you lookin' all sexy and shit, a brotha's gonna have a rough night." He swallowed and looked at my mouth. "Especially with those shiny ass lips of yours."

As I broke out laughing I hit him with my clutch. "You so nasty." I laughed. When I looked into his lustful eyes I knew he was serious. I stopped laughing and just smiled. "You know I'll leave."

He looked me up and down. "Why'd you wear a dress?"

"You told me to dress up."

"You got on panties?" I shifted my weight to one hip. He looked over his shoulder then back at me. "Alright. Guess I better let you in before I burn my damn house down."

He stepped to the side and opened the door. I put my hands to my face. "Oh my goodness Sincere."

I walked into absolute warmth.

He'd removed all his living room furniture and created a zigzagged walkway of candles with rose petals scattered between the candles that led to his dining room.

"Sincere?"

"This way madam." He bent at the waist and swung his arm in the direction of his dining room.

I curtsied and clumsily made my way to the dining area, lead by candles and rose petals, then I stopped. I turned around and walked back to the front door. Once outside, I turned and looked into the living room. I realized that the candles glowed in the shape of an "S". A big smile spread across my face.

"I'm glad you noticed." Sincere called from the dining room. "It was hard getting those angles just right to make that letter."

As I looked I felt like little red riding hood in the forest. I resumed my adventure admiring the array of candles on either side of me.

When I got to the dining room table, he was waiting. "For you." He said. As I lay my clutch on the table, he handed me a glass of white wine, and with a glass in his other hand, proposed a toast. "To us Sabrina."

He touched his glass to mine and we drank.

I looked at Sincere over the rim of my glass, awed at this beautiful gesture. As wine bubbles cascaded down my throat, the gleam of something in his glass caught my eye. When I saw what it was, I choked on my wine.

"Oh shit Sabrina! Are you okay?" Sincere put his glass down, took mine out of my hand, and smacked my back as I went into a coughing fit.

My drink had really gone down the wrong tube.

"Slow down baby and take some slow breaths."

I gagged every time I breathed, feeling like something was lodged in my trachea.

Sincere tried giving me words of comfort, big hand still hitting my back, "Take ya time. Remember what we learned in school. It'll come out." That was easy for him to say. Fluid wasn't stuck in his windpipe. It took a good three minutes before I was able to get my airway cleared. "Girl you scared the hell outta me."

As Sincere held me close, I wiped my eyes with the napkin he gave me. I took a seat. "I scared myself." I said. I kept my eyes on his glass, not believing what I was beholding.

"Oh, here you go." Without a second thought he dipped his finger into his glass and took out the ring. He popped it in his mouth to suck off the excess wine and took my shaking hand. When he got on one knee, my hand started trembling.

"Sabrina baby, it would make a brotha proud if you would do him the honor of making him the happiest man in the world. Since you've been in my life you've given me breath, a reason to wake up in the morning. For the rest of my days, I want to wake up next to you."

He placed the ring on my finger. I didn't bring it to my face because everything I needed to see shined brightly. I knew that ring set Sincere back a lot of money. To think that he found me worthy of such elegance was overwhelming.

I started crying, "Oh my God Sincere."

He took my shaking hand and pulled me into his arms. "I love you Sabrina. Because you chose me I plan to give you nothing but the best. You deserve it." We danced to soft music I hadn't noticed was playing. "Do you know what I want from you Sabrina?" I was speechless so I just shook my head no.

"I want a whole lot of little brown babies."

When he said that I froze.

He pulled back from me, "What's wrong baby girl?"

I sat down, shook my head and closed my eyes. It was hard for me to open them. "Sincere."

He pulled up a chair and sat in front of me. After taking my hands and placing them into his I took them back. He'd been leaning towards me but sat up straight after I pulled away. I looked into his eyes and that's when it registered.

"Spill it Sabrina."

There was no way I could tell that man I didn't think I could have kids.

"So what? You cain't have kids?" The way he said it made my stomach turn. "I thought you said you've never been with anybody, so how do you know?"

"I've never told you that I haven't been with anyone Sincere."

He acted like I'd slapped him. "So what the hell you tryin' ta say?"

I could tell I was being misinterpreted. "Calm down."

He stood, eyes flashing in anger, "Calm down? I don't think so."

"Sincere! The only person I've ever had sexual contact with is my father. Please remember that I was a child. A grown man's dick was not supposed to be inside of my little body."

He got the gist of what I was saying and took his seat. "Oh."

"I'm not saying that I can't have kids Sincere but I'm damn near thirty and never had a period. I've been going to a gynecologist for years and taking hormone therapy, but nothing has stimulated a cycle. He messed me up on the inside."

He looked at me with a blank stare.

I hung my head, "I'm so sorry I didn't tell you sooner. And to be honest it never really crossed my mind until now. I resigned myself to being childless a long time ago, never really giving it a second thought."

My words brought him back into focus. "Well," he said, "This is what we're going to do. Since you don't know whether you can or can't, we gonna make a whole lotta love after we're married to see."

Those word caused more tears to drop. When I looked down at the ring he'd placed in my finger I knew, that for the first time in my life, a man truly loved me.

"I love you Sincere."

He pulled me close and lay my head on his chest.
"I love you too baby girl."

I told Sincere that I never thought of myself as being a parent to my own child.

Although not always under the same roof, I always felt like a parent to my younger siblings. I was content with that.

I felt bad for not telling Sincere what I'd always assumed about my body, but the subject of kids was never mentioned. Therefore I never thought about it.

I absolutely detested my father.

Chapter Seven

Sincere...

Sabrina potentially not being able to have kids really threw me for a loop.

I envisioned us losing our minds trying to keep up with a house full of little 'me's' and little 'hers'. The possibility of that not happening didn't sit well, especially since I didn't have any biological kids of my own.

A man wants his seed planted, wants to watch as his lineage is expanded. Because of Sabrina's past, I might get denied that.

Instead of dwelling on "what if's", I went home and studied for my nursing license. It was an accumulative test; I had to pass to get a full time position at the Wiz. Pondering not being a biological parent would have to be addressed on another day.

Scared we'd do something she didn't want, Sabrina still refused to come to my house until we were married. I was cool with it. I knew she could be real anal when it came to her boundaries and chastity, so I respected her wishes and stopped asking her to come over.

Hell, we'd be married soon and it wouldn't be an issue. I waited all these years, a few more months won't hurt.

But since becoming engaged, she was always calling. Every time I turned around she was ringing my phone, like she just got a new toy.

"Hello?"

"What colors do you want?"

I smiled into the phone. "I'm leaving all of that up to you baby girl. It's your day so do what you want." She got quiet.

I had two weeks before my test for boards. Wedding plans were not on the top of my to-do list. "Okay Sabrina. What did you have in mind?" I logged off my computer and gave her my undivided attention.

She still didn't say anything. Every moment of my time was precious and she was wasting it; I started getting impatient. "Sabrina?" I said her name in a way that let her know I had a calm look on my face.

"Sincere?"

I sighed, "Yes…Sabrina."

"You don't have to say it like that."

"Yes…I do. Now what?"

"Remember when we first started talking on the phone and you told me that you wanted to take me out. I told you in your dreams?"

I started logging back into my computer, "Yes I remember."

"Well, do you remember telling me that you had a dream about taking me to dinner on a sandy beach?"

"Mmmhmm."

"Are you paying attention to me?"

"Of course I am. You asked me if I remember telling you about taking you to dinner on the beach. I told you I was paying attention." For some reason I couldn't log on and I was getting even more frustrated.

"Well I had an idea."

"Shoot."

She knew I was preoccupied, "I need you to pay attention Sincere!"

"I told you I was. Now say what you gotta say." I was still trying to log in.

"Okay, I was thinking that maybe we should skip the wedding and just go somewhere to get married. Me and you and nobody else. We find a sweet location, jump the broom and have our honeymoon while there."

I didn't say a word.

"I mean, I know you wanted your mom and Brice to attend but we can have a nice reception with both our family and friends when we get back."

I was still on mute.

"It's just something that popped into my head. We don't have to do it that way. If you want to have a big wedding, we can, I just thought we'd make it simple and intimate."

Still nothing from me.

"Sincere? Are you there?"

"Girl that's why I love yo ass. Smart and sexy as hell."

She started giggling. "I've already started searching."

"Well you keep on searching 'cause I gotta study for this test. And Sabrina?"

"Huh?"

"I absolutely love the idea." I could feel her smiling through the phone. I closed my computer, "And you know what else?"

She whispered, "No what?"

"I'mma tear yo' ass up."

She started laughing and hung up on me.

Mrs. Fleming...

I was hurt when Sincere told me they were having a private ceremony. He was my only child and this was a monumental moment in his life. I wanted to be a part of it.

"Look Mom, we're going to have a nice get together when we get back. It's no big deal."

"What do you mean no big deal? You're about to have a life-changing moment take place son. That's a big deal. And what about Brice?"

"What about him?"

"I'm sure he wants to share that moment with you as well."

"Mama, Brice don't care about no wedding. As long as he's able to get a piece of cake he'll be cool."

"Now that's not nice." I didn't laugh. Brice was getting bigger by the minute.

"Look ma. I promise to take loads of pictures. I know that doesn't take the place of you being there but it'll have to do. We just want to share this time with each other without the hustle and bustle that comes along with a wedding."

Lord knows I did not want to submit to my son's desires.

"Alright baby. Just make sure you bring us back some souvenirs." I had to get off that subject. I was about to burst into tears.

Sabrina...

We were on the plane headed to our wedding destination. Yep, two weeks after his proposal.

"You have your vows?" I asked.

"Of course I do." He sat beside me with his eyes closed.

We decided to leave our past behind the day following Sincere's test. Of course he passed, but it had been taxing on his brain. I took his hand into mine, kissed it, and held it close to my chest, scared about our wedding night.

Sincere left everything up to me as far as location and told me to spare no expense. I picked Cap Juluca. It was a random choice. From the pictures it was absolutely beautiful and received great reviews.

After landing and getting our luggage, we were driven about an hour to our very own private beachfront suite. We said nothing along the way, holding hands and delighting in the beauty of the Island.

When we got to our suite we were breathless.

The furnishings were sparse but enough for two people. The colors were inviting with bold cultural stitching and design. It was an extremely intimate atmosphere that afforded us our very own private pool, and breakfast area with a separate dining area. The ambience of the Island screamed luxury.

"You did good baby girl. You did real good."

I got so caught up in my surroundings that I forgotten Sincere was there. I turned, "Thank you. I hoped you would like it." The way Sincere was looking at me caused me to swallow. His desire for me was so thick it was almost suffocating.

"Which room do you want?" I asked. My question was like a scratched record in his ear.

With a scrunched up face he barely got out an audible, "What?"

I laughed. "It has a guest suite. Let's take a tour." When I grabbed his hand he was still in shock. "We're not married yet Sincere." I again tried leading him on a tour, he wouldn't budge.

"Matter of fact when are we getting married?"

"Tomorrow."

I was finally able to pull him along but the he stopped walking. "Tomorrow? Then why the two rooms?"

I didn't answer and resumed our tour. As we went from room to room all I heard from Sincere was "nice, nice." Every time he said it my heart swelled. When we got to the master suite Sincere pulled me into his arms and walked me backward until the back of my knees touched the bed.

"You got on panties under that sundress?" Before I could answer he held me close around the waist with one arm. With the other he lifted my dress.

"Sincere?" While looking in my eyes he opened my legs with his knees, kneeling between my thighs with his knee on the bed. I whispered his name again.

He smiled, and bent towards me, bringing his mouth to my ear. "I love you Sabrina. I love you so very much."

He inserted a finger into my moist pussy.

I wrapped my arms around his neck but he stood, leaving my embrace. I watched as he licked my juices off his thumb.

I felt his hard dick and knew that he was about to eat me alive. Instead he took my hand.

"Come on, let's finish this tour, get cleaned up and hit the Island. It's time we enjoy each other baby girl. We deserve it. Especially you."

I followed behind him like a lost puppy, wanting his finger in me again.

Sincere...

My brain was way fried after taking my test which made me appreciate Sabrina's suggestion of a private wedding all the more. I needed to get away from everything. The past few months had been stressful so a secluded getaway was welcoming.

Although I knew my mother wanted to be present for my special occasion, I really wanted Sabrina's day to be everything she wanted. Since her dad's passing, her nightmares had become more frequent. Sabrina didn't inform me. Walter had.

He told me that in the past Sabrina would climbed into his bed at least once a week. Since her pop's death, they'd increased to at least three.

I knew I needed to get her out that crib. Her ass didn't wear panties and if my dick got hard every time she climbed into bed with me I knew his did too. I didn't like that. Besides, I needed to be the one who comforted her.

But mostly I wanted to see her have a break from life's stressors. Sabrina wore plenty of hats. Although The Dicks took care of her psychologically, she took care of them on more levels than one. I wanted to take her away from all of that.

When she asked me where I wanted to go to get married, I told her to surprise me. I must admit, my baby didn't disappoint.

Thanks to my mom, I'd traveled around the world. She said my dad would have wanted it that way. I think she did it more for herself than me. It took her mind off the realities of her life.

Because, as an adult, I'd never been in a real relationship, I'd never been on any romantic expenditures. I'd gone on weekend trips, but nothing like this.

The Island brought me peace. Nothing about the atmosphere implied the hustle and bustle of everyday life. Just quiet, love, and unlimited possibilities. When I read the Cap Juluca sign that led to our retreat I knew Sabrina put a nice dent in my bank account. As I looked at her during the taxi ride to our suite, it was worth every red penny.

We changed and headed to our private oasis. On the beach, the staff already had a candlelit dinner prepared.

"Did you plan this?"

"I surely did." I looked around. The wind was gently blowing, the sun was setting, and the ocean waves played us a soft symphony. I held her hand tight, pressing it against my lips. When we got to the table I pulled out her chair. I damn near pulled a muscle; They were heavy as hell. They probably had to be weighted because of strong winds. But damn!

"Don't hurt yaself baby."

"Oh I'm not. Gotta save these muscles for tomorrow night."

Sabrina looked sexy as hell in an orange strapless sundress and no shoes. She had her toes and nails painted in a pretty orange and black which complimented her dark skin. I also kept things simple with a pair of white shorts and a tan tunic shirt. I was shoeless and enjoyed the white sand as it squeezed through my toes.

The food was already on the table. We lifted the lids and found loads of fruit and raw vegetables under one, grilled fish, roasted potatoes and fresh-picked green beans under another. I didn't ask if she'd planned the menus because I was sure she had.

I couldn't help but think that what she was doing for me, she'd done for The Dicks for years. I shook my head.

I poured us some red wine. She stood to fix my plate, but I told her to have a seat so I could serve her like a queen. After saying grace, we ate in silence, basking in the beauty of our surroundings and each other. When our wine bottle was empty a server appeared out of nowhere and replaced it.

I watched as Sabrina meticulously ate one item at a time. I longed to switch places with her meal that passed her sweet lips.

Everything about our first night was perfect.

After dinner we stood to take a walk on the beach. Before she could take I step, I removed a flower from a vase that was on the center of the table and tucked it into her Afro-styled hair.

I pulled her close and let her feel my semi-hard dick. "You know I'mma tear yo ass up tomorrow don't you?"

She laughed.

The glow from the candle, the Island, the water, the sand and Sabrina. She looked at home, like an Islander herself.

"You've told me a thousand times. Just don't hurt me."

I stepped back and looked down at my future wife. "Never that."

"I've heard THAT before."

I tried to not spoil the moment with my past indiscretions. It was time to switch gears. I took her by the hand and started walking away from our suite. We didn't get far.

"What time is the wedding?" I asked.

"Eight o'clock."

I stopped walking. "In the morning?"

She laughed, "Yep. I'm ready to be Mrs. Fleming."

A huge smile spread across my face."That's what's up. What do you have planned for the rest of the night?"

"Nothing. We're just gonna relax and enjoy each other. We need to be heading back though. The staff and minister will be stopping by to go over everything for tomorrow."

"You remember to pack all of the paperwork?" I don't know why I asked her that, she didn't forget a damn thing. The reality of what was about to happen hit me. "Are you ready for this?" I asked.

"Of course I am," she said, "I wouldn't be here if I wasn't." We said nothing for a little while before she asked, "Are you?"

My life was about to change forever. There would be no more dipping and dabbing into other women's treasure chests. No more extra long looks at women I found attractive. No more silent 'I wanna get with you' signals. No more being mad at Ramona. No more having one chick over one night and another over the next. No more eating April's pussy. No more excuses for not being faithful and you know what? I was okay because I'd set all that shit to the side a long time ago.

"Of course I am. I wouldn't be here if I wasn't."

She hit my shoulder. "Don't be stealin' my words."

We laughed and started back to our suite. We had a wedding rehearsal to attend.

The minister and staff came by and went over the next day's events. It seemed simple enough.

From what I could tell it was going to be short and sweet and that was definitely cool by me.

I took out my camera and started taking pictures. I wanted to make sure I got as much of the wedding festivities as possible. Moms wouldn't let me live it down if I didn't.

After everyone left Sabrina and I went out onto our private terrace and took a seat. I offered Sabrina another glass of wine but she refused.

"Gotta have a clear head in the morning. I don't want to miss a moment of it."

"That's totally understandable." I poured myself a hearty glass and got to sippin'.

"Sincere? Can you believe it? In a few hours we're going to be husband and wife."

I looked over the rim of my wine glass at my future wife, and wished I could marry her at that moment. Instead of answering I looked out into the dark ocean. We said nothing for a long time, just held hands, individually swimming in our own thoughts.

After about an hour Sabrina spoke, "Sincere?"

"Mmmhmm?" She got quiet so I looked her way. The look on her face worried me. "What's up baby? What's wrong?"

I turned my chair toward her, and scooted her between my legs. When she put her hands on my thighs I looked down. "You might not want to do that. I haven't masturbated today." She moved her hands like she'd been bitten.

"Hey, hey relax Sabrina. I was just kidding with you." It was hard to believe but she actually looked scared. "What's wrong?"

"Well, that's kinda what I want to talk to you about."

She paused and licked her lips. I wanted to tell her not to do that either, but didn't want to push it. "What is it Sabrina? You can tell me anything. You're about to be my wife so don't ever think you can't come to me about what's on your mind."

She took in a deep breath and let it out slowly. "Well, you know I've never been intimate with anyone right?"

"Yeah, yeah, right, right. So?"

"Soooo, that basically means you're going to be like my first."

"And?"

"Aaaaand I'm kinda scared."

"Scared of what?" She looked down at my crotch. I started cracking up, "You should be."

She hit me upside my head. "Sincere! I'm serious!"

It was hard for me to stop laughing but I eventually did. "Girl ain't nothing to be scared of."

"Yes there is. I mean…"

I stopped her, "Look baby girl. I don't ever want you to be afraid of my touch. I'm a man, and although you haven't had any experience in that area, I have. You are a beautiful delicate rose, and I'm going to take good care of you. All I need you to do is trust me."

With a worried look on her face she turned and stared at the water. I used my finger to turn her head back towards me.

"Sabrina, I got this okay? Don't worry about it, don't become consumed by it, or get anxious. I know this is a new experience for you, but you were a new experience for me. I know you better than you know yourself, baby girl." I looked deep into her eyes. "Because shit, on the real, after that bathroom incident I realized you's a quiet freak."

She punched me on my shoulder. "Shut up! No I'm not!"

"Oh yes the hell you are. Hell, I'm the one who should be afraid."

I pulled her onto my lap and she gave me a token struggle, not really trying. I kissed her cheek, held her close, thankful she chose me.

"We should probably be heading to bed Sincere. We've gotta get up early in the morning."

I didn't want the moment to end but she was right. After downing the rest of my wine with my arm around her, I placed her onto her feet. We closed up the suite, took showers and said our goodnights.

Neither of us wanted to separate, but soon sleeping in different beds wouldn't be an issue.

I could barely sleep under the blankets. Because of the coming hours my mind was in a million places. After thinking myself into a restful slumber, I woke to her screams.

I climbed out of my bed, confused by my surroundings. Once I remembered where I was, her cries guided me toward her.

When I got into her bed I held her close "It's okay baby girl. I got you." I kissed her sweaty forehead and listened to her anguished moans. "I'm not going anywhere Sabrina. You never have to sleep alone again. I'll always be here for you baby girl. Always Sabrina, always."

When I woke the next morning Sabrina was nowhere to be found. It was still dark outside. When I looked at the clock I saw I'd only slept a couple of hours.

She couldn't be far so I went into the bathroom, brushed my teeth, and hit the beach. I saw her on her way back.

"Where the hell you been?" I demanded.

She laughed but I didn't see a damn thing funny. "I just took a walk baby. Needed to clear my head." She draped her arm around my waist and led me back to our room. When she saw the look on my face she knew I wasn't pleased.

"Look Sincere," she sighed as we walked, "I had to make peace with my anger, fear and hatred. From the time you asked me to be yours I've been having this internal battle. Whether you know it or not, a deep-seeded evil I need to tame lives inside me. Hate is the main culprit."

She took my hands. "I'm not where I used to be but I'm certainly not where I want to be."

"I see where you're coming from," I said as reasonably as I could muster, "But we're on an Island where we know absolutely no one. I don't feel comfortable with you being alone. But dig this, although I can't take away what you've been through I do hope that I can be a sounding-board."

When we got to her room, I kissed her cheek. Still holding her hands, we sat on her bed.

"We're in this together," I said, "There is no me without a you and I hope the same applies with you. Do you realize you're about to be my wife? Not my girlfriend, but wife. That takes our relationship to a whole 'nother level, and it's a level we've gotta take together baby girl.

Now, I don't know what it's going to take for you to know for sure that I'm in your corner. But we ain't gonna have no more midnight walks, jogs, runs, skips or nothin'. Not without me by your side. With that being said we need to take our black asses back to bed. We only have two hours and a brotha is saving his energy for the marriage bed."

She snatched her hands out of mine and pointed to the door, "Get out."

I was in shock. "Huh?"

She started pushing me towards the door. "Out mister. You're not supposed to see the bride before the wedding. I heard it's bad luck."

"Yeah right. We been around each other already."

"I'm serious. Goodbye!"

I did as instructed and went to my room. I didn't sleep a wink. Instead I thought about my future wife. Sabrina was some kinda special. She was sweet and gentle, but still tart and aggressive. She had a magnetic sexual intensity I'd experienced firsthand in her bathroom.

And she was fragile. I got to see just how fragile at the hospital. We'd been around each other a lot but I'd never seen her behave like that. Her little ass was on fire and it was well-warranted.

Her heart was as big as the ocean that was outside my bedroom door and although trampled over time and time again she was forgiving and left room for others to step in and possibly take advantage of what she had to offer. She was damn-near genius who shared her knowledge with anyone.

Sabrina told me when she loved, she loved hard and she wasn't lying. Whomever she chose to love, that person had nothing to worry about when it came to fidelity. That was exactly what I needed.

Trust was an emotion I never wanted to have to worry about. My first and last heartbreak may have been the reason for my lack of past commitment, and why I chose the women I did. I knew those chicks were either after dick or dough. Desire was the only thing they were faithful to. And I was cool with it. They got what they wanted and so did I with no strings attached. Excluding Veronica.

With Sabrina I didn't have to worry. Even with her living with The Dicks.

Sabrina was a good, pure and innocent young lady, something I'd never had before. I was glad I hadn't. Although not fair, I know I'd have compared her to a previous 'good girl'. Along with that, her flaws would have been magnified. I'm afraid I would have broken her heart.

And she knew not to pressure me about my past. She accepted the lack of knowledge. My mom's business is not for everyone to know about. I was sure one day I'd tell Sabrina and let her completely into my world.

The memories of my mom's anguish damn near killed me the one time I talked about it with Ramona, I wasn't ready to put myself out there like that yet. One thing is for sure, whenever I opened up and told my wife about my past, I knew that she'd be there to wipe every tear dry.

I heard a soft knock outside my door. "Sincere? Are you awake?"

I smiled. "Awake and dressed future Mrs. Fleming."

There was silence on the other end of the door so I walked over and placed my ear against it.

"I love you Sabrina." I looked down and saw her shadow so I knew she was there.

"I love you too Sincere." She didn't move and I hadn't either.

"You nervous Sabrina?"

"No. I'm ready to be free."

At that moment I knew that all was well. "Me too baby girl. Me too."

"They're here."

"Who?"

She giggled. "The staff. Remember what they said. No peeking Mr. Fleming."

Her shadow moved so I opened the door. "Okay, future Mrs. Fleming."

She'd been headed to her room but turned when she heard my voice. Her surprise caused my heart to skip a beat.

Sabrina didn't wear makeup. She was an all-natural kinda girl. Today she wore light splashes of blush and eyeshadow, and long lashes. She was all kinds of beautiful.

"Damn!"

"Sincere!" I started walking her way. "You're not supposed to look." I ignored her. "I'm serious." When I stood in front of her she swallowed whatever words that were going float out of her throat. "Sincere?"

"Can we skip the ceremony?"

She was looking up at me. For the first time I saw the same desire that I possessed in her eyes. Her voice was thick. "What about our written out wedding vows?"

"We can say them in the privacy of our room." I bent down and placed my face into the crook of her neck. "Damn you smell good."

She wore a pretty cream-colored dress with an orange belt. I put my big hands on her pantiless ass and squeezed.

She took ahold of my shoulders, "Sincere," she breathed.

As soon as she said my name I took a step back. She looked confused and disappointed. I put my head down. "Girl. You gonna cause me to lose my mind."

When I looked up her cheeks were a lot rosier. All I could do was shake my head. She was absolutely breathtaking, "We need to go Sincere."

I looked down at my big, erect dick, then back at her. "Okay. After that goes down, and yes, I think we need to skip our vows." Hard dick and all, I took her by her hand and we made our way to the beach. I could wait no longer.

The day was so damn pretty I almost regretted cutting out some of the wedding ceremony. Almost.

The staff had the setup on point. There were rose petals on our private patio that led the way to the beach. All the windows were open, and the breeze pushed me forward. It was like the forces that be were aware of the gift at the end of the rose petal trail, just as there was a ring at the end of the one I'd set up for Sabrina in the day I proposed.

She requested no one attend the wedding except the witness, the minister and someone to take pictures. That's exactly how it was. There would be no music to announce the bride, just the sound of the ocean and its welcoming mist.

We walked hand in hand. When we reached the preacher, he smiled as if we weren't the first couple to abandon the particulars of a wedding day.

The night before, he'd given us instructions on how the ceremony would be performed. I was to be outside standing next to him when Sabrina walked out. As soon as he saw us walking towards him hand in hand he knew that there had been a change of plans.

He greeted us with a deep Caribbean accent. "Good morning Sabrina and Sincere. Are we ready to get started?"

"We surely are. And if possible, can we expedite it?" I looked down at Sabrina who, with a smile on her face, was looking up at me.

"Of course of course." The minister said.

I couldn't take my eyes off of her, and in a flash, the witness tapped my shoulder. So that there'd be no nervous fumbles on my part during the ceremony, I'd already given the rings to him. I was glad of my foresight because I was nervous as hell.

As he handed me the rings my damn hand shook. It was like I was in a dream, functioning strictly off emotions. I didn't even realize that I'd said 'I do' and put the ring on Sabrina's finger. I was aware when his ass said I could kiss my bride tho.

With the ocean in my ear, Sabrina within my grasp. I was in heaven.

I gently brought my wife close to me, and as her husband, kissed her softly for the first time. She held me so tight I didn't wanna let go.

Then my stomach growled.

She pulled back and laughed. I pulled away as well, mad that I hadn't eaten. I was starved to be inside of my wife but knew I had to feed my body first. I looked at preacha man; he smiled, got the hint and motioned for his partners to leave.

"We'll do the paperwork later," he said.

As they quietly made their exit, the photographer snapping away, Sabrina and I went to the patio and found our breakfast. She'd planned that too. Sadly, I was so hungry that I couldn't really appreciate the kind gesture. As soon as we sat, I shoved a piece of bacon in my mouth.

"Can we at least say grace?"

I looked up, impatient but when I saw her concerned face I straightened up. "My bad. Please bow." I took a sip of orange juice then took her hand in mine, "Thank you Lord for this food. Amen."

She chuckled and sipped on some water.

"Are you going to eat?" I asked as I dug in. I was surprised by her response.

"I only have an appetite for one thing."

As I sliced into some French toast I looked up and saw desire. I wasn't going to be worth shit in the bedroom if I didn't eat, but she was making it hard. "Did you eat something earlier?"

"Nope, just waiting on you."

Blood rushed to my dick. I knew a subject change was in order. I tried not to talk while chewing but couldn't help it. She was horny and made it very clear that only one thing was on her mind. With a mouth full of food I asked, "Were you pleased with the ceremony?"

She stood and started walking away. "Of course. I'll be even more pleased when you stop asking me questions and eat."

Her wish was my command. I took a few more bites, drowned down some more juice. I then rushed into my bathroom, brushed my teeth, then went on the hunt for my wife.

As I walked into her bedroom, she was exiting the bathroom. She jumped back and closed the door. "Go back out. Go back out. I'm not ready yet."

I was confused. "What?"

"Just stand by the door. But close it first. I'll tell you when I'm ready."

I rolled my eyes up in my head. "Shit. You better hurry up." She snickered but I didn't find nothin' funny. A few seconds later she called out my name. "That was quick."

I opened the door and found her under the covers. "Naw baby girl. You gotta come up." I took off my shirt, shorts and underwear. When she saw my hard dick her eyes got big. I was swinging as I walked over to the bed. When I tried pulling back the blanket it wouldn't move. She had a death grip on it. "Let go Sabrina."

For her to have been so hot and horny she was really killing the mood.

"Nobody's ever seen my body."

I barely heard her ass so I put my hand up to my ear. "What was that?"

"My body. No one has ever seen me naked."

"So what was all that shit you were talkin' at the table? I have seen you naked. Remember the bathroom?" My dick had gone soft and I was annoyed.

"I still want you, but you gotta get under the covers."

I could not believe my damn ears. Butt-ass-naked I took a step back and looked at her like she was crazy. "Sabrina. You walk around with those tight clothes and say that nobody has ever seen you naked? You really don't leave much to the imagination."

She turned into a little mouse. "Pleeeease."

I sighed loudly and got into bed. Her whole attitude changed. She let go of the blanket, leaving little room between us. She got on top of me. "Thank you."

I kissed her head which was on my chest and rubbed her up and down on her body. "No problem Sabrina."

She leaned up and angled her head over mine. When she did I felt her kitty hair scrape across my belly. "You know you can't hide from me forever."

"I don't plan too. I just need to be more comfortable around you."

I gripped her butt. "We lived together Sabrina. You should be used to me. And I saw all yo' shit over your house."

I lifted my head and caught her mouth with mine. I was tired of talking. I wanted to be inside my beautiful wife. Her kiss and touch was sweet as she held my face in her hands. She spoke into my mouth.

"I love you Sincere."

I spoke with my movements. I gently flipped her onto her back. Her legs spread automatically and I fit between them perfectly. Everything about her felt good. Her hands, her breasts against my chest, her flat belly, her hairy pussy.

Her eyes were closed when I removed my lips from hers and sat on my knees. She had to be out of her damn mind if she thought I wasn't going to look at her bangin' ass body. The blankets fell to uncover her flawless frame. She opened her eyes at the absence of my touch. She covered her breasts.

"Sincere!" She tried closing her legs but I held them open. "Sincere!"

"Be still." Although I couldn't see all of her body, I saw enough. "Don't move Sabrina."

With her legs opened, her scent rose and hit my nostrils. My mouth automatically watered.

She looked me in my eyes and knew I was serious. I sat back on my haunches and looked at her beautiful pussy. When I glanced up she was still looking at me. Her breathing had increased. The wind was blowing, the ocean was singing and my brain could barely decide on what to do first. I wanted all of her and I wanted her all at once.

Swallowing hard, I looked at what had caused my thirst. While still on my haunches, I took my hands and opened her flower. It was shiny and juicy.

"Your shit's perfect."

I bent down and pulled her closer to me. I wanted to dive into her essence. Instead I smelled that shit and blew on it. I had barely touched her ass, and she was going crazy.

"Ohh." I licked my lips and blew again. "Yes. Yes. Yes." Every time I blew her legs shook. "Oooh. Yes."

When I looked up she still had her stupid hands across her chest but her eyes were closed tight. I watched in amazement as her clit got hard then placed the tip of my tongue on it.

"Ooooohhhh yeessss." She opened her eyes and grabbed the blanket. "Oh Sincere."

Mission accomplished. I got back onto my knees. She tried hiding her breasts again but I wasn't having that. My expression halted her movement.

"You're flawless Sabrina and I'm your husband. Don't be ashamed to show me what's mine." She bit her bottom lip. "You hear me? Even if your ass had one tittie you'd be perfect."

She nodded.

I leaned forward, placed my hands on either side of her head and looked down upon her. With my knees I opened her legs wider. "I love you baby girl."

"I love you too Sincere."

I got to my elbows and started kissing her all over her face. "I love you more than life itself."

She opened her legs wider. "Me too Sincere. Me too."

I took my dick and started rubbing up and down her wet hot spot. "I promise to never, ever, hurt you Sabrina. Never."

She grabbed me around my neck and I felt her fast beating heartbeat. "Please don't."

I slowly put the tip of my dick into her tight heaven and thought I was gonna embarrass myself. "Ooooh shit!" She tried to wrap her legs around my waist but I wouldn't let her. "Not yet baby girl. Let me get some more in."

I slid out and had to start over. I got all of the head in and again thought I was going to find myself being ashamed.

She tensed.

"Relax baby girl. Just relax." She didn't. With my neck in a death grip I could barely move. When I put a little more in I felt her legs shake. "It's okay Sabrina. I'll be gentle. Just try to relax." Her stuff was so damn tight that it really felt like it was her first time. I wanted to make sure she enjoyed it.

Instead of putting more of my dick inside of her, I started going in and out with what was in there. She finally started to relax. It wasn't much, but some was better than none. "That's it baby girl. Let me do this. Aww shit!" The more that I stroked the better it got. "Oh shit Sabrina."

Her grip around my neck loosened and I looked down at her. Her lids were closed. "Look at me Sabrina."

She frowned and shook her head. A tear was gliding down the side of her face. I kissed it away. Although I was causing her pain, that I was the one doing it must have been a turn on because her shit was wet as hell.

It had been over two years since I'd had any pussy, and the wait was well worth it. The depth of her pool was so heavenly. I wanted to squeeze her tight and never let go.

It took a minute but I was able to get my entire dick inside of her. Once I got my rhythm going she started to enjoy it. I had to concentrate to control myself. Besides having some good pussy, the fact that she'd chosen to save herself for her wedding night was a huge turn on. Her ass didn't disappoint.

"Look at me Sabrina."

She blinked her eyes open and then slowly closed them. When she let out a small moan I thought I was going to lose my mind. I took her hands into mine and started dicking her down with slow, long strokes.

"Mmmmmm. Sincere."

"Look at me Sabrina." She bit her bottom lip and opened her lids halfway. "I love you baby girl."

While arching her back she squeezed my hands. As I looked into my wife's eyes, my strokes got faster. She started rolling her hips.

When Sabrina let go of my hands, placed hers on my face, and brought my head close to hers and started tonguing me down, shit got intense.

She started off kissing me really soft but then she got aggressive. The more aggressive she got the more aggressive my dick strokes got. She welcomed them. She gave me more room by spreading her legs wide open, and I took total advantage of it.

"Oh yes Sincere. Fuck this shit."

I stopped mid-stroke. I could not believe what I'd just heard. Sabrina's ass didn't curse and the fact that she had shocked me shitless.

She frowned, not appreciating my cease in motion. With her lids still closed she scooted downward in the bed, trying to get me to move again. Her titties shook, reminding me of the task at hand. I bent down and took a nipple into my mouth. She placed her hands on my butt, prompting me to start pumping again. After getting back into rhythm I looked down at her pretty brown face. I was still a little surprised at what she'd said.

"What do you want me to do Sabrina?" She didn't respond, just started biting on her bottom lip. "Say it again."

She opened her eyes. "Make me."

I smiled and started long strokin' her ass again.

"What? Like that?"

She moaned, "Nope."

Her lips were so thick with lust that I licked them and as I did I increased the speed of my strokes. "You like that shit?"

"Mmmmmm." That wasn't the response I was looking for so I started giving her the entire dick but a little harder. "Oh yes. That's what I like. Yes baby." Her titties shook enticingly, so I grabbed one and squeezed hard, "Yeeeeees! That's it. Squeeze that shit."

When she said that I lost it. I sat up, placed her legs over my shoulders and went to town. "Oh yes! Sincere! Yes baby! Fuck yo pussy. Fuck yo shit!"

That was it. My whole damn body got weak as I pumped one last time into her warmth, releasing a moan from deep within my chest that was more like a growl. It was the longest orgasm of my damn life. "Oh shit!" I was certain that the billion little Flemings I deposited were going to cause her to look pregnant. "Awwww shit Sabrina."

I was in pure ecstasy.

"Oh girl, shit!"

She drained me dry.

When I finished my whole body felt like a damn noodle. I didn't want to but I plopped my ass on top of her, exhausted. When I woke I was still in the same position. I looked down at her pretty chocolate face, and gave my Sleeping Beauty a kiss.

I eased out of bed, I was starving. As I made my way to her bathroom I looked over my shoulder, amazed that I'd been given such a gift.

Chapter Eight

After a shower I walked naked into the kitchen and ate some fruit. I knew I'd need more than that to satisfy my hunger, so I called room service and placed an order for myself and Sabrina for lunch.

I was on my third banana and sipping some grape juice when I decided to dive back into the fruit of my woman. When I got to the door of her bedroom I stood and looked at my new soulmate. She was still in the position that I'd left her, legs gaping open so I could see her treasure.

It was real tempting to dive in tongue-first, but licking my seed off privates was not my forte and I wasn't going to start either. I got between her legs and softly licked her clit. Her ass was out cold, so I watched it get hard and swollen. Being able to arouse her made my dick hard, and since she was already in position, I sat up and gently worked my dick back inside. She closed right back up. I guess she was sore down there because as I started making my way deeper into her goodness, she grimaced and woke.

"Ouch Sincere. It hurts."

"Okay baby. It'll start feeling better." My shit was hard and needed to be satisfied.

She placed her hands on my chest as if signaling me to slow down but I was already going slow as hell.

"Open your legs."

She didn't want to but did, and the fact that she wasn't wet probably didn't help. I kissed her neck and made my way to her plump breasts. I nursed on them both, rolling my tongue over her nipples until they got hard. She moaned lightly and I knew I was in. I started slowly rolling my hips. "You feel so good Sabrina. So soft." I leaned forward and lay on top of her. When I felt her hands on my broad back I placed my head between her neck and shoulder. "You still smell fresh."

Her legs had been tense and stiff but as I whispered in her ear she loosened up.

"Yeah baby. Let daddy in." Her shit got wet so I knew she was into it.

"Mmm yes Sincere."

Hearing her say my name tickled my ears, "Say my name again." She didn't so I lightly bit her ear, "Say that shit."

Wrapping her legs around my waist, she submitted. "Sincere."

My dick got harder so I ground into her pussy but not too hard. I didn't want to give her a reason to ask me to stop. "One more time baby girl." My dick was all the way in her so I rolled my hips.

"Mmmm Sincere. Yes baby." My arms were under her shoulders and hers were gripping my back. I started kissing and sucking on her neck. "Oh yes Sincere. Yes baby."

I grunted and grind, grunt and grind. Although trying my hardest to make it last, she was making it damn near impossible.

"Gimme that dick." I increased my speed and felt her breast shaking against my chest. She held on tight. "I feel it Sincere. Oh shit. I feel that pressure. Oh shit." She squeezed me so tight that it felt like she trying to make us become one. Her shit clamped on my dick and that was all she wrote. I groaned loudly. Her ass was going to kill me because my second orgasm felt just as wonderful as the first.

"Sabrina!" I didn't think I had that much damn sperm left in me but I did. "Yes baby girl. Oh fuck!"

It felt like that shit lasted a whole minute and again my whole damn body felt like a noodle. I didn't pass out this time. Instead I kissed, and kissed, and kissed her. The damn bed was soaked and when I moved my knee it came across the cold wetness. While kissing her face she sang a melody into my ears.

"I love you Sincere. I love you so so much."

I was ready to listen to that song for a lifetime.

Following round two there was a knock at the door. It happened so fast that I started looking around the room for cameras. I kissed the top of Sabrina's nose, climbed off my wife, and slipped on some shorts. When I looked through the peephole no one was there just a tray with our food. I opened the door.

After lifting a lid I saw a salmon, then pulled the cart into our suite. After locking the door I took the contents off the cart and place them in the kitchen. I went to tell Sabrina that the food had arrived but didn't find her in the bed. I did see that big-ass wet spot and made a mental note to call housekeeping. Then I heard water running from the shower.

Although I was damn near starved, I took my shorts off and joined my wife. When I pulled back the glass shower door she jumped back and covered her body.

"Don't even start that shit," I said.

"Sincere. You scared the hell outta me. You could have at least knocked."

"For what?"

"For what? It's rude not too."

"Whatever. You're my damn wife so there's no need to knock. Hell, your ass keeps the damn door cracked even when takin' a shit so what are you talking about?" She hit me on my chest and then turned her back towards me. "Turn around Sabrina."

"Sincere. I have got to get used to this. To us. Will you please be patient with me?"

"Girl, I just saw your ass spread eagle. You ain't got shit I ain't seen." She put her head down and when she did I rolled my eyes up in my head. "Your tail is real sensitive."

"No, just aware."

"Aware of what Sabrina? I'm your husband. That's the only thing you need to be aware of." I showed some mercy and grabbed a face towel and started washing. My stomach was on empty and needed immediate attention. I'd have to deal with Sabrina on a full stomach.

After showering I wrapped a towel around my waist and made my way to my bedroom. I dressed and made another mental note to merge our stuff in one of the rooms. As of today there would be no separate beds.

Once in her bedroom I found her putting on her pants. I poked my head in the door, "I'm about to get lunch ready so I'll see you when you come out."

Her fat ass jiggled under her linen pants and my dick jumped. I would probably never get enough of Sabrina. I repositioned my dick, made my way back into the kitchen and got our plates together.

Salmon, grilled asparagus, hand-whipped potatoes, caesar salad, and a nice bottle of wine were on the menu. As I placed asparagus on Sabrina's plate I popped one in my mouth. That shit was hot as hell but with my stomach touching my spine, I tolerated the pain and enjoyed its saltiness.

"Couldn't wait for grace?"

I looked over my shoulder and beheld absolute perfection. After drinking some water I responded. "Naw baby girl. You wore a brotha out. I need fuel for round three."

I wiggled my eyebrows up and down. As I did Sabrina placed her hands over her private part. She was walking slow, "I don't think so," she said, "Not tonight anyway."

When I saw that I felt bad about round two but I couldn't help it. Her apple bottom was more than tempting. To make it up I catered to her every need. I pulled out her chair then poured her some wine. After tossing the salad I placed some in our bowls and sat.

I placed my hands into her outstretched ones and said grace. "Thank you Lord for this food. Amen."

She giggled.

I put a piece of asparagus in my mouth, held it with my teeth. "Come here. I've seen white people do this corny shit."

With a big smile on her face she placed her mouth on the opposite end of the asparagus. Then we chewed into a kiss, but just a peck. I didn't want her food swishing through my mouth.

"Damn we gotta do that again. Forgot to take a picture for Mom and Brice."

With our heads tilted in a weird angle and big smiles we took a picture. Afterward we ate in silence.

We spent the remaining days sightseeing, shopping and went on a few excursions. I moved my things into Sabrina's room and whenever she had nightmares she had easy access to my loving arms. I held her tight, kissed her tears away and assured her that I was there for her always.

Sabrina eventually got used to being naked in my presence. I took full advantage by slapping her ass whenever she walked past me or by softly squeezing one of her breasts as she lay in bed.

It turned out that my wife, who was a lady in the streets, was a straight up freak in the bedroom, and wanted the dick all the time.

Just because she wanted the dick did not mean she knew what to do with it. She lacked experience and I had no problem being her instructor.

"Now put your tongue on the tip and roll my pre-cum around it." She wore her regular everyday lipstick with the gloss on top. "Yeah that's it baby girl. That's it. Just like that." I thought I was going to nut in her mouth. "Now. Put just a little bit of your lips on the head and then lightly suck." When she did that my damn toes curled. "Oh shit. Not so hard. Oh shit!"

She learned how to satisfy her husband; she wasn't the only one getting schooled.

"Sincere. I don't like when you do that."

I was fingering her. "Since when?"

"Since now."

"Well you sure didn't have any complaints when I did it to you in the bathroom at your house."

"Well I hadn't felt your big fat dick inside of me either. Nothing compares and your finger is just a tease. If it ain't your dick or tongue I don't want it in me."

That settled that.

Our trip was seven nights, but after our first night of sexual exploration Sabrina was sore and couldn't take the dick. Instead of making love physically we made love to each other's minds and enjoyed that we were now one. But, as soon as the pussy was healed I beat that shit up on a daily. What tripped me out was the fact that no matter how many times I touched my wife I felt like I could never touch her enough. Our last night let me know why.

"Close your eyes Sincere."

Instead of closing them I rolled them up in my head. As I lay in bed my dick was standing at attention. I was ready to get busy but she told me that she had a surprise for me.

"Are they closed?"

"Yeah!" They weren't but when she opened the door I hurried up and closed them.

"No peeking."

"Mmmhmmm."

"Now put the headphones on."

I did as I was told and waited. About twenty minutes later I felt my wife straddle my lap. She took the headphones off and I heard soft jazz playing. When she placed something over my eyes I took ahold of her wrist.

"Don't you dare open those eyes Sincere!"

"I'm not but what the hell are you doing?"

"Don't worry about it. Just obey."

As I removed my hands a small smile danced crossed my lips. "Is that riiiiight?"

She tied the garment around my head, covering my eyes. "That's riiiiight." I felt her climb off of me and the bed. "Sincere?"

I turned my head to the left. The direction of her voice. "Yes baby girl?"

"Do you love me?"

She was on my right so I turned my head in that direction. "You know I do."

She hesitated. "How much?" Straight ahead at the foot of the bed.

"More than life itself."

I could feel her smile. "Do you trust me?" She was still in the same spot.

"Always."

"Come here."

I raised my arms to uncover my eyes.

"Find me Sincere. I need you to find me with the blindfold on. I promise I won't make it hard." My dick had gone down but the way she said that last statement gave it a little life. "Follow my voice. I'm not far Sincere. I'm right in front of you." I got on my hands and knees and cautiously made my way to the end of the bed. When I felt nothing but air beneath my hand I sat on its edge. "Now reach out and touch me."

I did and that shit was sensual as hell. It was kinda weird at first because I didn't know what part of her body I was feeling. What I thought was her thigh was actually her arm. My thumb touched her breast, and that was all the lead I needed.

With her arms being my guide, without taking my hands off of her, I made my way to her face. My fingers traced her eyebrows, her closed lids, her nose and her mouth. Then I followed her cheekbone to her ears and made my way to her neck. I placed my hand on her pulse. It was beating fast and hard.

I continued my journey to her shoulders and around to her breast. My hands lingered there for a long time, playing with her nipples, making sure they got erect. My big hands trailed down to her small waist, then she moved.

I reached out for her and felt nothing. In that instant I missed my wife.

"Sincere?"

I stood.

"Did I tell you to stand?"

I smiled and sat my black ass down. "Yes Sabrina?"

"Do you love me?"

"You know I do."

"How much?"

"More than life itself."

"Do you trust me?"

"Always."

"Come here. Follow my voice. I'm not far Sincere. I'm right in front of you."

That was a damn lie. I could tell that she was in another room but followed her voice anyway.

With my arms outstretched and walking hella slow, I know I had to have looked crazy as hell. I wasn't trying to stub my toe while playing Sabrina's seductive game. Because a brotha was concentrating, my dick had gone soft again, I couldn't think about pussy and my final destination at the same time but I knew that somehow my baby was going to make it rise once more.

"Follow my voice. I'm not far Sincere. I'm right in front of you."

I did as instructed and knew I was in the kitchen.

"That's it. Almost there."

"Almost where?"

She didn't answer.

"Now stop!"

I froze like a statue which caused her to suppress a laugh. "Reach out in front of you and take ahold of the chair. Once you have it, take a seat."

Using my knee I found the seat and slowly sat down it in. She'd placed a towel on the seat. Her ass don't miss shit.

"Now reach out and touch me."

As before, I did as was told. The first thing I felt was air and had to lean forward to feel flesh. I touched her breast and was happy. As I rubbed on her soft skin my dick rose and so did the speed of her breathing.

"You like that Sincere? You like the way I feel?" Instead of answering I traced my hands over her body and made my way to her round butt. "Now open your legs and pull me close."

It started to rain. That and the subtle sound of the jazz with the scent of the ocean and the closeness of her pussy caused me to damn near yank her towards me. I tried pulling her onto my lap but she wasn't having that. She placed her hands on my chest and pushed back.

"Not yet big boy. Not yet."

I was disappointed.

"Now, if you're good I'll let you smell it. Are you going to be good?"

I smiled and nodded. I could hear her moving around but didn't have a clue as to what she was doing. I heard the table being dragged across the floor.

"Scoot up to the table Sincere. It's time for you to smell your dinner."

A big fat smile spread across my grill. I loved my wife.

After getting close, I was given more instructions.

"No touching."

All I could do was shake my head.

"Now slowly lean down."

Even with my eyes blindfolded I could picture Sabrina with her legs wide open, leaning on her elbows, looking down at me making sure I obeyed.

"Right there."

Her voice was husky and as I smelled her succulent scent I knew why. She was just as aroused as I was.

"Are you touching yourself Sincere?"

Guilty as charged. I place my hands on my lap, wishing I could lap up her juices.

"Smell that shit." Her ass was trying to get into trouble. With my face so close to her pussy, her hairs were tickling my nose. I wanted to lick her so badly I almost started drooling.

"Yes baby. Smell it. You like that?"

My throat was so thick I barely got my yeah out. I inhaled deeply and hated that I had to exhale. The fact that I knew she was looking was such a turn on that my dick started hurting. Something on my body needed to be inside of her.

"Since you've been such a good boy you get one..." She had me messed up. I draped my arms around her thighs, pulled her to the very edge of the table and dived in. "Sincere! No not yet!" She tried getting up but I had her in a death grip. "Sincere! I had a surprise for you at the end!"

I lifted my head. "This is all the surprise I need."

She placed her hands on my head and started rolling her hips. "Oh shit Sincere. Oh yes baby. Eat that pussy."

I had her clit in my mouth and sucked on it tenderly.

"You're squeezing my legs too hard Sincere." I let loose of my grip. "Ahhh yes that's it. Mmmmm." She pressed hard on my head. "Yeah baby. Right there. Right there. Right there." I pulled Sabrina off the table onto my lap and started sucking on her titties, nursing off one then the other.

"Sit on this shit."

She reached around rose up on her tiptoes and then eased down onto my dick. She held onto my neck and squeezed. "Oooooh yesssssss." And then she started slowly going up and down. "Oh yes Sincere. Mmmmm yes baby." I knew that her head was back so I blindly took total advantage of it by licking and sucking her erotic neck. "Yes baby. Make this shit wet." My hands were on her butt and I gripped it as she glided up and down my pole.

I still had the garment over my eyes, but knew her body and movements as if they were my own. "I want you to give me that feeling again Sincere. Make me feel good baby." I pushed her down on my dick, found her lips and kissed her hard.

"You better stop talkin' that shit."

"Please baby please."

My hands went to her hips. I sat back and started slowly rocking her back and forth. "You like that baby girl? Huh? You like ridin' this big dick?"

All she could do was moan. The sound of the rain, the music, the ocean, the swishing sound of her juices as I rocked her back and forth, the flesh to flesh contact of her titties touching my chest, and her mouthwatering scent were magical.

"Take my blindfold off. I wanna look at your ass."

She removed her hands from around my neck and took it off. It took a minute for my eyes to adjust because Sabrina had the whole suite black except for the candles she had throughout the house. I stopped moving her hips. Once my vision was straight I looked into her eyes.

"Surprise." She slowly rolled her hips. "I did all of this for you."

She took my bottom lip into her mouth. "Because you found me."

She pecked my lips. "And because I love you."

She lightly bit my neck. "And because you've brought something good out of me."

She took ahold of my shoulders and squeezed. "That I didn't know I had in me."

She sucked on my ear. "And I want you to bring it out again."

She rolled her hips a little faster. "And again."

She threw her head back and with closed eyes touched her breasts. "And again. Mmmm."

As she rolled I grabbed ahold of her neck and licked it down to her breast. "Yes baby. Yes. Like that." I went from one to the other and then squeezed them together and sucked on both those bitches. "Mmmm. Be gentle."

Everything about her made me excited. Everything.

As she rolled I lifted my hips. I don't want nothin' separating us. "Do that shit girl."

"I want that feeling baby. Make me feel good." With my hands on her hips, back and forth, back and forth back and forth I went. The scent of our sex entered my nose.

"Get on the floor baby." She said, "I wanna feel that entire dick."

She didn't have to tell me twice. I stood and her legs automatically went around my waist. I threw the towel to the floor. A brotha was not tryin' to get no splinters. We plopped down kinda funny but without incident.

"Ride this dick Sabrina. Ride this dick." I was still in the sitting position and she still had her legs wrapped around my waist.

"Yes Sincere. Yes." She held onto my neck as if for dear life and as she rocked back and forth I helped her out. The sounds around us accentuated the moment. Even with the breeze coming through the windows we started sweating. With the candle light, her skin glowed royal black. A small glistening drop slid down her neck, and I licked it up.

"Even your sweat taste sweet." I kissed the spot.

"Hold me tight Sincere and never let go." Our wet sticky bodies came together and I rolled my hips in sync with hers. "That's it Sincere. Oooooh. Yeah."

I pulled back to give her a passionate kiss. She moved her face, threw her neck back and rolled her hips faster. "It's coming Sincere. I feel it. I think I feel it." She tried to hold onto my shoulders but they were too slick. She placed her head into the crook of my neck and held on tight. "This is it! Oh shit! It's happening. Sincere! Sincere! Sincere!"

When she screamed my name I pushed her down onto my dick, lifted my hips and then damn near broke her in half as I held her in position around her waist.

As her pussy gripped my dick, I placed my face between the crook of her neck, sucked hard and let loose in tenor. That shit felt so good I sound like a yowling cat. "Shit!"

I eventually let Sabrina go and as I lay back onto the cool floor, I pulled her down on top of me.

"I love you Sincere."

I breathed hard. "I love you more Sabrina."

Before driving us home I stopped by Mom's to get my mail. I let myself in and went straight to the refrigerator. There was something about my mother's house that always made me feel safe. Like no matter what life threw my way, I could always go back there and know that in her arms I'd be comforted.

I fixed myself a healthy glass of milk and as I drank, flipped through my mail. I put my glass down when I came across a letter from the Wiz.

I walked to the front door, looked out and saw Sabrina with her head leaned against the headrest, eyes closed. I slowly closed the door, walked over to the couch and sat down. Before opening the letter I took a deep breath.

As I scanned what was written, a big smile spread across my face.

I was in! Hell! I was actually in that thang!

As I put the letter between the rest of the mail I quickly came up with a solution to a problem that didn't yet exist.

The Wiz had offered me a full time position on nights. I knew Sabrina's ass was not going for that. I could barely take a shit without her wondering where the hell I was. As I washed my glass and locked Mom's house, the thought of periodic, twin house guests danced through my head.

Sabrina officially moved into my house as my wife. The crib was ours. Although she'd lived there before, this was totally different.

We were having sex everywhere and made sure we christened damn near every room in the house. I said "damn near" for a reason.

Before she slept in my bedroom, Sabrina, in her own whack way, let some things be made known. At first there were subtle signs. But then she got bold.

After getting most of our things unpacked and situated, we were exhausted, and decided to turn in early.

As usual we showered together. When exiting the bathroom, Sabrina went in the opposite direction of the master bedroom. I stopped her in the hallway.

"Hey baby. Come on. We don't sleep in separate rooms anymore."

"I know Sincere. But is there any way that we could sleep in the spare bedroom? Your mattress is too firm for my liking."

To my knowledge, she'd never lay in my bed. I was extremely tired so I didn't argue and took my happy butt to the guest bedroom, following right behind my wife.

The next night she said she didn't want to agitate her back by lying on a hard mattress. The night after that she went to bed early and was asleep before I could say anything.

When the next night came, I didn't ask any questions and just eased in next to my wife and held her when she woke screaming.

A couple of days later I noticed that none of Sabrina's belongings were in the master bedroom. She'd placed all of her things into the room we'd been sleeping in, so I asked her about it.

"Hey Sabrina. Why are all of your clothes in the other room? There's plenty of closet space in the master."

I knew my wife was a bit peculiar so I didn't want to rock the boat. But there seemed to be a problem with the room itself, not just the bed.

"Well Sincere. I've thrown out most of the things that you had over here, it made more sense to keep things uncomplicated by leaving what I wanted in there and adding my new stuff to it. It's no big deal. I'll move them into the master when I have time."

I raised an eyebrow. "We ain't doin' shit right now."

I rose to go move her belongings but she grabbed me by my arm. "I don't feel like it right now," she protested, "There's no rush. I'll get to it."

After I sat back down I gave her a crazy look. She smiled, placed her hand on my zipper and with those sexy ass glossy lips of hers diverted my attention.

About a month later she let the cat out of the bag. We were at the grocery store when she made an offhand statement.

"I need you to get rid of that bed."

That was random as hell. "Huh?"

I'd paid a few grips for my bedroom suite and was not going to just give it up without a fight.

"How many women have you slept with on those mattresses?"

Damn!

She had a box of cereal in her hand and was acting like she was reading the back label.

I dodged the question. "How about I just get rid of the mattresses? It's better than throwing away a perfectly good bed."

I stood with my hands on the grocery cart, waiting on her to throw the cereal box in. Sabrina turned around put it in the cart and walked down the aisle.

"Matter of fact," she said, "How many women have crossed the threshold of your home?"

We made it to the fresh fruits and vegetable section and I watched her delicate hands picked up broccoli stalks. She wasn't really paying attention to what she was doing, her mind was elsewhere.

"Not many."

"Hmmm." She put the broccoli down and walked to the dairy aisle. "You want some Butter Pecan ice cream?"

"That shit's for old people. I'm good." I knew the conversation wasn't over and watched as she stared at her options. "We need a new beginning Sincere."

"How 'new' can we get? We been married two months."

She picked out two gallons of different brand ice cream, shut the freezer door, put them in the cart and started for the checkout. "I need a new beginning. Every time I walk into your house it feels trampled on."

"You didn't have a problem being in 'our' house when you lived there before we were married."

She put items on the checkout counter. "I wasn't your wife Sincere. I feel like the other woman."

Her comment pissed me off. "What the hell you mean the other woman? Shit, you're the only woman that has ever lived under my roof."

She slammed the fresh salmon on the counter. "But I'm not the *only* woman who has 'been' under your roof."

We said nothing as she paid for our groceries. I put our items in the cart and made my way to the car. I didn't wait for her to finish the transaction. By the time she got to our vehicle, everything was in the car including me.

I knew where Sabrina was going with her statements and wasn't feeling it.

When I turned eighteen, I had my house built to my specifications. My shit was tight. Although it had originally been my bachelor's pad, Sabrina's touch was making it into a real home. The stainless steel pots and pans, the dishes that had pretty designs on them, the plants. It was the little things that signified her gentle presence. Things that welcomed me every time I walked through the door.

She got into the car and looked out of the window. I sat on the driver's side and looked at her.

"We not getting another house Sabrina. The shit we got is just fine."

I started the car and drove us home. As I opened the door to step out of the truck, she remained seated.

"You coming in?" I said with a little more attitude than I'd intended.

"It reminds me of my father." She said that shit so low that I put my hand up to my ear.

"What did you just say?"

When she turned and looked at me my damn heart broke. "It reminds me of my father. I've always seen myself as second best. Like I wasn't good enough to be number one. He rejected me at eight years old, Sincere. I've been feeling that sense of rejection ever since.

Every time I walk into that house I feel the ghost of women from your past. It's so damn weird. It's like they've already walked on a journey that I'm just embarking upon which means that I wasn't number one."

I turned facing her. "You are number one baby girl."

"It's different for you Sincere. You're a man. I'm number one to win your heart, but not number one in every other area of your life."

"My heart is all that matters. Everything else is obsolete Sabrina."

"There's no way you can possibly understand what goes is on in my psyche. Just know that, when I walk over that threshold." She pointed towards the house. "I feel as if I'm stepping on another woman's crown. They beat me to the throne. It's not the throne of your heart, but it's something that belongs to you. I feel as if I wasn't worth waiting for."

All I could do was turn forward, place my hands on the steering wheel, look out the window and shake my damn head.

That shit didn't make crazy sense to me and I wasn't about to wreck my brain figuring it out. I got out of the car, walked around to her side and opened her door. I led her to the porch, let her inside, then took care of the groceries.

She patiently sat on the couch while I put the groceries away. When I finished I sat next to her.

"I'm sorry Sincere," she said, "I really am but I can't help it. It's like when I took the place of my mother as his lover, I'm taking theirs as yours and it's disturbing to me. Please try to understand."

A tear slid down the flawless cheek of my gorgeous wife. I wiped it away with my thumb and kissed her on her pouty lips. I sighed deeply. She was right, there was no way I could understand where she was coming from. I said the first thing that popped into my head.

"Let me think about it baby girl. Just given me a few days."

Another tear slid down her cheek. "Thank you Sincere."

There were some things from my past that Sabrina didn't know, so I used that moment as an opportunity to let her in, just a little bit, "Sabrina?"

"Yes?"

"I'm going to think about it, but I want you to know that it's not going to be an easy decision to make."

"I understand."

"No, you don't." I looked around my crib. "Look baby girl. This place holds extreme sentimental value to me."

I paused, making sure I didn't divulge too much information. I wasn't ready for that talk and wanted to make sure Sabrina didn't have a window to start asking questions. "I was able to get this place because of a trust my mom set up after my pops died. Although I never met him, I feel that he's been with me throughout my life. Especially here. I just need you to understand way I find it hard to part ways with this place. I love you so much, it hurts. I also love a man I've never had a chance to meet. I don't want to resent you because you made me leave. Give me a while to process what a move may mean for me and we'll go from there. Okay?"

Sabrina took ahold of my hand and nodded her head in agreement. "Will you do me a favor?"

"Anything for you. What's up?"

"Could you make me a bowl of ice cream please?"

As I rose up off the couch she sat back. "Which one?"

"Doesn't matter."

I went into the kitchen and made her a hearty bowl of Ben and Jerry's ice cream. I tasted some just to quip my curiosity. The shit even tasted old. After handing her her snack I sat next to her and put my hand on her thigh.

"Baby girl. You were eating good on that trip. Looks like it's starting to catch up with you."

"So what you tryin' ta say?" She had a mouth full of ice cream when she asked, looking real cute. I kept my hand on her thick thigh, ignored her question, picked up the remote and found something for us to watch on TV.

I wasn't watching it. I couldn't believe that Sabrina could be selfish enough to ask me to leave my crib. It wasn't her fault she didn't know how sentimental the place was. I thought once she found out, that she'd be a little sympathetic and change her mind. When she didn't it made me feel some kinda way.

The money used to purchase my house was birth through my father's death. It would take death for me to part from it.

It took a month for me to make the decision to move. I watched as Sabrina turned into an emotional rollercoaster. It seemed the smallest things caused her to burst into tears.

She was on winter break from her job as a damn career student. All the schools were out, so we took Brice to Christmas at the zoo.

Sabrina had been doing good until we got to the penguins. As soon as we walked into the exhibit she burst into tears.

What! In! The! Hell!?

Brice got excited and tried consoling his new mommy, but nothing worked. When I walked up to her and wrapped my arms around her waist she shook them off.

"This reminds me of Happy Feet. It's one of the movies my brothers and sisters loved."

What was crazy was it wasn't our first time at the damn zoo. I'd owned a membership since Brice was born and we'd taken him numerous times. In fact, penguins were what Sabrina enjoyed the most.

"It's okay baby we can go."

"Yeah, I can't take it."

Brice and I were confused as hell. Sabrina was a strong woman. Outside our home she rarely let her emotions show so this shocked me shitless.

Another incident happened at the movies. During previews she let loose again. The shit was so random that I thought something was actually wrong with her ass.

"Baby what's wrong?"

When she pointed to the screen I scrunched up my face, "What?"

"Tha tha that's horrible."

I turned and looked at the screen but the preview had gone off, "What was horrible?"

"I'll be back." She got up to go to the bathroom. All I could do was shake my head. When she returned and sat, I took her hand and kissed her forehead.

Butter Pecan

The last straw came when we'd gone on a weekend getaway. Walter had found a new lady friend that he was really feeling and wanted to do a double date. I really wasn't feeling that shit but Sabrina insisted. She took any opportunity to get out of the house. Since I knew the reason, I didn't complain.

We decided on French Lick. Sabrina based most of her travel and restaurant decisions based off online reviews so we stayed at the Cornerstone Inn in Nashville, Indiana. Everything about the trip was on point. It was a well-needed getaway, and it was nice to spend time with another couple.

Walter was into his lady friend and she into him. I was happy for homeboy. I didn't want brotha man to try to get close to my wife. I worked hard to get her away from The Dicks. She wasn't easily persuaded when one wanted to visit.

The four of us walked around town. A lot of the little shops were closed for the winter, but we came across a small, family owned store. Sabrina was happy as hell when she saw that they sold homemade, Butter Pecan ice cream.

"Do you guys give out samples?" That was Sabrina's butt hovering over the options.

Walter looked at my wife, "You've been puttin' on the pounds little lady."

He immediately regretted his words. Everybody but Sabrina looked over at him. She was still looking at her selections. But when we heard the sniffles our little group shifted gears and placed our attention on her.

"I'll take two gallons of the Butter Pecan please," she gave Walter a look that could kill.

"Where in the hell are we going to put two gallons of ice cream Sabrina? And how do you know that it tastes good? You haven't even tried it yet."

She acted as if I hadn't said a word. That shit was funny as hell. You could hear the light-ass snowflakes falling it was so quiet. They packaged her two gallons and as she walked out she called for me to pay. The three of us started cracking up. We knew that she was on edge so chilled when we walked outside.

"Y'all don't think I know I've gained weight?" She barely got the statement out before she burst into tears. It wasn't even that deep.

I pulled my baby into my arms but knew we were going to have a serious talk when we got home.

The rest of the trip was cool. Because it was winter, Sabrina had no problem preserving her ice cream.

When we got back on the home front I sat Sabrina down for a talk.

"What's been going on with you? You cryin' at the drop of a dime. Extra sensitive about simple shit. And you have emotional outbursts that ain't even called for. I know you don't like the house but I got the feeling this has nothing to do with our house. It's a little deeper than that."

We sat on the couch. I took her hands into mine and scoot closer to her. The shit had to stop but I couldn't be insensitive, especially if her fits had to do with her past. But damn, the shit was getting out of control.

"I don't know Sincere. I really don't. It just happens automatically. It's like I have no control over it." She gave me a strange look and then put her head down. "It started about a month ago. I've been keeping it in check. When I was looking at a Hallmark commercial and started crying I thought my reaction was silly."

I lifted her head to look at her pretty brown eyes. "But then it happened when I was in class. I mean, it was out the freakin' blue. What's messed up is I don't recall what triggered it. It's really weird." A tear rolled down her cheek and I couldn't help but roll my eyes. "I'm sorry Sincere. I can't help it. It just happens."

She got up and ran to her room like a two-year-old. I followed and found her laid across her bed crying her eyes out. I wanted to laugh, but didn't. Instead I lay with her, held her while she cried and decided to call a realtor the next morning.

The following weekend we were house hunting. I wanted it to be a family decision so we picked up Brice. As he skipped out to the car I noticed he was getting more chunky. I made a mental note to talk to Ramona about that shit.

Our realtor found us three ranch style-homes to look at.

Sabrina and I agreed a big house wasn't necessary. If down the road we decided to have, or adopt kids we'd decide on a larger home. Until then we settled on a four bedroom, full basement, in case one or two of her siblings needed a place to stay.

The first two homes we looked at were cool, but we didn't feel they were worth our coins. Both were beautiful, but the square footage for each fell short. Although surrounded by million dollar homes, neither made us oooo or awww while taking the tour.

But the third house was on point.

It was all-brick, over five thousand square feet, four bedrooms, with five full baths. Hardwood and carpet. The home housed a fully finished basement with a wet bar, wine cellar, home theatre, recreation room, hot tub, gas fire pit and deck. I specifically told our realtor I didn't want to live in no 'ville, town or field', as in Martinsville, Whitestown or Greenfield. I wanted to stay as close to Indianapolis as possible. He didn't disappoint.

The house ran just below our five hundred thousand budget in Fishers, Indiana. When I saw the smiles on Brice and Sabrina's face, I knew we'd found our new home.

"Can we watch a movie when we move in dad?"

We were on our way home. "We surely can."

"How about some ice cream to celebrate?" asked Sabrina. I looked at her out of the corner of my eye.

Brice's fat ass said excitedly, "Oooooh, I like ice cream."

I looked at him through my rear view mirror and shook my head. But, because I was able make my wife smile, I figured a type of celebration was in order. We made a pitstop at Baskin Robbins. Sabrina ordered her old folks ice cream while Brice tried ordering a double dip of chocolate on a waffle cone.

"That'll be one dip please, and put it in a bowl." I corrected. His big butt didn't need any extra calories.

We sat and ate our celebratory snack and I'll be damned if, halfway through our family moment, April's ass didn't walk in.

The world was too damn small!

I was facing the door so Sabrina didn't see her grand entrance. April and I made eye contact and when I saw her eyes shift towards the back of Sabrina's head I lost my appetite. As predicted she got messy.

"Sup Sincere?" She stopped at our table and looked down at Sabrina. "Nice running into you again."

I prayed Sabrina didn't burst into tears. Like a champ she didn't. Instead she kept eating her ice cream and paid April no attention.

With her hand on her hip she looked from me, to Sabrina and then Brice. "Now ain't this one little happy family." She put her eyes back on Sabrina. "It's about time Sincere had his own fuckin' baby, 'cause everybody and they mama know that THAT ONE ain't his."

I quickly looked at Brice who had his face in his bowl. For the first time I was glad that he was greedy.

Just as I was about to stand and slap the shit out of April, Sabrina grabbed my arm. "Sincere?"

April used that moment to make a quick exit. It wasn't until I felt Sabrina's nails digging into my arm did I pay her any attention. She was crying, but tilted her head towards Brice.

His head was still in his bowl, but he had tears streaming down his face as well.

The celebration was over. We drove home in silence, and every time I looked back at Brice I saw him quietly wiping tears from his eyes. When I looked over at Sabrina she too was silently crying, but I noticed that she kept her hands on her stomach.

Before we dropped Brice off at home, although my tank was full, I went to a gas station. I needed to have a talk with Ramona without Brice hearing. I got out of my truck and called her.

"Hello."

"That hatin' ass April told Brice that he wasn't mine."

"What? When? How?"

I exhaled long and hard. "We found a house and went out to celebrate. We got ice cream and she walked in. I cannot believe she would stoop that damn low."

"Oh my god! Oh my god! Oh my god! What exactly did the bitch say?" I told her word for word what April said and she was not happy. "Her ass is grass the next time I see her." Ramona didn't play.

Although educated and makin' bank, on the low, Ramona was extra ghetto. "Sincere, what are we going to do?"

"Shit, we gone sit down with our son and tell his ass that I'm his father and always will be. That's what the hell we gonna do!" I stood at the back of the car as if pumping gas. I looked inside my ride at my boy and could tell he was still crying. "Look Ramona. I gotta go."

"Hold up."

I waited for her to speak but nothing was said. "Spill it Ramona. I ain't got all damn day!"

She cleared her throat, "So when were you going to tell me?"

I frowned in frustration at her question. "What the hell you mean? I just told you what went down. What more is there to tell?"

She was real quick with her response. "About the baby, nigga!? About the fuckun' baby."

"I know you better calm the hell down!" I took another quick look towards my truck and saw Brice turn in my direction. I walked away and headed towards the inside of the gas station.

"So Sabrina's pregnant?" Ramona asked.

"Hell naw. Her ass cain't even have kids."

As soon as I said it I regretted it. That was none of Ramona's business and I couldn't believe I let it slip.

"So what the hell that bitch April mean? Talkin' bout it's about time you had your own baby? Where the hell that come from?"

It took a moment to register, but when it did I took the phone from my ear, stopped walking and looked back towards my truck. As I did my heart started beating really hard and fast.

What the hell?

I could see the back of my wife's head and wanted to damn near cry. Ramona called my name so I hung up. My stomach turned as the past three months started making sense; The weight gain, the emotions, the Butter Pecan ice cream and the bomb ass pussy.

I had to clear my head so I made my way into the gas station. Moving on automatic I made my way to the pop section, opened the door and stuck my head inside. I had to cool off.

Am I about to be a dad again?

The thought was exciting and scary.

Is my wife really pregnant?

Like Ramona, Sabrina must have caught onto what April had said. She'd already figured it out.

When I heard somebody behind me clear their throat, I knew it was time for me to pull myself together. I paid for a Coke and then made my way back to the car.

Once I was secure in my seat belt, Sabrina reached over, grabbed my hand and squeezed it hard.

When I looked over, the most beautiful woman in the world was looking out the window, biting her bottom lip.

I raised her hand to my lips and gave it a loving kiss. As we drove to Ramona's, I prepared for a talk I never wanted to have with my son.

When we pulled up to Ramona's Brice hopped out of the car and sprinted to the front door.

His ass had gotten so big that I didn't know he had it in him.

Ramona was at the door waiting. Before I got out of the truck I gave Sabrina a synopsis about what was about to go down.

"We are going to go in here and have a talk with Brice."

"I understand." She turned and looked out the window.

"I don't think you do. 'We' are going to have a talk with Brice. All three of his parents."

When my wife turned and looked at me I saw 'pregnant' written all over her face. She glowed like a new woman.

Her hand was still in mine so I brought it to my lips. Overwhelmed with emotions, I grabbed the back of her head and kissed her lips. With my hand on her neck, I placed my forehead on hers.

"I love you Sabrina Fleming. I love you to death." I gave her one more kiss, got out of the truck, ran around to her side and helped her out. Ramona was waiting.

I held the front door opened, and as soon as Sabrina walked in, Ramona looked at her stomach. The shit happened so fast that I'm certain Sabrina didn't catch the shade. The two women embraced and said their greetings.

"He's in his room."

"I'll go get him." I said. As I passed Ramona I gave her a real calm look. She better not say one word to Sabrina about being pregnant. Her fake smile let me know that she got the message.

When I got to my son's room he was sitting on his bed, looking out of the window. "Come on Brice. Your moms and I need to have a talk with you."

Without hesitation he climbed off his bed and led the way to the living room. He took a seat between his two mothers on the couch and I pulled up a chair. I placed his plump hands into mine.

"Son, I know you heard what that woman said at the ice cream shop. I want you to know that no matter what you hear, or what anyone tries to tell you, you are, and will always be my child."

A tear glided down his chubby cheek. "Why did that lady say what she said?"

"Because she's a stupid bitch!"

"Ramona! Don't be talkin' that shit around my son!"

"Well she is Sincere! And like I said, when I see her ass I'mma fuck her up!"

I wanted to slap the shit out of Ramona. She knew how I felt about that kind of talk around Brice. I'd deal with her later. I turned my attention back to my son and continued.

"Look Brice, ain't no sense in us acting like nothing that woman said was true. You're way too smart for me to play with your intelligence like that. Just know that you are my son, I was there when you were born, and the moment I saw you I fell in love. I fed you, changed you, was there when you took your first steps, did something your mama couldn't do and that was potty-trained yo butt. And when it's time for you to learn how to drive a car I'mma be right there. I'm going to teach you about the birds and the bees, when you graduate high school and college I'm going to be right there too. Those are the things that make a man a father Brice. We're not blood but blood don't make a daddy, actions do."

I paused to let what I said sink in. Sabrina scoot to the edge of the couch. "Brice?" She asked gently. He was looking at the floor with his head leaned against Ramona's shoulder, "Am I your mom?"

He took Sabrina's hand. "Yes."

"Did I give birth to you?"

"No."

"But you still see me as your mom?"

"You are my mom. You're married to my dad."

When he said 'dad' he looked at me. I wanted so bad to choke April's ass!

"Well just as you see me as your mom, I see you as my son. The only thing we have in common is your dad." I saw Ramona swallow. "But I love you just the same Brice." She looked up at me and then back at Brice. "Let me ask you something. Have you ever had an animal as a pet?"

"Yeah, I won a fish from the fair."

"Did you feed it and take care of it?"

"Yeah, every day."

"How long did you have it?"

"For a little while but then it died."

"How did you feel about the fish? Did you name it?"

"Yeah, I named it Buster. And I liked it a lot."

"You liked it a lot. How did you feel when it died?"

"Real sad and I missed it a lot too."

"The same way you liked your fish is the same way your dad likes you, except a hundred times more. And just like you liked your fish, you liked it for what it was to you, not necessarily because of what it is. You're not a fish but you still liked it. Sincere is not your biological dad, but he still loves you the same. There's nothing that could ever change that. Nothing."

I loved my wife. I absolutely loved her!

We said our goodbyes to Ramona and Brice. Because emotions were high, I made a mental note to talk with her about his weight later. When we got into the car, we sat in Ramona's driveway for a few minutes.

"When are you going to make your doctor's appointment?" I asked my beautiful queen.

"First thing in the morning."

"How do you feel?"

"Scared."

I smiled. "You ain't the only one." I started the car and put it in reverse.

"Can we stop and get some ice cream on the way home?"

My smile broadened. "Shit! You can get any damn thang you want!"

She laughed and I held her hand all the way to the store.

When we got home that night I followed Sabrina around the house like a lost puppy and got on her very last nerve.

"I can't breathe Sincere. Will you please give me room?"

"You wasn't sayin' that last night."

She laughed and then gave me a serious look. We still hadn't moved her things into the master bedroom, so she went into the one we shared and changed into a tee-shirt. Without panties of course.

"What do you think?"

"I think you're wonderful and magnificent and beautiful and fantastic..."

She cut me off. "I'm not talking about me, I'm talking about us possibly being pregnant." She walked into the kitchen and started doing busy work and I was standing right behind her.

"Oh yeah definitely. My boys told me about how sweet that pregnant pussy was."

She reached behind her shoulder and hit me with the dishtowel she held. "Is that all you think about?"

I held her from behind and placed my hands on her belly. "Yep." I rubbed my semi-hard dick against her fat ass. "You got that goody-good good girl. And I cain't get enough of it." She turned in my arms and placed my hands back on her stomach. We looked down at the little round lump. "Do you think that this is the reason your titties been so sore? Cain't remember if I learned that in school or not."

"I'm certain that's the reason. I looked it up when we were at the gas station."

"Is that right?"

"Yeah and the cravings along with my crying and sensitivity."

"How can I help you with those things? More ice cream? More dick?"

She started laughing then lifted her head and looked me in my eyes. "Thank you Sincere. Thank you so much."

I scrunched up my face. "Girl please. You've made me the happiest man in the world. Since April opened her big mouth my heart hasn't stopped pounding. Naw baby girl. Thank you."

I put my lips on hers. It was a slow sensual kiss, wanting to enjoy the totality of each other. When my hands took ahold of her butt and I squeezed she pulled back.

"What if I'm pregnant Sincere? What about the baby?"

I raised an eyebrow. "Sabrina, we been sexin' each other down like teenagers for the last three months and ain't nothin' happened." When I bent to kiss her neck she dodged and went into the living room.

"But how can you be sure? You know I'm not right in there. The fact that I've never had a period confirms that."

I could not believe what I was hearing. As I followed her I watched her butt shake and got hard as hell. "Well obviously you're not as messed up as you thought. Periods or no periods ya ass is pregnant."

"But it's not confirmed…"

I shut her up with a kiss. What she was saying was going to have to wait. With my hands back on her butt I lifted her with one smooth swoop. Her legs automatically went around my waist. She felt my hard dick and started slowly rolling her hips. Her scent ascended to my nose and I was placed in a zone. Her ass was just as horny as I was.

As I walked over to the couch I unzipped my pants and brought out my dick. I took a seat and as I did I held on to her tight. My sitting broke up our kiss.

"I love you Sincere." Her hands were all over my rock hard chest. As she searched my black skin with her touch she sucked on my neck.

"I love you too baby girl." She got on her knees, took off my shirt, lifted herself up and sat on my dick. I closed my eyes in total ecstasy. "Oh yeah baby." She hadn't even started riding the dick and my toes were curling. In slow motion she started gliding up and down my plank. I wanted to eat her alive. I lifted her shirt and sucked on her breast.

"Please be gentle Sincere."

Cautiously rolling my tongue around her nipple and started moving her hips. She placed her hands on the back of my head and threw me into confusion. She'd told me to be gentle yet smashed my head into her breast.

"Fuck this shit Sincere. Fuck this pussy"

As soon as she said that I knew she was wanting a quickie. Who was I to deny my sexy wife her request? I lifted my head off her tittie and scoot further down on the couch. I had to be careful though, didn't want my zipper snapping onto my dick.

Once in position she wrapped her legs around my waist and went to town. "Mmmmmmm."

While her eyes were closed I kept my eyes on her and watched every facial expression and movement she made. She was so damn sexy!

Her breasts shook and bounced as she rolled her hips. It didn't take long for a light sweaty mist to cover her already glowing body. Her lips were open and her head thrown back.

"Yes baby. Yes," she moaned.

I looked down at her beautiful flower and her wetness that covered my pole. The smell of her arousal was intoxicating. As I watched new liquid form on my dick I wanted to drink her dry.

"That's it Sincere. That's it." She rolled her hips a little faster and as she I did I kept my eyes on the show. I placed my hands on her pussy and opened until I saw her clit. "Touch it baby. Touch it." The hip action increased in anticipation of my touch.

With her own juices I wet my finger and gently placed it on her clit. I looked at my wife's face, contorted with her bottom lip in her mouth. "Mmmmmmmmm!"

I put my eyes back on my personal porn movie, shocked at how that one touch caused her to get more wet.

"You like that shit Sabrina? You like when I touch you?"

She grabbed the back on my neck and pulled me close. I kept my hand in place but added more pressure. It drove her crazy. "Give me that feeling baby. Give it to me." She moaned into my ear.

I turned my head and kissed the shit outta her lips. With my hand still playing with her pussy I used the other to pull her down on my dick. She was so slick my finger kept slipping and it was hard to keep rhythm, but I worked with it.

She sang into my mouth and started grinding onto my dick. When she could take it no more she placed her face into the crook of my neck. "It's coming Sincere. I think I feel it. I think I do."

She said the same shit every time and I loved it. When her pearl gripped my dick I removed my hand, placed both of them on her hips and started slamming into her ass.

"Oh shit Sabrina! Give me that pussy. Give me that shit!"

Her stuff was contracting on my dick and I lost my damn mind. Every time I made love to my wife it felt like the first damn time.

Sabrina made her appointment the next day. It was a late afternoon visit. Her doctor was already booked but squeezed her in where she could.

"Well little lady. Contrary to what we thought about your ability to conceive, you have contradicted us. My dear Sabrina, you are exactly three months pregnant."

Her doctor had just finished a pelvic exam. When the results came in Sabrina was still on her back. With her legs in the stirrups she looked over at me. As she did a trail of tears crept out of her eyes.

"Did you hear that Sincere? Did you hear what she said?"

I love me some Brice. He's my first born and always will be, but I'd be lying if I said the news of having a child with my blood didn't affect me in a whole different way. Especially since we thought Sabrina couldn't have kids.

We'd briefly talked about babies, but decided to wait until later to consider trying, or possibly adopting. The confirmation of Sabrina being with child nulled the subject.

As my blossoming butterfly looked at me in awe, I kissed her tear-stained lips.

"You're going to be a mommy again Sabrina."

"And you're going to be a daddy again Sincere."

As the doctor finished her business between Sabrina's legs we looked into each other's eyes with so much love that the shit got emotional.

"So." I started, " What's up with our sex life doc?"

With big, appalled eyes Sabrina hit my arm. I needed to break up the moment. Sabrina looked between her legs. "Please excuse him. Sometimes he has no tact." She looked at me with a frown on her face, moving her lips silently. I ignored her and looked down at the doc. I needed answers.

Sabrina's physician laughed.

"There's nothing to excuse, Mrs. Fleming. To answer your question Mr. Fleming, there's nothing up with your sex life except that it's a healthy one. From what I can tell from my examination, all is well."

She shifted her attention towards Sabrina. "Because of your past abuse I want to see you every two weeks for the next couple of months. We need to immediately stop your hormone therapy. I want to do an ultrasound to make sure all is well with the baby. Otherwise, you're good." The doctor popped off her gloves and started washing her hands. "I'd like to start you on some prenatal vitamins..."

I cut her off. "We don't have to worry about that." I said, "I'll be making sure she has all the essential vitamins and iron she needs. Sabrina is a career student and doesn't work."

Sabrina didn't like that, "I'm about to graduate from the nurse practitioner program." She argued, "I don't want to not work after I'm through. I need to be hands-on and get out into the workforce..."

I cut her off too. "No need for those things. We'll take care of it all."

The doctor looked from me to Sabrina as if trying to choose which one to listen to. When Sabrina saw my face go from frustrated to calm she shut that shit down.

"We'll take care of it. Thanks anyway."

"That's fine." The doctor said, "Just check with the nurse on your way out to set up your next appointment. And once again, I'd like to congratulate you both."

As soon as the doctor walked out of the room Sabrina turned towards me. "Do you have to be so damn controlling? Is that not something we could have discussed together?"

"You gotta be out yo mind if you think I'mma let you put that synthetic vitamin shit into my child."

She sat up and burst into tears. "Don't you fuckun' talk to me like that!"

I knew Sabrina was upset but I didn't give a damn. I kissed her on her forehead, helped her off the examination table and then handed baby girl her clothes.

"I love when you talk dirty. Now get dressed while I go set up our next appointment."

I left Sabrina staring at my back as I walked out of the room.

One thing was for sure, she was out her damn mind if she thought I was going to allow the state to nourish my child with their chemically made essentials. Not on my watch.

Chapter Nine

To lift the thickness in the car on the way home, I pulled into a Baskins Robbins. That cheered her ass up. To cheer her up even more I ordered us both Butter Pecan ice cream.

"You can be so sweet sometimes."

"Mmmhmm"

We sat and dug in. I had my reservations about my ice cream choice, but to get some brownie points I indulged. "Okay," I admitted, "This isn't too bad."

She clapped like a first grader. "Told yooooou." She sang her words which meant she was happy, but it didn't last long. I was starting to enjoy my ice cream when she started.

"Sincere?"

"Yeah?"

"You know I didn't go to school to just sit around the house, get fat and do nothing. I would like to get a job."

"I don't know why. You haven't had a job in years and now all of a sudden you want to work? You got all those degrees and ain't done nothing with them."

"I never knew my purpose, but now I do."

The only purpose Sabrina's had was to keep our baby and I happy and healthy. "You can always work after you have the baby. Besides, the doctor said that she wants you going in for a checkup every two weeks. That means you're high-risk."

She chuckled. "She ain't said nothing about nobody being high-risk."

I needed to change the subject, "So when are you going to tell The Dicks?"

"I already did. I sent them a group text."

I sat back in my chair. I didn't appreciate them knowing before the people who were our flesh and blood knew, "Now why you go and do something like that? I ain't even told my mama yet and you dun run off and told those jokers?"

She sat back as well, "Those jokers are my friends, and have been better to me than my own flesh and blood."

"What if I told your ass that I'd text one of my ex girlfriends to tell them the good news. How you that make you feel?"

She got quiet.

"That's what I thought." I watched as she toyed with her bowl of ice cream.

"My dear, you knew, from day one, who and what those men were to me. I would not appreciate it if you text or told one of your ex's about the pregnancy but I'm not you. Unlike you, I haven't slept with any of those guys. I love them all in my own special way and they love me too. They have been with me through some horrid things in my life, and I will forever appreciate them for that. Just like our marriage is a milestone, this too is a milestone. I want to spread my joy to everyone I care about, and that includes them."

I was not trying to hear that shit, "So who congratulated you on your good news?"

She paused. She wanted to lie and say they all wished her well, but I was just as aware of those men's mentalities as she was.

"Everyone except Cyprus."

"That's what the hell I thought. And you wonder why I don't like being around they asses." I stared her down. "At least Cyprus is honest and silently makes his dislike of our relationship known. I can't say that for the rest of The Dicks." I knew I was being a crab but didn't care. Sabrina needed to know that whether she'd slept with them or not, her move was foul play.

"I'm ready to go Sincere. You're stressing me the hell out."

Without saying another word, I got up, threw my half eaten ice cream away and went and sat in the car.

I watched her order two gallons of ice cream and wondered if Sabrina would ever allow our relationship to be between just the two of us. Since being married I noticed some characteristics I didn't know I had. I'm certain it was because the only real relationship I'd been in was with Ramona. That was years ago.

I was real possessive of Sabrina, but I couldn't help it. I've never had anyone around to tell me how a man is supposed to treat a woman, or how a husband is supposed to act.

I think Mom used to sneak out and get herself a little sumthin-sumthin on the side, but she never brought a man around me. Not once. According to my mother the only man she would ever love was my father, and she meant that. To her their love affair never came full circle, and wouldn't until she was laid to rest.

I suppose being an only child had something to do with my possessiveness as well. Although caked up, my mother didn't really spoil me. I had to work for what I wanted, but she made sure I had opportunities available to get my hands dirty, with my first job being at her store. I clocked in like everybody else and I wasn't paid a higher salary because I was her son. I was treated just like every other employee, which allowed me to appreciate the value of a dollar earned.

As I watched my wife walk towards the exit of the ice cream shop I knew I needed to lighten up. I was stressing her out.

When she got to the store door I hopped up, ran and opened it wide for my baby to walk out. I ran to the car door and did the same. I then made my way to the driver's side, got in and put on my seatbelt.

Just as I was about to start my truck I heard sniffles coming from Sabrina's side of the car. I turned her direction. Her face was towards the window, looking out, not paying me any attention.

I rolled my eyes, started my truck.

It was going to be a long ass six months!

Ramona...

When Sincere told me what April had said about Brice and about Sabrina being pregnant, the pregnancy was all I heard. I should have been more concerned with the fact that our son had learned that Sincere wasn't his biological dad, but damn! Brice could look in the mirror and come to that conclusion.

I could not believe that Sabrina was pregnant! Sincere never told me anything about her, I got most of my information from Brice. From what I could tell, all she did was go to school and study. But pregnant? That bit of information made my ovaries jump. That they thought she couldn't get pregnant meant their baby was extra special. Their miracle child.

After their ice cream excursion, when they brought Brice home, I noticed how pretty Sabrina looked. She had that pregnancy glow. I was jealous.

I knew I had no right to be jealous but I couldn't help it. Sincere loved Brice, but he wasn't his flesh and blood.

Brice was a good kid and I didn't want the news of a new baby, and that Sincere wasn't his real dad to haunt my son. My past indiscretions had placed my baby in a peculiar situation. I needed to make sure things were going to remain the same. I had no doubt that, if he was alone, Sincere wouldn't shift, but I wasn't so sure about his wife. I needed a face to face with Sincere and pronto.

"You have nothing to worry about Ramona. She loves Brice just as much as we do."

No he didn't!

How in the hell could he say something like that? She was new to the scene and only saw Brice when Sincere picked him up. That was pretty damn often, because she was always with Sincere, but still.

He made it his business to drop by on a daily even if it was for just a few minutes. But that's Sincere, not her.

I didn't have anything personally against Sabrina, I just didn't want her messing up what Brice, Sincere and I had. And although Sincere had women come and go, I knew Sabrina was different.

Except for Sincere taking the dick away, he hadn't changed. That was before marriage and a baby.

"I don't know how she feels about Brice, but what I do know is that y'all change when a chick is having your seed."

"Who the hell is y'all? Have you forgotten you had me believing a baby was mine that wasn't? If a brotha did throw shade when a woman pretended to be pregnant by him, I would totally understand. But I'm not that dude so don't start with your conspiracy theories 'cause it's not going to work. And Ramona?"

Aww shit!

The way he said my name let me know that he was kinda pissed so I tried to play hard.

"What Sincere?"

"Sabrina ain't some chick. She's my wife, and I expect you to respect her. Now, as far as my wife and I are concerned Brice is, and always will be, our first born. I'm not about to tell you Sabrina's life story, but know that that woman has a heart that spreads so deep and wide for others, I'm not sure that she'll have room to love the child she's carrying."

Yeah right!

"And furthermore. Name one thing that would cause you to think that I would shift in my love for my son. On the real, your statement is quite insulting especially under the conditions that I allowed Brice into my heart. I'mma keep bringing that shit up. As long as you keep micromanaging my love for my son I'mma keep reminding you that my love for him has nothing to do with you, but everything to do with the relationship I have with my boy."

I started blinking my eyes really fast trying to stop the tears from falling. Sincere sat next to me on the couch and held me in his arms.

"I ain't goin' nowhere Ramona. Brice is my son. It seems the only person who has a problem is you. Stop worrying about shit that don't matter. Shift all that energy towards our son having a well-rounded life and future." He sat back and got that stupid calm look on his face. "And speaking of well rounded. His ass is getting mighty fat..."

I rolled my eyes up in my head and listened to him lecture me about Brice's weight for damn near an hour. I loved every minute.

Sincere...

I'd gone through the pregnancy thing with Ramona when she was pregnant, but she hadn't been my wife. Sabrina was totally different.

I wasn't technically with Ramona when she was expecting. I was around, but we weren't a couple. I'd been sleeping with her, so the probability of Brice being mine was a high, but her whoreish ways caused me to keep a little distance. With Sabrina, shit was different.

I found out during clinical that PEDS were not my cup of tea, and chose to work with the elderly. No kids my way. Listening to the doctor explain our unborn child's gestational age and weight while at Sabrina's appointments peaked my interest, but what I really paid attention to were Sabrina's lab results.

Since I'd refused vitamin and iron pills, we made sure she had the proper food to make up for what the doctor said she needed. The doctor was extremely pleased with her lab levels.

Her shit was always within normal range, and although she was gaining hella weight it was well-balanced.

Sabrina wasn't a skinny chick - Thick in all the right places. She ate healthy, but her elbows stayed on the table like she couldn't get enough. Fine by me. As along as my two babies were happy, I was happy.

Eventually Sabrina and I got into a routine.

She graduated with her master's degree at six months pregnant. I was a stickler about her not working while pregnant, so we compromised.

Without much resistance Sabrina agreed to help my mother at the clothing store, which was an all-around win for me.

I'd already let Mom know that I didn't want Sabrina doing any real work; She was at the store so she wouldn't die from boredom at home.

Mom was all for that. She'd be able to spend quality time with her new daughter in-law, and watch the slow growth of her second grandchild.

I was working a full-time night shift at the hospital. Although new to the job, Sabrina and I agreed that I would take maternity leave. If my leave wasn't granted I'd just quit. We weren't hurting for cash and bonding with our child outweighed any amount of coins.

The twins were on hand to be with Sabrina on the nights that I worked. It was a win-win situation for both Sabrina and myself. Surprisingly, they'd really gotten themselves together while living with The Dicks. Sabrina couldn't have been happier.

As newlyweds about to become new parents, I wanted to share every precious moment of change with the woman I loved. Since I'd never lived with a newborn, I was embarking on unfamiliar terrain. To make the transition smooth, we set our house in order and got ready for the next chapter of our lives.

Moving day, we hired packers but it didn't leave our hands empty.

My priority was Sabrina. At eight months pregnant she was not to lift a finger. To make sure, I paid Brice to be at her beck and call.

"I know how your mother is," I told Brice, "she's going to ask you to do something and when she sees you're not doing it the way she wants, she'll say she'll do it and try to push you out of the way. If that happens, you come get me immediately. You hear me?"

"Yes Dad."

I barely got shit done. After two hours of running back and forth, telling her to sit down, I finally had a talk with her.

"Look baby girl. I don't want you hurting our unborn child over some stupid shit."

"I'm not disabled Sincere..."

I didn't let her finish. "Today your ass is. We've got a lot of stuff to do and I can't be babysitting you while trying to tell these men how to pack our shit."

"I don't know why you wouldn't just let me call the boys. They'd have willingly helped."

As soon as she said that my mood shifted. I was tired of Sabrina throwing those Dicks into our life. When my frustrated frown disappeared, replaced by calm, she knew I was done.

I don't know why Sabrina couldn't realize she was the one who had needed those men, not me. That she always called upon them to do my job did not sit well with me.

"I work every damn day to make sure we don't want for shit."

"You don't have to cuss Sincere."

"Yes the hell I do! You fail to realize that I'm a man and don't need them for shit. Not for a damn thing Sabrina. Not for you. Not for my house. Not for my damn kid, not for nothing! If you wanna call them to move your shit go right ahead, but I'm telling you you'll regret it."

She had the nerve to get an attitude. "So what in the hell is that supposed to mean?" She snapped.

"Just what the fuck I said." I was pissed and walked away before I said something I'd regret. Her wobbling butt had the gumption to follow me. I turned and was about to go off but saw Brice walk into the living room so I stopped myself.

"You sonovahbitch!" Sabrina slapped the hell out of me. That shit stung so bad, like a little bitch, my hand automatically went to my cheek. "My muthafuckun' father is dead you asshole. You don't have the right to talk to me like that!" She was crying which meant our baby was stressed. But so in the hell was I. "What is it about them that cause you to act the way you do? Huh?"

She took two steps and was in my face. "What is it Sincere? Why do you hate them so much? They've been nothing but good to me. They comforted me, sustained me and protected me. What's so damn wrong with that?"

I clicked.

"That's my damn job!" I yelled, "And you know what? Just like you don't like this damn house because of the women who have been in it before you. I don't they asses for the same reason. They had you first and they asses still got you!"

"How in the world could you say that?"

"If they didn't you wouldn't use every opportunity to invite them into our home, our marriage, our life. The people they were for you in the past you constantly bring into your future and I'm sick and tired of it."

I turned to leave, but Sabrina grabbed my arm, "Don't walk away from me," she snarled, "I'm still talking to you."

I looked down at her hand as if it was diseased. "Let me go Sabrina."

With more tears streaming down her face she shook her head. "Never Sincere."

She walked into my chest, wrapped her arms around my waist and held me tight. I didn't hug her back.

"Why didn't you tell me that's how you felt?"

"I've been telling you for years, but you never listened." I tried removing her arms but she held on tighter.

"I'm sorry Sincere. I never knew."

"That's because you didn't want to know Sabrina. You wanted your cake and to eat it too. Look baby girl, I gotta lot of work to do. We'll talk about this another time."

I again tried leaving but she wouldn't let me. I released an agitated sigh and waited.

The hired help knew not to speak unless spoken to; Instead of asking us to move out of their way they worked around us.

"Look at me Sincere."

I didn't want to but I did.

She was so damn beautiful!

"It's over."

"What is?"

"Me talking to them."

"Yeah right. Man get out of here with that." I still couldn't get out of her embrace.

"I'm serious. I'll do it right now." She pulled out her phone.

"Naw, you don't need an audience to do what should have been done a long time ago. I'm good."

"Don't do this to me Sincere."

"I ain't done shit to you Sabrina. You did this all by yourself, so handle it by yourself."

"Dad?"

That was Brice's big ass. It wasn't my intention but I clicked on him too. "WHAT?!"

He said nothing for a few seconds. "I don't feel so good." He said in a small voice.

I watched in horror as my son dropped to the floor. "Brice!"

I sprinted to my son, got on the floor and felt for a pulse. "Thank you Jesus! Sabrina call 911! Brice! Brice!"

After Brice passed out Sabrina called 911. I sat and held my son, shutting down the house and dismissing the workers.

After watching the drama with me and Sabrina I'm sure the workers had no problem leaving. A couple of the guys stayed until the ambulance got there. I made a mental note to personally thank them for their concern, later.

I dealt with stat, adrenalin-filled days at work all the time, but this was different. This was family.

The EMT's got there and did a quick assessment. They took his vitals and asked me a thousand questions that I could barely answer. All I could really do was look down at my child. I had to make sure he was alright.

Without hesitation Sabrina answered what I couldn't. I didn't know how much I'd appreciated her until everything was over.

At that moment, Brice was the only thing on my mind.

They put my boy on a gurney. When I told them that I wanted to ride with them in the ambulance they shut me down.

Firstly, there was no room; Secondly because Sabrina, under the circumstances, did not need to be driving a car in her condition.

Sabrina and I followed the ambulance to the hospital. To my surprise, Sabrina was calm and hadn't shed a tear.

As I drove behind the vehicle that held a piece of my heart, my mind was all over the place.

"Calm down Sincere. He's going to be alright."

"How do you know?"

"I've seen this before."

I looked over at my wife. "What you mean by that?" She was beating around the bush and I needed to know what she was implying.

"The clammy skin, the scent of his breath, and before today, his constant thirst. I'm leaning towards diabetes."

"Diabetes? Where the hell he get that?" I knew where he got it and I was going to get on Ramona's ass. For years I'd been telling her about his diet. I always took healthy shit over to her house and she continue to feed him pizza, ding-dongs and cupcakes.

Sabrina didn't answer. She knew I knew the answer to my own question.

"Call his mother Sabrina. Shit! Call her and let her know that we're on our way to the hospital."

"Already done," she said.

I looked over at my wife who was looking out of the window.

"Your mother too," she said calmly.

I put my eyes back on the road and my mind back on Brice.

Sitting in the hospital waiting room were Sabrina, Mom, Ramona, her dude and myself. We hadn't heard from the doctor. When Ramona had initially walked in, I gave her a look that caused her to hold onto her man tighter.

She knew I had a cake baked for her ass.

Ramona and her man greeted everyone. Then we waited.

After an hour a nurse told us that we could go back to visit. The five of us surrounded his bed, looking upon this innocent child.

The doctor confirmed Sabrina's suspicious, and again I gave Ramona The Look.

"Diet and exercise are key. When it comes to kids and diabetes there's only one place to look, especially if it could have been prevented. That's the parents. Because you buy the food, you control what goes into your child."

I wanted to choke Ramona.

We asked numerous questions which he gladly answered. "He'll have to stay overnight for observation but otherwise you have a healthy son." He looked at Brice. "You guys are lucky. This could have turned out very bad."

All I could do was shake my head. Before leaving the doctor shook our hands. "I'll print off some literature for you to read over, and please, watch his diet." As the doctor left, Ramona and I gathered at the head of Brice's bed. He was asleep and looked so pure.

As I watched my sick son all I wanted to do was protect him from this cruel, sick world. But how could I do that when I couldn't even protect him from his own mama.

After a few minutes a nurse asked us go to the third-floor waiting area. Brice was ready to be transferred to his private room.

While we waited I tried to use the opportunity to talk to Ramona. She knew what was up and tried blockin' it.

"You wanna go get something to drink Ramona?"

She scooted closer to her man and laced her arm through his. "I'm not thirsty."

I stood and started walking towards the vending machines that were located down the hall.

"What kind do you want?"

"I said..." I cut her off and gave her The Look. She turned to her man. "You want something to drink baby?"

I didn't stick around to hear his response. I'd just hit my selection when she approached.

"I've been stupid Sincere and I am so sorry. But he's my baby, my only child..."

"Do you know that he could have died? Huh? I spend good money buying that boy food, healthy shit, and this is what I get in return."

"I know Sincere..."

"Obviously you don't know shit! You weren't there when he called my name. You didn't see his ass pass out. You weren't the one feeling for a pulse. Ramona? Shit!"

I pulled her into my arms and she burst into tears. "I'm so sorry. I didn't know. I just love him so much."

"You're about to love him to death girl."

Both of our emotions were high. We could have lost our son. We would have been devastated. "You've gotta do better Ramona. You've just got to do better."

I heard Sabrina behind me. She cleared her throat, "We can see him now," she said.

I turned and looked at my wife. She gave me a look of understanding and walked away. I stepped back from Ramona, took out my handkerchief and dried her tears. "He doesn't need to see you like this." She took it and blew her nose. When she tried handing it back to me I jumped. "Ewww!"

She chuckled. "Look at your dramatic ass."

As I put my arm around her shoulder we started laughing, and walked to the waiting room to snatch up our family.

Sabrina and I sat with him for an hour and then left. Ramona was staying the night and said she she would keep us updated. That was fine and dandy with me. The day had been long and strenuous. I was dog-tired.

Tension from our earlier discussion about The Dicks had dissipated, but I knew Sabrina hadn't forgotten. "Thank you for today Sabrina. You helped a lot and I really appreciate it."

"No problem Sincere."

I took my wife's hand and kissed it. "I love you Sabrina."

She didn't respond and I didn't expect her to.

I took a detour and made a run to a fast food restaurant. I knew that if I was hungry Sabrina had to starving. We ate in silence all the way to the crib.

When we got home we felt defeated. The house was a wreck.

Our bedroom furniture had already been broken down and was at the new house.

"Shit! I forgot to lock up the other crib."

"It's already done Sincere. I asked one of the workers to do it." She sounded exhausted. When I went to grab her around her waist she dodged my efforts. "I'm tired Sincere."

She maneuvered throughout the house trying to get to the bedroom. There was no way my pregnant wife was sleeping in that mess.

"Come on Sabrina. We're going home."

With a funny look on her face she turned. "We are home."

Walking through the maze I strolled over to my sexy ass wife. Despite being big as hell I scooped her into my arms. "What are you doing?"

I kissed her forehead. "Taking you home."

She was heavy as hell. "Put me down Sincere. You're going to drop me."

"Girl! You didn't know? I'm Superman, I got this."

I might've dropped her big behind. She was heavier than I thought. Sabrina wrapped her arms around my neck and used her feet to kick the screen door opened. When we got to my vehicle I gently placed her on her feet. I was happy. "Watch your step, beautiful."

Once Sabrina was inside the truck I ran back into the house, turned out the lights and locked up the place.

Before heading to our new home I stopped at a twenty-four hour Walmart. "I'll be right back."

Before she could protest I hopped out. Snatching up a cart, I rolled through the store like a madman picking up all the essentials for our sleepover.

I was in the damn store for almost an hour. The time flew by so fast that I hadn't realized it. Sabrina let me know that she didn't approve. "Did you really leave me out here that long?" She turned and looked at all the packages. "Did you have to do that tonight? Looks like you bought the whole store."

As she turned around I caught her face in my hand, leaned over and gave her a kiss. "It's all for you."

She raised an eyebrow and sat back in her chair. "Whatever."

I smiled and made my way to our new crib. When I pulled into the driveway Sabrina livened up. "I just love this house!"

I looked at the manicured lawn, the solar, LED-lit pathway that led to our front door and had to agree. "It is beautiful." We sat in the truck for a few minutes, taking in the beauty of our new purchase.

"Can't you envision Brice and the baby playing out here? I wonder what kind of brother he's going to be. Sincere? Do you think he's going to be okay?" I saw her vision. Brice holding his baby brother or sister. Teaching his younger sibling how to ride a bike. I also wondered if our son would be fine.

"Well, considering that he'll probably be discharged tomorrow makes me believe he'll be just fine. It's what's going to happen when he gets home that I'm worried about."

Sabrina let that statement hang in the air. She very rarely butted in when it came to how Brice was reared. She left that up to me and Ramona. When Sabrina reached to open her door I stopped her.

"I got that." Instead of running to help her out of the vehicle, I ran to the front door of the house, unlocked the door and positioned the screen to stay open and hurriedly turned off the alarm. I then went inside and turned on some lights. After making sure all was well, I opened the truck door for my wife, took in a huge deep breath, lifted her out of the truck and walked her to the threshold of our new resting place.

"Sabrina Fleming."

She turned her head towards me. "Yes Mr. Fleming?"

I took a step over the threshold of our house. After placing her onto her feet I pulled her into my arms. I looked down into her beautiful brown eyes. There was such profound joy on her face that I was glad I made the choice to heed my wife's needs.

"Welcome home baby girl."

She draped her arms around my neck. "Welcome home Sincere."

Although we'd been out all day and hadn't freshened up, our kiss was sweet. It was a long welcoming kiss, our very first in our new abode.

She pulled back. "I gotta pee. You got any toilet paper in those bags?"

Before I could answer she started making her way to the bathroom.

I ran out to the car and made three trips bringing in the bags. By the time I'd finished I was exhausted. When I heard the shower running I took some items into the bathroom.

As was her habit, Sabrina had the bathroom door cracked. Although I wanted to desperately slide in there with her I had too much shit to do.

"Here." I handed her a face towel and some soap. My dick immediately got hard.

"Thanks baby." She took the items and acted like I wasn't there. Her ass and titties were huge, and looking at them made my mouth water. Because of her protruding belly I couldn't see her pussy, but had that shit memorized in my head.

Before I got caught up in the moment I made my exit. At the entryway of the house I stopped and looked around.

"Damn this shit is sweet!"

I could not believe I gave up my place. It held so many sentimental memories, with the main one being my pops. That he'd never lived there didn't matter. He was the reason for me having it, that's what I held dear to my heart.

Instead of dwelling on my previous crib, I looked around and appreciated my blessings, happy to share a new chapter of my life with the person I loved.

Forcing myself to move, I took the bags to the kitchen and placed my purchases in their new home. By the time I got the air mattress blown up Sabrina was getting out of the shower.

"Don't even put on any clothes." I said. I wanted her prepared for what was to come.

Most of our belongings were in the three-car garage, and there was no way in hell I was bringing any of it into the house. After our long day that extra could wait.

"I wasn't getting dressed anyway." She walked out of the bathroom butt naked. "This carpet feels good." She stopped walking and stretched her toes into its softness. My eyes were on her sexy body.

"Not as good as I'm about to feel."

I turned my attention to the task at hand and placed the pillows and blankets on the mattress.

"Did you get any deodorant?"

"Shit! I knew I was forgetting something."

She slowly lay on the bed. "No big deal Sincere." After looking down at my hard dick she smiled. "Hurry up." She said. She need not say another word.

I was tired mentally and physically, but it didn't stop me from desiring my wife. I high-tailed it to the shower and washed faster than ever. When I walked out with a towel wrapped around my waist she whined.

"That's not fair." She complained.

I didn't know what the hell she was talking about. When she opened her thick legs I didn't care. I dropped to the carpeted floor, and pulled Sabrina to the edge of the mattress, dragging the blankets with her. Once in position, I placed her thick thighs on my shoulders and dove face first. Her hands automatically went to the side of my head. Her belly prevented her from grabbing it on the top.

"Oh shit Sincere!" She was already moist I therefore swirled her nectar around my tongue. "Oooooh baby, baby, baby!" I lay flat on my stomach giving me a better angle. I licked her from one hole to the other. The only sound was my slurping and her sounds of pleasure. "Yeeessssssss." With the heels of her feet digging into my back, I used my fingers to open her flower and sucked on her hard, erect clit. She tried closing her legs. "Mmmmmm! Yeeeeeessss! Suck on that pussy!"

When she started talking freaky I knew what time it was.

Lately it hadn't been taking Sabrina long to reach her peak and then pass out. When her legs started shaking I rose on my knees. My towel now on the floor, I dove into her warmth and immediately heard my heart beating in my ears. Her shit was so creamy and wet it felt like I was swimming in warm honey. I'd barely got in two good dicks strokes when her pussy started to clamping.

"Damn already Sabrina." As I dicked her down, I watched as my beautiful puffy faced wife closed her eyes.

"Give me that feeling Sincere. Yes baby. Give it to me." I wanted to bend down and kiss her so bad but her big stomach had me second guessing that move. "Yes baby! Yes baby! Yes baby! Right there. Pleeeeease! Please! Please!"

The weight of the whole day was in my entire body. As I gave my wife what she wanted, it drained me of everything I had left.

She felt my momentum slowing. With her legs wrapped around my waist, she pushed me forward, "Look at me Sincere."

I hadn't even realized that my eyes were closed. I opened my lids and looked at my stunning wife. As I slowly ground into her warmth she took ahold of my arm on either side of her and squeezed them tight.

"I love you baby."

I took a chance and bent down to kiss her. "I love you too Sabrina."

A tear slid from her eyes and she squeezed my arms tighter. "Yes baby. Yes baby." She bit her bottom lip and that's when I lost it. I took a chance and place my elbows on either side of her and kiss the shit out of her ass. "I love you Sincere. Oh shit!"

My hips rose and felt like a see-saw pounding into her fresh pussy. With renewed strength I stopped stroking and went for a nipple.

"Don't stop! Don't stop! Don't stop!"

I didn't. I leaned back onto my knees, held her legs opened, then fucked into her hard. "You don't want me to stop? Huh? You want this dick?" She's gripping. Her juicy peach is gripping!

"Yes baby! Yes!" And as she gripped I ground. "Give me all that shit. I want all the dick."

Her pussy started contracting on my cock. I looked at the most stunning woman in the world.

She moaned, groaned and growled and soon I was behind her, coming with my whole body.

I grunted loudly. My body was so weak I started to shake. "Oh! Oh! Oh! Shit! Girl!" I wanted to squeeze her tight. "Oh baby! Damn! Shit!" But I didn't.

My body melted into nothingness, and I caught myself before falling on my wife. Five minutes later we were both knocked out.

At three in the morning Sabrina nudged me. I reluctantly opened one eye.

"Yeah baby?"

"Feel this." She placed my hand on her stomach, I closed my eye. When I didn't respond she nudged me again. "Sincere? Your baby wants some ice cream."

I could not believe her. I felt weak and fragile.

"I know it's early but we haven't eaten in hours." When I opened my eyes my lids were like sandpaper. That shit hurt so I closed them again. Her stomach growled. All I could do was shake my head. This wasn't my first midnight run to the store for my two babies, and it wouldn't be the last.

"Is that all you want Sabrina? Don't you think you should get some food?"

When she didn't answer, I, with dread, opened my lids and looked at my beautiful Sabrina. She'd fallen back asleep.

I looked down at her stomach. Her hand was still on top of mine. When I felt my seed kick my hand three times in a row, I was sure he or she was telling me to take my black ass to the store.

I removed my hand and rubbed my eyes. Although tired as hell, there was no food in the house. I'd planned to take Sabrina out for an early breakfast. Why I hadn't purchased any snacks earlier I don't know.

After taking another shower, I got dressed and made my way back to Walmart.

I sleepily made my way through the aisles, making sure I picked fruit, vegetables, shrimp, seasoning and virgin olive oil. Brotha-man was going to make us a nice lunch later in the day.

As I checked to make sure I wasn't forgetting anything I made my way to the checkout. What's funny is the cashier from earlier in the day was still working for this three am run.

"Back again?"

As he rang up my items I smiled. "Yeah. Wife is at home getting her beauty sleep while I'm out here purchasing her her midnight craving for our unborn child."

"Well congratulations. Wish you both the best."

"Thanks man. Appreciate that. Be careful going home. I know all about working that night shift."

"Thanks you too."

As I was walking out of the store I watched as someone in uniform walked towards me and I'll be damned if it wasn't Cyprus, dressed in blue.

"Hey there Sincere. Outta your neck of the wood aren't ya."

I raised an eyebrow and kept it moving.

"That shit for Sabrina?"

My hands were full of bags and although I shouldn't have entertained his ass I couldn't help myself.

I stopped and turned. "And if they are?"

"Hey man. No offence." He held up his hands as if surrendering. "I wish you guys nothing but good vibes. She seems happy which makes me happy."

Although he was wishing us good vibes I wasn't getting any from him. I gave him a head nod and kept it moving. "Thanks."

He couldn't leave well enough alone and followed me to my truck. "So when's she due?"

"None of your business." I was pissed and that uniform was a little too close for my liking. "Look Cyprus."

"Don't you mean Officer Boss?"

I looked at him like he was crazy. "Look Cyprus. I'm about to go home to my beautiful, pregnant wife. I'm about to feed her this now melting ice cream and handle my business as a man. If you have questions about what goes on in my marriage direct all your inquiries towards Sabrina."

I turned but thought better of it. "And Cyprus never forget that she's my muthafuckun wife."

"She sure doesn't have any trouble hanging on to old flings."

No the hell he didn't!

"That's because all y'alls asses are weak. She's there for y'all, not the other way around." I walked up to Officer Friendly. "Don't get shit twisted Cyprus, just as she gives y'all tad bits of what goes on in her life, I know all yall's shit." We were eye to eye. "I know how you begged her not to marry me."

I saw his blue eyes twitch.

"Shit! You didn't know? What? You thought I was on the sidelines just allowing y'all to have your way with my damn wife? You gots'ta be out ya damn mind! Every ounce of that woman is mine. Do you hear me? Every ounce. I let her keep in touch with you out of courtesy. She needed you dicks at one time, but that's no longer the case Cyprus. I'm all the damn man she needs. Why do you think I'm out here at four o'clock in the damn morning? Now, I'm about to take my conquering black ass to my muthafuckun castle and make love to my beautiful pregnant wife."

I started for my truck but stopped. "I'll make sure she sends you an announcement when she has our muthafuckun baby."

As I stormed off I could have sworn I heard his ass tell me good luck. I turned back around, disbelief on my face. "What the hell did you just say?"

Cyprus smiled, tilted his hat in my direction, and walked away.

I was heated. I could not believe that he'd had the bold audacity to question me about me and mines. He was way out of line and knew it. He just didn't give a damn.

With my anger at the top of the scale, my body was drained. I pulled out of the parking lot and started making my way to the crib. I replayed our conversation over and over in my head. As I did, I became more and more angry which made me angry at Sabrina. That incident had just confirmed all the shit I'd been telling her, which pissed me off even more.

I did not want to go home with my emotions on my sleeves.

Sabrina was damn near due. With the previous day being so draining I didn't want to add to it. Once on familiar terrain, I pulled my truck over to the side of the road to get myself under control. I was a couple of miles from the house which would give me a short distance to drive once I'd pulled myself together.

I turned off my truck. I couldn't help going back to the incident with Cyprus, which did nothing for my temper. I had to think of something other than his punk-ass so I shifted my thoughts to names for the baby Sabrina and I had been talking about.

If a girl, Sabrina wanted to call her Samantha. I did not like that name, and when I told her so she started crying. As soon as I saw that tear slide down her puffy cheek I started cracking up.

"Nothing's funny Sincere."

"Girl you crying over a name? I dun seen it all."

"I like that name. Besides it starts with 's' which is in both our names."

"Well hell. If that's the case why cain't we name her Shaquasha." My wife looked at me like I was cra-cra. When she realized that I was serious she started laughing. I didn't see shit funny. "What's wrong with Sahquasha? You still get your 's'."

She ignored me and wiped the tears that now flowed from laughter. "If it's a boy do you want him named after you?"

I answered that real quick. "Hell no!"

She was taken aback. "Why not…"

I cut her off. "My name has a meaning to it and it's not a good one. What about Sidney?"

I knew I'd hurt her feelings but didn't care. There was no way in hell I was going to name my child after me. Never!

Her head was down. "I guess Sidney is fine."

There were things Sabrina still didn't know about my past. I was going to tell her real soon though. Our child needed to know its history. I kissed Sabrina's forehead. "Good."

As I thought on that conversation, I lay my head back on my headrest. Without any prompting from me my lids got heavy.

I told myself that I'd close them for five minutes. An hour later I opened them to blue and red lights.

"Put your hands where we can see them."

We? What?

A bright white light shined into my truck, blinding my eyes. I placed my arm over my face, blocking the light. "Put the gun down!"

Gun?

I shifted my arm and looked at my hand. I saw that I was holding Sabrina's melted Butter Pecan ice cream.

Sabrina!

#BLM!

#BLM!

#BLM!

#BLM!

#BLM!

#BLM!

#BLM!

Chapter Ten

Sabrina...

It was like my baby was fighting itself, but that wasn't what woke me up. It was the persistent banging and ringing of the doorbell. I picked up my cell phone. It was five o'clock in the morning. I was naked so I rolled off of the air mattress and wobbled my way to the kitchen counter.

"Sincere?" I called his name but got no answer. The ringing and banging continued.

"Sabrina! Open the damn dooooooor!" My cousin. My heart skipped numerous beats.

"Sincere?!"

After finding the Walmart bag with clothes Sincere had purchased I dressed. I realized later they were Sincere's.

"Sabrrrriiiinnnnna!" I could tell she was crying. "Open this fucking door!"

After getting dressed I walked throughout the house calling his name.

The first bedroom.

"Sincere?"

The second bedroom.

"Sincere? Where are you baby?"

Third bedroom.

"Sincere?"

Fourth.

I started crying and wobbled my way down stairs to the basement.

There was no Sincere.

My baby was kicking. Our baby knew.

After I made my way through the house, I slowly made my way into the entryway and stood in front of the door. They don't give up.

"Sabrina baby open the door, baby." Said Malcolm's voice, "Please."

Malcolm?

With outstretched arms I opened the door. They were all there. Walter, Malcolm, Cyprus and Rusty. My cousin was on the ground dry-heaving. I guess her man of the month came to give support.

"Sabrina?"

They started walking towards me but I stopped them. With a raised hand and closed eyes I shook my head. "No, no, no, no, no, no, no, no, no, no please no, no, no, no, no, no, no, no."

My hand went to my thigh and started beating it.

"NO! NO! NO! NO! NO! PLEASE! PLEASE! PLEASE! NO! NO! NO!"

A hand touched my shoulder.

"NOOOOOOOOOOOOOOOOOOOO! NOOOOOOOOOO! PLEEEEEEEEEEEASE NO!"

Three bodies surrounded me.

"JESUUUUUS!"

I shrieked. As I drop to my knees they held me up. "Oh my God! Oh my God! Oh my God!" My anguish became a melody. "OhmyGodohmyGodohmyGodohmyGodohmyGodohmyGod!"

And then I became weak.

"Nooooo Sincere. Please don't leave me. Sincere please don't. Please baby don't leave me alone please. Please baby pleeeease. You promised me. Sincere you promised!"

I couldn't believe I was saying those words.

"NOOOOOOOOOOOOOOOOOOOOOOO! NO! NO! IT'S NOT TRUE! NOOOOOOOOOOO! PLEASE TELL ME IT'S NOT TRUE!"

I opened my eyes and looked at them all. They were so broken. Every last one of them pained.

I balled up my fist and bit into it hard.

Walter grabbed my hand. All of them spoke. "Don't do that Sabrina. Please baby don't. Don't hurt yourself."

On and on they went. Their words sounded like a thousand needles being pricked into my eardrum.

They carried me to our makeshift bed and gently lay me down. When they tried sitting on it to comfort me I shooed them away.

"He was just here!" I picked up the blanket, put it up to my nose and took in a deep breath. "See?"

I held it out for them to smell.

"See he was just here. He was right here."

The tears were like Niagara Falls. Never-ending.

"He was just here. Right here."

When I hit the bed to prove a point, my hand bounced back at me.

"I'm telling you. There's no way he's gone. No waaaaaay."

Rusty excused himself. Although they were a blur I knew they were crying.

My cousin fell onto the bed next to me. We held each other close, like when we were kids. And just like that time, we didn't want to let each other go. When we were young we were traumatized by our fathers. Now I stood alone and just like then, I knew I would never be the same.

I asked Sincere why his mother never opened another store. I recall him telling me she never had a reason. He also told me that he didn't know why his mother called her shop Justice. Now I know better.

Two weeks after my husband was murdered by police, I delivered our little boy. Although devastated and heartbroken, Mrs. Fleming was front and center to welcome her new grandson into the world.

After my little man was cleaned Mrs. Fleming burst into tears.

"Oh my God! He looks just like him! He looks just like his daddy!"

The staff knew who we were. Everybody knew who the woman due to give birth on any given day, whose husband was slaughtered over ice cream, was. All because a white woman, on her morning jog, saw a suspicious black man in the neighborhood.

No one said a word.

As the doctor closed me up and the tears streamed down my face, all I could do was lay back and shake my head.

I screamed "They killed my husband! Those bastards killed my fuckun' husband!" My dam broke and the staff was there. I held one nurse so tight I know it had to hurt. "I'm sorry. I can't help it. I'm sorry."

"Nothing to apologize for baby. Nothing at all." She didn't resist me, and an hour later I was still holding her tight.

I was placed in my private room and had so many flowers from well-wishers I had to ask to have most of them taken out. Although I'm certain they were beautiful, my world was a single shade of gray.

The birth of my son made headline news, and the world wanted me to know they were by my side.

When I held my son for the first time my hands shook.

"Oh my goodness. Oh my goodness."

He was perfect.

I counted his toes and fingers. When all were accounted for, I cried.

"Sincere. Oh Sincere."

My emotions were on volcano, so the staff took him from me.

My hospital stay, too, was a blur.

It took months for me to get to living. My baby boy forced me into life. I'm sure I would have died.

Mrs. Fleming helped me too. "You cain't let them win Sabrina."

We were at the new house. Although everything was where it was supposed to be, every time I walked inside I saw Walmart bags on our kitchen table. The very table where Mrs. Fleming told me what my husband hid from me for years.

"They tried to kill me right along with my husband but I didn't let'em." Her eyes got misty. "Take charge of your life girl." She sounded like an old Negro slave trying to give me instructions on freedom. "The first few years are going to be hard."

She looked down at her grandson who was feasting on my breast. "But he'll get you through."

I shook my head and broke down. It didn't take much. My whole heart was broken. I couldn't understand it. It didn't make any sense to me. My husband was gone. All over some damn ice cream!

As I cried, my anguish was transferred to her.

"Do you know why I gave him the name Sincere?"

I shook my head no.

"Because that's all they kept saying. 'I'm *sincerely* sorry for your loss.' 'We *sincerely* send you our condolences.' 'We *sincerely* apologize for this tragedy.' 'It is with *sincere* sorrow that we have to inform you that your husband was killed by friendly fire.'"

"What?"

"Yes child. My husband was a policeman but he was a good one. Not like these gutter cops today."

My tears dried up.

"Wait a minute. Are you telling me that Sincere's dad, your husband, was an officer?" I couldn't believe my ears.

As she wiped her face a crooked smile came across her lips. "He sure was. Fought crime the same way he fought for our love; With all of his heart." She stared into space "There was an internal affairs investigation. Seems that there were some crooked cops on the force."

She looked at me. "Can you imagine that? Crooked cops. Anyway, Charles was a witness to everything and was due to testify. He died before he got the chance. How convenient."

The things she said caused my head to hurt.

"Yeah, Officer Boss got away with it again."

"Boss? And what do you mean again?"

"Oh, Charlie wasn't the only one who was going to testify. There were two more officers. Black officers. After the first one was found shot in his patrol car the other backed down. Charles refused. He said he witnessed his comrades slaughter a group of young drug dealers like they were on a pig farm. Boldly too. Didn't even try to hide it from the honest cops. I guess they knew they didn't need to."

As I listened intently I lightly shook my son.

She sighed.

"Anyway, Charlie said 'wrong is wrong' and that those young men deserved justice just as anybody else would. Just as they slaughtered those young black men, they did the same to my husband. Making sure justice would never have her day."

As I shifted my baby to my other breast, I wondered how she could be so damn strong.

"How in the hell is being shot five times by two different guns friendly fire? Everybody knew that it was a setup. And Boss, the main culprit in the whole operation, four of the five bullets that hit my husband came from his gun."

"Is that why your shop is called Justice?"

"Oh hell naw. It's called Justice because I wouldn't stop until I got justice for my husband. Honey, they picked the wrong wife."

She looked at her grandson. "Why do you think Sincere wanted so badly to work at Wishard?"

I had a blank look on my face. "He never told me." I said. "He rarely told me anything about his father. He always told me that he would tell me in time, so I stopped asking. But we ran out. We ran out of time Mrs. Fleming." Saying those words made me sick at the stomach, and once again I broke down.

She moved to my side of the table and held me close. "It's okay Sabrina. Let it out baby. Let it all out." As she held me close she spoke.

"My son was determined to get his hands on copies of his father's medical records. You see, although my husband was pronounced dead at the scene there were a few officers who said he'd actually been grazed by most of the bullets and was alive, calling out for help. They also said that while faking cpr, Boss had somehow suffocated my husband to death. I don't know Sabrina."

I'd calmed, so she took her seat.

"That boy was obsessed with the events surrounding his father's murder. Can't say I blame him. What they did to his daddy was filthy. He never found his father's records though. Somehow they'd been sealed. From and by who, I don't know, but he never got them. I'm sure he'd have never stopped trying."

When she gave me a look I got her silent message. I got her message loud and clear.

Once she realized her unspoken words were understood, she placed her eyes back on her grandson.

"Just like you, I was pregnant with Sincere. Do you know how much sympathy that garnered? Not just from this city but all around the world. Number one, because my husband was a policeman, but my being pregnant topped the cake. I even got a letter from the President of the United States talking about how *sincerely* sorry he was for my loss, thanking me for my husband's ultimate sacrifice.

The platform was set for me to stand, and I stood. I stood for the injustice of our people who are harassed and murdered by law enforcement like it's training day. The same platform my beloved husband stood on. I just took his place, advocating for our people."

Mrs. Fleming looked at me with a sly eye. "They thought they killed their witness by getting rid of my husband, they just didn't know that they'd just created one."

She smiled.

"My husband had all of his testimony against those cops recorded and written down. He hadn't even told me he'd done that. I found those things years later. I suppose he was trying to protect me and Sincere. But, that's neither here nor there. Just know that I got'em. Every last one of those bastards. The ones who pulled the trigger on my man and the ones that killed those boys. That's why my shop is called Justice. Because I was able to get it for my husband. Nothing more, nothing less."

Mrs. Fleming sat straight in her chair and asked me a question that sent a small chill down my spine.

"How do you know CJ?"

At first I didn't know who the hell she was talking about but she surely clarified it. "Cyprus Boss Jr. how do you know that man?"

My eyes got big as plates. I thought I was going to throw up. "What?"

"His daddy murdered my husband."

Two Years Later

Whoever said time heals all wounds lied. My emotions are just as raw as they were two years ago, but some things have changed.

My little man has gotten so big. I know that Sincere would be proud and bubbling with joy. He's the spitting image of his father.

It pains me every day to look at him. Especially when he smiles! He's got our deep dimples.

It's a constant reminder of what was, and what is. I *'was'* happily married, on the threshold of embarking on a new journey with my new husband. Instead, I'm a single mother who has had to accept the fact that that's the way it *'is'* always going to be.

Sincere and his dad both married women who were committed to them until the day we died. It wasn't because of Mrs. Fleming I made that choice, but my heart. Sincere was my *'first'* everything and I wanted to keep it that way.

And speaking of Mrs. Fleming, she has done something that I never thought she'd do. She's opened another store; Justice2.

The circumstances of her opening the new one were the same as the first, except we're still waiting for justice. She is confident that we'll get it.

She gave me words of wisdom, "Don't let them forget Sabrina. The moment you do, you've lost the case and the cause has been forgotten."

And I haven't. Every invitation extended to me to speak, I accept. I speak at those engagements with conviction, anger and love. Never faltering on my agenda.

Using my unwanted platform I brought up cases that went all the way back to 1987, up to the present day. And not just for my city either. I've spoken of the murders of numerous African Americans by the police throughout the country. Murders that nations watched take place, then gasped when the police weren't convicted, giving the next crooked trigger-happy cop the green light to shoot at will.

There were times when I didn't want to go an event. When all I wanted was to curl in my bed. My cold bed, always empty on the other side, and scream. Then I'd hear my son whimper or trying to talk. That was all the motivation I needed to roll myself out of my coffin of sorrow.

What the police did to my husband was not to be forgotten. I was going to make sure of that.

Working at and managing Mrs. Fleming's second store was a constant reminder of why I had to push forward. It was well worth it.

We're at the grand opening of Justice2. A few of my siblings, my cousin Shanika and her man of the month. Malcolm, Walter, Rusty and Cyprus. Ramona, her boo and Brice were there as well.

We are all one big happy family, there to celebrate a special occasion and remember a sad one.

Before the cutting of the ribbon Mrs. Fleming said a few words.

"I would like to thank each and everyone of you for supporting Sabrina and me in this monumental endeavor. Although it's under dire circumstances that I'm opening a new store, it's also a day of celebration."

She held out her aging arms and my baby boy ran into them.

"This is the day that God blessed me with an extension of both my husband and son. The day that our little Sincere Jr. was born."

She kissed him on his fat chubby cheek.

"A day that will stand as a reminder that there is life after death. A day that signifies new starts and clean slates. It's a day of new beginnings. New beginnings don't constitute forgetting. Naw, on the contrary. They signify hope and healing. So, as we continue on that journey I'd like to welcome you to Justice2. A place where hope lives and giving up is never an option. Justice will be served, but in the meantime, and in-between time, let us bask in such a time as this."

She put Sincere Jr. down and handed me the scissors.

"Welcome to Justice2!"

I took the hand of the small replica of my husband and with my hand on top of his; Together we cut the ribbon to a new chapter of our lives.

About the Author

Angela Moore has worked as a Respiratory Therapist at the VA Hospital for many years. The biological mother of three (but mother of many) is a faithful member of her church and the grandmother of three.

In her spare time, she enjoys roller skating, swimming, and fellowshipping with friends and family both far and near.

Other Works

Conversion of A Pimp: Joseph

Conversion of A Pimp: Joanna

Conversion of A Pimp: Joanna Book II

Conversion of A Pimp: New Beginnings and Sad Endings

Coming Soon!

Conversion of A Pimp: Family Ties

Conversion of A Pimp: Judgement Day

Conversion of A Pimp: Salvation Has Been Brought Down

Moments in Time (An accumulation of short stories)

www.ingramcontent.com/pod-product-compliance
Lightning Source LLC
Chambersburg PA
CBHW051249260626
47162CB00002B/683

* 9 780990 990345 *